THE RUMBA

OF THE

BEAST

By

Ian Jarvis

Paperback ISBN 978-1-80424-235-3
ePub ISBN 978-1-80424-236-0
PDF ISBN 978-1-80424-237-7

Published by MX Publishing
335 Princess Park Manor, Royal Drive,
London, N11 3GX
www.mxpublishing.co.uk

Cover design by Brian Belanger

Chapter 1

Oliver Tarrant rarely ventured far from his Northumberland home and his familiarity with foreign weather was limited, to say the least. He'd expected Mexico to be hot, but not *this* hot. Twenty-four hours ago, when he stepped from his airplane into the sky bridge tunnel, he'd felt a scorching draught tussle his curly blonde hair. Mystified as to why such a warm country would install airport heaters, he'd glanced up and realised his mistake. The tunnel's rubber seal had failed to make full contact with the doorway and this was just the daytime air wafting through from outside.

No, these temperatures were very different to the climate Tarrant was accustomed to back in northern England. Stepping out of his air-conditioned hotel in Mexico City felt remarkably similar to opening an oven to check on the progress of the Sunday roast.

At least it was cooler here in the mountains, he mused.

Sitting in the rear of the police car, Tarrant turned from watching the passing countryside. "I have to say it," he murmured, nervously. "I don't like this."

"Why am I not surprised?" snorted his colleague. "You want to be careful you don't piss your pants. You haven't liked *anything* since we arrived and most of the time you're scared of your own shadow. I can't believe the Laird sent you with me."

Tarrant gritted his teeth, but said nothing. Richard Brunton had always been an arrogant bastard and he detested the man, but their somewhat unique situation meant they were forced to get along with each other. Attractive, with shaggy black hair and a fashionably unshaven square jaw, Brunton stood a few inches over six feet in height, a good eight inches taller than the slender Tarrant. His muscular stature was intimidating, which, along with his aggression, was the main reason the Laird had long ago appointed him his Head of Security. Out here in the wilds of Mexico, however, Brunton's size and violent nature wouldn't count for much if things turned bad.

Tarrant swallowed uneasily. *When dealing with drug cartels like this, things could often turn very bad indeed.*

Wearing a pale blue civilian suit, Eduardo Garcia, the district Police Chief, sat in the front of the patrol car beside the uniformed driver.

"A smooth road, I think you gentlemen will no doubt agree?" He spoke perfect English and gestured to the winding route through the woodland ahead. "Believe it or not, this has nothing to do with our Highways Department. No, we have Senor Blanco to thank. He paid for the repairs and the resurfacing of the entire road between the city back there and his home. Presumably he doesn't like bumps. I should say: he *didn't* like bumps." Garcia laughed. "He won't be disliking *anything* anymore."

Tarrant peered out over the lush landscape of forest and rugged mountains. He'd assumed Mexico would be an arid desert, a preconception shaped by countless movies featuring dusty towns with men in sombreros lounging around during siesta. Presumably some parts were like that – maybe around the Texas border – but he hadn't realised the size of this place, some eight times larger than his native Britain. This was the south of the country, fifty miles west of Mexico City on the edge of the Cumbres Sierra Nevada National Park.

"Is this it?" asked Brunton, leaning forward.

"This is it," confirmed Garcia. "The Aztec Palace."

Tarrant gazed at the building complex ahead, an isolated collection of white towers and red-tiled rooftops, all enclosed behind a high wall. Constructed atop a rugged hill, it did indeed resemble a palace, with a helicopter pad, a private reservoir to supply water, and several machine gun turrets to supply security. An inconceivable amount of money had clearly gone into this *residence* and it was safe to say that the owner, Francisco Blanco, wasn't short of pesos.

"Welcome to the headquarters of the Muerte Blanco Cartel," said Garcia.

"Muerte Blanco?" Brunton translated the name and laughed cynically. "White Death?"

"Er, yes." The Police Chief pulled a sour face. "I have to say, Francisco Blanco was somewhat theatrical. Until last night he was one of the biggest players in the world of narcotics. I think this palace speaks as to just *how* powerful he was."

Tarrant remembered once reading why footballers were paid such obscene wages – they needed those hundreds of thousands every week because their sporting careers could be relatively short. They might be out of a job in their mid-twenties and thirty million in the bank would protect them from the nuisance of having to find another line of work. Blanco's people were similar. A career in a drug cartel *also* paid quite well, but it too could be short-lived and the severance package often left much to be desired.

The electronic gates were open and the patrol car drove through to enter a tiled plaza decorated with huge Aztec statues and a central fountain complex. Circumnavigating the latter, it pulled up outside the main doors beside a small fleet of police vehicles and forensic vans. Clambering from his seat, Garcia beckoned to his guests.

"Gentlemen, please..." He nodded to the entrance. "My people are working inside, but it's quite safe to go in and explore. Feel free to report anything you see in your magazine story, but I'll need to personally vet any photographs you take."

The two men had no intention of taking pictures, mostly because they weren't journalists. A lucrative bribe had ensured the Police Chief hadn't bothered to verify their false story, or check the fake credentials.

Tarrant gazed anxiously around the courtyard. The stone

walls were painted gleaming white and festooned with the red blossoms of climbing plants. Some areas were covered in a very different shade of red; a dark congealing red that seemed to be highly popular with clouds of buzzing flies. Beneath the crimson splatters and arterial sprays lay the mangled bodies of seven or eight men.

Tarrant gulped. *Or maybe nine or ten – with the state they were in, it was difficult to be sure.*

"So which one is Blanco?" he asked.

"Oh, no, my friend." Garcia shook his head. "These are just a few of his men. There are many more like this inside, but you'll find Blanco, or rather various pieces of him, out back by the main swimming pool. Just be careful you don't slip in the blood as we go through. By the way, it's perhaps a little late to be asking, but I hope you aren't squeamish?"

Brunton grinned. "Not at all," he said, truthfully.

"Why is everyone wearing a white suit?" asked Tarrant, still staring at the corpses. "It's like a uniform."

"I suppose you could call it that," explained Garcia, leading them into the palace. "Blanco insisted that all his foot soldiers dressed the same. It ensured that, whenever they killed, the terrified witnesses would know who was responsible. Murderers in *your* country strive for anonymity, but these people like to advertise their power."

Tarrant walked slowly through the opulent interior of marble columns and expensive artworks, gaping around in wide-eyed horror. Blanco's men had indeed been outfitted in white, but their clothes now resembled blotchy camouflage attire, if ever camouflage attire were needed for a bizarre environment of scarlet and white. Floors, walls, and even ceilings, were splattered with blood and torn corpses were strewn everywhere, many having been literally ripped apart. The air conditioning was switched off and a sickly, almost metallic, stench filled the rooms and corridors.

Tarrant knew that blood contained metal, probably iron, if

4

memory served, but surely there shouldn't be so much iron that it actually stank?

"I'm afraid this isn't a rare scenario," said Garcia, noticing his pale features. "Over two-hundred thousand people have died in the drug wars. Blanco originally had an alliance with the Delgado Cartel in the north, but recently they had a falling out."

"Er..." Tarrant looked around at the carnage. "This is the result of a *tiff?*"

Garcia shrugged. "These people don't fool around. Angel Delgado, the cartel head, obviously decided to remove Blanco from the picture and send a definite message to the other players in this business. God alone knows how many he sent here to inflict *this* sort of damage."

Brunton and Tarrant exchanged knowing glances. It had taken far fewer assassins than the Police Chief believed, but both men had to agree, it *did* look as if an army had gone through the place, a crazed army wielding chainsaws.

They walked out through open rear doors to a large swimming pool where Garcia headed to speak with a group of his officers.

Tarrant turned to Brunton. "There are bullet holes everywhere," he whispered. "How come the guards all missed her?"

"Don't be stupid," sneered Brunton. "They almost certainly *didn't* miss. No, the information was correct; this is definitely the person we're looking for."

Like the building interiors, the swimming pool area was lavishly decorated with Aztec tiles and large statues, but the overall aesthetic was ruined today by the arms, legs and intestines floating in the murky red water. Green hummingbirds whirred between pots of begonias, their emerald beauty incongruous beside the visceral devastation. Some of the more stupid ones hovered briefly over mutilated bodies, mistaking the ghastly wounds for the bright red flowers. A marble nymph poured an endless torrent into the pool from the upturned urn she carried. Tarrant stared at the giant water feature, his mouth falling open.

"My God," he croaked, seeing the human colon draped over its head like a red wig.

Garcia strolled back to his side. "It's doubtful that God was present last night," he said, pointing to a pile of offal. "Blanco is over there. His head has been taken, presumably as a trophy for his rival. I'm told Senor Delgado preserves them in bottles of formaldehyde to decorate his study."

"Each to their own," murmured Tarrant, dryly.

The knowledge that just *one* assassin had done all of this terrified him. Moving away from the Police Chief to walk around the pool, he took a small hip flask from his jacket pocket and sipped.

"Take it easy with that," snapped Brunton, following. "We have a limited supply and you don't *need* it."

"This woman..." said Tarrant, quietly. "Like you said, they were correct about her, but are we really sure she's the right one for us. Maybe we could find a..."

"What?" scoffed Brunton. "A less dangerous one? I think *dangerous* kind of goes with the job description. Besides, we don't have the time to *shop around* as it were."

"But the risk..."

"Everything is a risk. Just our being here is a risk. Imagine finding ourselves in a Mexican prison for whatever reason and being separated from the Fountain for too long."

Tarrant winced, That was something he *definitely* didn't want to imagine.

* * * *

The Four Seasons hotel stands in the heart of Mexico City on one of the central tree-lined avenues. Entering the main lobby, Tarrant and Brunton discovered an oasis of coolness and calm, quite a contrast to the endless cacophony outside where Latin American temperaments were paired with loud vehicle horns. Grateful for the air-conditioned breeze, the two men took one of the elevators to the top floor where the most expensive suites looked out over the rooftops. The subdued lift music was supposed to soothe the guests, but it did little to calm Tarrant's nerves. He hesitated as the doors slid open.

"What's wrong now?" snarled Brunton.

"I can't help thinking..." Tarrant swallowed and took a few deep breaths. "If she should suspect we're lying to her... If she suspects that this is just a ploy to..."

"Come on." Grabbing his arm, Brunton marched him to the suite at the end of the corridor and rang the bell. "You might not like this, but you know there's no other way. The clock is ticking and we have to get this done."

A middle-aged woman in a white towel robe answered the door. Strikingly attractive, with dark shoulder-length hair, a black silk patch covered her left eye. Tarrant was momentarily taken aback. He'd never given any real thought to such things, but he'd expected top assassins to have *two* eyes. With this particular woman, however, he didn't suppose it mattered much.

"Miss Crane?" asked Brunton. "Maria Crane?"

"That's the name I currently use." The woman looked him over, smiling at his muscular frame. "How can I help you?"

"We know you're here in Mexico on business." Brunton lowered his voice. "We have a proposition that we hope will interest you – a *business* proposition."

"I see." Crane paused for several seconds, which felt like minutes to Tarrant. "Then you'd both better come on in, hadn't you?"

They followed her into the plush suite and she closed the door behind them, smirking at Tarrant.

"No need to be so frightened," she said.

"Er, no..." He looked confused. "I'm not..."

"Your breathing is rapid and your heart rate is elevated; the pulse in your rather appealing throat is pumping much faster than it should. Don't worry, I won't bite."

"He knows what you're capable of," explained Brunton, grinning. "We saw your handiwork at the Aztec Palace this morning. It scared the shit out of him, but I found it impressive."

"Is that so?" She stared for a few moments. "I see."

Tarrant had the distinct impression that she was considering whether or not to kill them. *With all the cartel warfare, finding bodies in a Mexican hotel room wouldn't be too unusual for Conchita from housekeeping. It was probably on a par with discovering a condom in the bed, or a stolen towel.*

"How did you find me?" asked Crane.

"We've been searching for... someone, er, like you," said Tarrant, nervously. "We, um, trade in a certain product and we asked some of our customers on the Dark Web if they knew of anyone like you who..."

"Angel Delgado, the cartel boss, is one of our clients," broke in Brunton, exasperated by his colleague's edginess. "He told us all about you; about what you are. He explained how he hired you to take care of Blanco and told us where you were staying."

"Did he?" Crane nodded. "My work is strictly confidential. I'll have to call upon Senor Delgado and discuss this before I leave the country. Just out of curiosity, what does Delgado buy from you?"

"Bottled water," laughed Brunton.

"Is that some attempt at a joke?"

"Not at all," Tarrant quickly assured her. "Shallow people will pay stupid money for water, but our product is *different* and it's actually worth the price." He took out his hip flask and warily passed it to her. "Um, this is it: *Ravenspoint Spa.*"

Crane sniffed. "Yes, this *is* water, but it's something far more,

8

isn't it? How much do you charge?"

Brunton winked at her. "We charge thousands, darling."

Closing her eye, she sniffed again. The liquid was odourless, but Tarrant guessed this woman's olfactory senses might be a little different to the norm.

"Interesting." She returned the flask and smiled thinly. "You mentioned a business proposition?"

Brunton nodded. "As I say, we've just visited the Aztec Palace. We have a similar job for you and we need your unique talents as soon as possible."

"Where?"

"The north of England, near Newcastle."

"I've visited Scotland." Walking to the glass balcony doors, she gazed out over the lush trees in the neighbouring parkland. "The weather is a little different to this."

"This is a nice view," said Tarrant, approaching her. "But allow me to show you a much nicer one." He took out his phone, tapped a banking app and held up a page of transfer details for her to read. "This amount is only a deposit and it's ready to send to the account of your choice. You just need to enter your details."

"I like you." Smiling at him, she took the mobile and transferred the money. "I can't say as I'm so keen on your big brash friend there, but I *do* like you."

"Um, very good," said Tarrant, nervously clearing his dry throat. Hopefully she wouldn't like him *too* much. "Now all you need do is travel to Britain and we can discuss the work."

"Who is it?" she asked.

"You mean the target?" said Brunton.

"I *mean* who just paid me that money? You're clearly representing someone and I want their name."

"Reginald Mulgrave," said Tarrant.

"I've never heard of him." Crane shrugged. "But fortunately

9

for you that isn't a problem. His money is good."

"The deposit is an incentive," said Tarrant. "You'll keep it whether you take the job or not. The remainder will be deposited after you visit Britain and speak to Reginald in person. I should point out that time is very much a factor here. It's less than two weeks to Christmas and the work needs to be completed before then. It needs completing before the 21st of December."

Crane laughed. "Christmas won't get in the way of anything. I'm not in the habit of celebrating such things."

Well, that's one less name on my gift list, thought Tarrant, nervously.

"I'll be there," she confirmed. "I have a loose end named Delgado that I need to tie up and then I'll fly out two days from now."

"Excellent," said Brunton. "I'll supply you with all the contact information."

Tarrant was still far from happy about this. Despite the air conditioning, rivulets of sweat trickled down his back.

"Yes, excellent," he agreed, his heart thudding. "We'll look forward to seeing you there."

* * * *

Chapter 2

Yorkshire, Britain's largest county, was named by the Vikings and sliced up by them into three manageable areas known as Ridings. After a thousand trouble-free years, the bureaucrats decided this was impractical and, in 1974, they changed the ridings to North Yorkshire, West Yorkshire, and South Yorkshire. The county of Humberside replaced the East Riding, but this was highly unpopular and, after much campaigning, it reverted back to its original name in 1996. No one was entirely sure why any of this disruption occurred, but it's generally assumed to have been some obscure governmental way of making wealthy people wealthier.

Hull is the only city in the East Riding, or Kingston upon Hull, to use the full title. The name was taken from the River Hull that flows through the centre, but where other cities, such as Newcastle upon Tyne have been simplified to just *Newcastle*, the people of Hull bizarrely discarded the obvious name of *Kingston* and went instead for *Hull*, or "Ull" as many there pronounce it. The city sprawls along the tidal banks of the vast Humber River, so why the nondescript River Hull was chosen for the name is anyone's guess.

Hull has undergone major changes in recent decades. Historic buildings received a facelift, derelict warehouses metamorphosed into upmarket dwellings, and the rundown waterfront was startlingly transformed into *the* place to be, a superb area of shopping malls, chic bars and eateries. On the western outskirts, surrounded by acres of parkland, stands the iconic Humber Bridge with its twin suspension towers soaring 500 feet into the sky and a single span of over one mile. When this engineering achievement was completed in 1981 it was the longest suspension bridge on the planet... then, a few years later, the Japanese built a longer one. Like old Mister Lennox, the Hull councillor famously said: "Bloody Japs. First Pearl Harbour and then *this*. You just can't trust the sly bastards."

Winding beside the wide Humber, the A63 road passes beneath the northern end of the bridge. John Watson peered up at the concrete span from the passenger seat as Bernard Quist sped towards the city in his blue Ford saloon. A lightning flash transformed the river into an immense sheet of silver, the night sky grumbled angrily and lashing rain bubbled on the tarmac ahead, reminding Watson of a boiling chip pan. The young man licked his lips.

A nice bag of hot chips would be great on a freezing December night like this, but he doubted his boss would indulge him by stopping outside a takeaway. They had a tricky job to complete and food would have to wait.

Christmas was only one week away, but the thunderstorm that tore in from the East Coast this Wednesday evening didn't feel particularly festive. The windscreen wipers whipped at the glass in a frantic effort to combat the downpour as the car entered Hessle on the city's western outskirts.

Watson didn't know much about Hull, but he did know *one* thing – this was the birthplace of William Wilberforce, the driving influence behind the abolition of slavery. Five years ago, Watson had been on a school visit to Wilberforce's museum house. He was the first to admit he hadn't listened much during lessons, but he'd certainly taken notice of *this*, probably because, two centuries ago, the dark colour of his skin would have made him a very desirable trading commodity.

Slavery was evil, but there was no escaping the fact that an attractive young black guy like him would be worth an absolute fortune, he'd decided, proudly.

Another booming thunderclap rolled and echoed between the surrounding buildings. Listening to music through earphones, Watson adjusted the volume on his phone and shook his head.

Importing the American practise of naming storms had to be one of the worst ideas ever. What was the point? Imagine your mum being killed under a tree felled by Storm Timmy, or having your home destroyed by Storm Trudy. If they had to have names, why the hell didn't they go for something more appropriate, such as Storm Stalin, Storm Himmler, or Storm Thatcher?

The young man smirked. *At least this storm had one benefit. His boss usually dropped the window and smoked in the car, but the driving rain made this impossible.*

"Raining cats and dogs?" He shook his head, puzzled. "Why do you reckon people say that?"

"Um..." Bernard Quist shrugged. "I honestly don't know."

"Really? I thought you knew everything."

"Apparently not."

"My cryptozoologist mate Barry makes me laugh. He always says it's raining wolves and pumas."

"*What?*" gasped Quist. "How come I've never heard about this *mate*? A cryptozoologist, you say? Someone who studies unusual and paranormal beasts? So what the hell do the pair of you talk about?"

"Relax, Guv," laughed Watson. "He isn't a mate as such and we don't actually talk. I just like to listen to him. He props up the bar in my local pub, the Duck and Diogenes, and tells everyone his theories about Loch Ness, the Beast of Barmston Drain, the fake moon landings and how vaccines kill everyone." He checked the dashboard clock; it was a little after seven. "So how long do you reckon tonight's job will take? I have a hot date later."

"*Hot date?*" Quist glanced at him. "Good Lord, do teenagers still use that phrase? Oh, my mistake – you're no longer a teenager, are you?"

Watson's recent twentieth birthday meant his teenage years were now behind him, but Quist still thought of his assistant as a *youth* - claiming the human brain doesn't fully mature until around twenty-five. Watson couldn't really argue. Although his boss now

13

operated as a private investigator, or *consultant detective*, as he preferred to call it, he'd once been a medical doctor. Over the years, Bernard Quist had been a great many things.

"Yeah, I'm practically middle-aged," laughed Watson. "But believe me, Guv, that won't affect the temperature of the date. Donni Patterson will be sizzling hot."

The detective frowned. "Forgive me, but isn't that a boy's name?"

"No, not like *Donnie Darko*; this is Donni with a letter I. Her mum says she got pregnant in a bus shelter after a girls night out in Doncaster, or Donni, as everyone calls it."

"Good heavens," muttered Quist. "It's as if I'm listening to the synopsis of a Jane Austen novel." He gestured to his assistant's phone. "What on earth are you listening to there? The singer with the shrill voice? I mean, I use the word *singer*, but…"

"Lorraine Quiche and the Flans," said Watson. "I turned it down so it wouldn't bother you as you drove."

"I possess exceptional hearing, as you well know."

"Yeah, in fact it's almost supernatural."

Watson grinned at the private joke. On meeting his boss, most people tended to notice his nose, not his ears. It was a large aquiline nose which the youth had always felt would look more at home on a long-legged bird fishing by a lake. People also commented upon Quist's deep, eloquent voice, the sort of voice that was ideal for reciting Shakespeare, or *that poncy crap*, as Watson referred to it. Attractive, with dark wavy hair and Devilish eyebrows, the consultant detective looked to be in his mid-forties, but he was much older.

"The point is," said Quist, tetchily, "we're on our way to an important assignment and, instead of concentrating upon the task in hand, you're listening to music and…"

"Hey, this shit could be dangerous and music relieves the tension." Watson grimaced as more thunder ripped the heavens like a salvo of battlefield canons. "I thought you liked to do the same?"

"Classical music relieves *my* tension and helps me to think, not the sort of..."

"Hey, the Flans *are* classic. Lorraine left them after this album to form the Hoovers. Surely you remember their big hit, *Crevice Nozzle?*" The young man grinned. "I could have bought you their CD as a present. Didn't you say it was your birthday this week?"

"I did." Quist checked the rear view mirror and narrowed his eyes. "It's tomorrow, actually."

"Well, let me be the first person to say happy birthday, Guv."

"Why thank you." He nodded. "First and, very probably, the *only* person."

"Yeah, knowing you, I don't suppose you'll be throwing a party." Watson looked at his employer's hand on the steering wheel and the gold signet ring with its initials RQ. He'd once been *Richard Quist* amongst several other names. "When did you say it happened? 1790, wasn't it?"

"I was born in 1745," said Quist. "But my rebirth, for the lack of a more suitable phrase, occurred in 1790..."

"Okay..." Watson counted on his fingers. "So that makes this birthday the big two-eight-nine."

"Give or take a few years, thanks to your somewhat shaky grasp of mathematics..." The detective glanced again in the mirror. "Wait a moment. We need to get away from this vehicle. It's been following me since this morning in York when..." He grabbed his assistant's arm. "No, don't look. Keep facing front."

Waiting until the last moment and swerving left without indicating, Quist turned off the A63 and saw that the car was still behind them. He took another sharp left into the next street, then turned right and accelerated, before turning again into a narrow alleyway beside a closed-down pub.

"What are you doing?" quizzed Watson. "Training for the

Dalby Forest rally race?"

"I'm evading them; I should have thought that was obvious." Quist parked and killed the lights, twisting to survey the street to their rear. The rain hammered a tinny staccato drumbeat on the roof. "Ah, here we go."

"The black Range Rover?" Watson peered at his passenger wing mirror, watching as headlights reflected on the waterlogged tarmac and a car sped past their dark hiding place. "Looks like you lost them, Guv. Are you sure it's the same one you saw earlier?"

"Positive," said Quist. "I saw the registration, and by the way, the car is dark red, not black."

"Ah, the trusty old night vision."

The detective smiled thinly. "Yes, my sight *is* enhanced during the hours of darkness, but it was daylight when I noticed the car in York and realised it was following me. Naturally I was curious, so I decided to take no action and see what transpired. Unfortunately, that's no longer possible here in Hull."

"Yeah, we can't have them tailing us to the girl's address."

Quist nodded. "Incidentally, I telephoned your friend Lestrade earlier and gave him the Range Rover license plate to check. Apparently, it's registered to a gentleman named Oliver Tarrant in Northumberland." He paused. "Strange though…"

"What's that?"

"To get here we travelled along those long country lanes through various villages. There were very few cars about due to the storm and this Range Rover certainly wasn't behind us back there; I would definitely have noticed."

The youth nodded. "But then, as if by magic, it turned up here in Hull."

"Exactly." Quist gave a wry smile. "I wonder…"

Watson watched as his boss took a torch from the glove compartment and grabbed his long leather overcoat from the rear seat, draping it over his head like a police blanket over a bashful mass-murderer.

"Seriously?" Watson looked bemused. "You're actually going out there in this crap weather?"

"Seriously." Quist gave one of his peculiar lopsided smiles. "I won't be long."

He jumped out into the downpour, crouching low beside the vehicle and quickly fanning the torch beam left and right beneath the chassis and wheel arches. Several seconds passed before the door opened and he reappeared, tossing his saturated coat back into the rear and holding up a small device resembling a black cigarette packet.

"As I deduced..." Quist examined the metal box. "We've seen something similar to this before, haven't we?"

"*Shit*," gasped Watson. "*This* is how they found you in Hull? Is that thing a tracker?"

The detective nodded. "A transponder secured by a powerful magnetic back plate. Someone secreted it out of sight above my rear wheel."

The youth shook his head. "Bloody hell, Guv. What's going on here? Who do you suppose they are?"

"I really can't imagine, but whatever their intentions might be, they're clearly serious." He jotted down the transponder brand name and serial number before crushing the casing between his hands, something which the majority of *normal* people would have found difficult, to say the least. "As you said, we can't have them following us to our destination."

"Whoo!" Watson laughed dryly. "That's quite the strong grip you have there."

Dropping the window and tossing out the broken device, Quist started the car and reversed out of the alley.

Once again, the thunder rolled and Watson looked up at the storm, tensely contemplating what would soon be happening. He'd seen it many times and, although it *did* get easier, it didn't get *much* easier. Somewhere above these black clouds, the moon was almost full and he wasn't too keen on full moons – they made his boss a little tetchy. Watson preferred *his* moons to be crescent-shaped, resembling silver toe nail clippings.

"You normally wear a jacket, shirt and tie," he said, peering at his boss's attire. "Tonight you're in a sweater and trousers. Is that because it's easier to undress?"

"Correct, it's for when I need to get into character." The detective turned to him with another lopsided smile. "So to speak."

* * * *

Chapter 3

As a child, Watson's grandma had often told him that thunder was nothing to be afraid of; it was just God moving his heavy furniture around upstairs. The youth glanced heavenwards as another crash rent the black sky, causing Quist's car to actually vibrate. This sounded like the Almighty had grown bored with rearranging wardrobes and, for some weird reason, was now detonating explosive charges. It was safe to say the storm was growing worse.

The main road through Hull changes from the A63 to the A1033 as it passes the city centre and continues out along the Holderness peninsula towards Spurn Point, Yorkshire's bleak answer to the Florida Keys. The detective had turned off this highway to drive through Fenbrook on the eastern outskirts. This small suburb presented a *very* different picture to the Tourist Board's preferred image of culture and family visits to the city aquarium and museums. Watson peered around dubiously. He couldn't be certain, due to the dark cloud cover and lashing rain, but he strongly suspected the storm made the area look *better* than it was. Quist parked at the rear of Spittal Court, a long, two-storey apartment block on the edge of the grim estate.

"Hey, *lovely* place," quipped the youth, climbing out of the vehicle into the icy downpour and zipping up his canvas jacket. "Do you reckon your wheels will still be attached to the car when we get back?"

Quist smiled. Although it was bitterly cold, he left his overcoat in the vehicle and pushed aside an abandoned shopping trolley to enter the lobby of the building. The main door had been smashed so many times, the authorities no longer bothered to repair it.

Although they categorically deny the practise, British councils have always grouped together certain types of individuals in their rental housing programme. Spittal Court housed Hull's 'problem tenants', the majority of whom had chosen a lifestyle that didn't involve work. Most partied, or slumped in front of loud televisions all night, and retired to bed at daybreak in a vampire-like existence of state benefits, cheap booze and strong weed. Watson walked with Quist along a graffiti-covered corridor, warily eyeing the doors on either side. Pounding music blared from many of the flats and the stink of ammonia suggested the passage was regularly mistaken for a lavatory.

"Here we go," said Quist, approaching one of the doors and ringing the bell.

Watson looked around as they waited. He wondered why a hosepipe lay amongst the human faeces, beer cans and other corridor litter, then realised the residents had ripped it from the vandalised locker of firefighting equipment. Most of the lights were also broken, but it would be difficult to break the steel-barred security gate that protected *this* door. Kareem Fadel lived in the more upmarket area of Kingswood, but this was the gentleman's business address.

A large Asian man appeared behind the gate. Around thirty years old, with engorged, tattooed biceps, he gripped a pair of chains restraining two huge dogs. The facial scarring suggested these muscular animals paid for their keep by maiming and killing other dogs in organised fights and, despite the bars that separated them, Watson moved back. He guessed they wouldn't be averse to also maiming and killing people. Pit-bulls have been illegal since the *Dangerous Dogs Act* banned them, but owners circumvented the law with false pedigree papers, or by simply not giving a shit.

"Yeah?" The thug eyed the two men curiously. "So what do you two want?"

"Good evening," said Quist. "Would I be correct in thinking you're Kareem?"

"No, I'm Hasan. You might say I'm Kareem's private security advisor. I'll ask again – what do you twats want? You don't look like customers or cops."

"Correct," said Quist. "No, our interests lie in the whereabouts of a certain young lady. We've been led to understand she currently resides…"

"You *what*?" snarled Hasan.

"Sorry," said Watson. "He talks a bit posh, doesn't he? We're looking for Jocasta Laine. We've heard she's here, so I'm wondering if we could speak to her and…"

"And I'm wondering if you could fuck off," said Hasan. "Right now."

"Honestly…" Quist feigned offence. "Well, that isn't very polite, is it? If you could just be good enough to let Miss Laine know we're here, I'd be…"

"Well if you won't listen to *me*…" Unlocking the gate, Hasan let the chains slip through his fist and allowed the dogs to lurch forward. "Maybe you'll listen to Lockjaw and Asbo?"

Watson had never been the bravest of youths and there was a time, not so long ago, when he'd have been petrified here. Potentially violent situations no longer scared him these days, at least, not whenever the boss was around. He took a step to the left, strategically positioning himself behind the detective.

Quist immediately dropped into a crouch. "Good doggies," he said, holding out a hand for them to smell. "Well, aren't you two good boys?"

Hasan watched aghast as the animals cautiously sniffed the fingers, then quickly bowed their heads, lowering themselves into a trembling, deferential posture. Most animals ran a mile whenever they sensed Bernard Quist, but the more vicious creatures didn't seem to mind his presence and always became submissive. It had been a long time since he'd been able to stroke a dog and he really missed it. Lockjaw noticed Watson behind the detective and began to snarl, eyeing the young man's throat the way some larger ladies eye the restaurant sweet trolley.

"No, no, no." Quist murmured into the animal's ear, instantly calming it. He softly stroked its neck. "He's much too skinny to eat, isn't he?"

"Wonderful." Watson shook his head in disbelief. "It turns out you're a monster whisperer."

"What the fuck, you stupid..." Hasan stepped outside the flat and booted the closest dog in the ribs. "Don't you dare lick him. Tear into the bastard like you're trained to do."

"Oh, dear," sighed the detective. Rising from his squat, he swiftly brought up his fist to slam the thug hard beneath the jaw. "I can't tell you how much I despise animal cruelty."

"Bloody hell, Guv." Watson winced to see Hassan lifted four inches off the floor. "Remember your golden rule."

"It's rather more than a *golden rule*, but don't worry. I haven't harmed him too badly." He grabbed the dog chains in one hand and caught hold of the man as he crumpled, sitting him in an unconscious heap against the passage wall. "You really shouldn't kick them. Now why not wait there and have a little nap?"

Watson quickly checked inside the flat to see if anyone had heard the commotion, but the dark room seemed to be empty. Quist led the dogs across the corridor to a broken door hanging from its top hinge and pushed it back to reveal a vacant apartment. He bundled the two animals into the kitchen and closed the door to pen them in

"There," he said. "I've no doubt your loving owner will find you when he awakes. You both have my deepest sympathies."

"Are you still planning to do what you said?" asked Watson. "It could be risky. The moon's almost..."

"Yes, *almost*." Quist gave him a reassuring smile. "It won't be full for three more nights."

Checking that Hasan was still out cold as they passed him, they quietly returned to Kareem Fadel's flat, or more accurately, *flats*.

Watson realised that two neighbouring residences had been knocked through into one, although the hole in the dividing wall, created by a sledgehammer, didn't shout out *council approval* or *planning permission*. The lights were off and metal shutters were fixed over the windows, but this lounge shutter had been prised loose providing a little illumination from a nearby streetlamp.

The room appeared to function as a security area, guarded by Hasan and his two canine pals. Visitors would need to pass through here to reach the merchandise and cash in the 'pharmaceutical business' next door. The grubby place was surprisingly warm, although drug dealers like Kareem and Hasan usually bypassed the electric meter to save themselves the petty annoyance of paying bills.

Sneaking up to the jagged hole in the wall and cautiously glancing through, Watson saw three naked people lying on a filthy inflatable mattress. Lit by the dim glow of a desk lamp, a sleeping Asian man sprawled between two extremely thin girls. The youth recognised the fair-haired, tattooed girl as Jocasta Laine from the photograph provided by her father.

"Unbelievable," he whispered, stepping back from the aperture. "Old Scarface in there has made himself a real fortune from drugs, but he's kipping on a shit-stained airbed. Hey, how the other half live, eh?"

"Yes, we appear to be in luck." Quist tugged off his sweater and passed it to his assistant. "The ideal time to do this is whilst Kareem is enjoying a post-coital doze."

Watson squinted in the darkness, collecting the clothes in his arms as his boss swiftly kicked off shoes and pulled down his trousers. This was something he'd seen many times, but he still felt weird and a little frightened whenever it took place. The fear had nothing to do with his employer's nakedness, but the knowledge of what was to follow this hurried striptease show. Criminal thugs and vicious dogs no longer scared him, but *this* still did. It would have

23

scared *anyone* – it was an ancient, primordial fear imprinted within the human genes.

The temperature noticeably fell and the revolting sound of crackling, twisting bones filled the room. The detective hunched over, grunting and gasping, as his naked form seemingly melted into the darkness, his pale skin vanishing beneath a covering of thick black fur. A lightning flash outside the broken window shutter momentarily revealed the huge creature that now stood in Quist's place, fangs glinting in its huge jutting muzzle. Watson was no stranger to this, but an involuntary crusting of goosebumps rose on his back. Yes, he'd witnessed the transformation on many occasions, but he still couldn't help feeling scared in the presence of a real-life werewolf. He'd just joked about Quist being a *monster whisperer* with the dogs, but his boss was an *actual* monster.

The young man's pulse raced. *Mythology maintained that werewolves only transformed on the full moon, but this was wrong. The lunar phases certainly affected his mood, but the boss and his kind were able to pull off this furry quick-change shit any night between sunset and sunrise.*

"Okay, Guv…" Watson swallowed dryly. "So what's the plan here?"

"Fear," growled the wolf, its amber eyes luminous and smouldering in the dark. The lightning flashed again, highlighting the enormous beast in silver, ironically Quist's least favourite metal. "Extracting the young lady from this undesirable situation would be simple enough, but judging from her father's past failed interventions she'd soon return. If *this* works, she'll hopefully be terrified out of her bad habits."

"A sort of werewolf aversion therapy?" The youth grinned. "Let's hope you're right."

He watched as Quist stooped to step quietly through the hole into the adjoining flat, his muscular bulk filling the opening. The wolf moved into the lamp light at the foot of the airbed, standing erect on two legs with tail swishing from side to side.

Watson noticed the shaggy testicles. *Balls supposedly descended as men grew older and the boss was well over two-hundred. These plums should be dragging on the floor by now, but the lycanthropy clearly spared him this embarrassment.*

Quist gazed at the snoring trio for several seconds. A detritus of empty cans, vodka bottles, cannabis stubs and other drug paraphernalia lay around the airbed, suggesting this would probably be a very *deep* sleep. Reaching down to grab the bottom of the mattress, he effortlessly jerked it out from beneath them, dumping all three on the floor.

"What the hell," yelled Kareem, sitting up. "Hassan, what's going on..." He saw the horrific black figure towering over him and the words dried to a strangled croak.

"I hunger," snarled the drooling wolf. "I've just feasted upon Grandma and now I'm looking for Red Riding Hood." He pointed a furry paw at Jocasta. "Where is she? Tell me NOW."

"*What?*" screamed the girl, her eyes bulging. "I don't know. I don't know. I don't know."

"Jocasta Laine?" Quist moved forward, his evil grin revealing razor teeth. "I like my dinner to taste of heroin. I think I'll eat *you* instead."

Watching from the hole between the apartments, Watson nodded as a combination of narcotics and sheer terror caused all three to pass out. "Nice one, Guv," he muttered. "Nothing sends a junkie to sleep faster than a werewolf sedative."

* * * *

Fully dressed and sporting a much smoother complexion than earlier, Quist drove north along the A1079, his headlights cutting through the torrential rain.

Watson turned in the passenger seat. "Yeah, she's out of it," he said, checking that Jocasta was still asleep in the rear. "Whereabouts in York does her father live?"

"Heworth Green," said Quist. "But we won't be calling on him tonight. I've found a private clinic in Bishopthorpe where she can receive the necessary treatment. We're taking her straight there."

"She certainly needs to receive *something*," snorted Watson. "What an arsehole. Just imagine injecting that shit into your body."

"Well..." The detective raised his eyebrows. "Ten out of ten there for understanding and compassion."

"Hey, I've met addicts with *real* problems, Guv." His assistant laughed cynically. "They came from the kind of crappy childhoods and backgrounds that you wouldn't believe. This is a good-looking, clever bird who went to a poncy private school. Her dad bought her a Porsche for her seventeenth and she *still* got herself hooked on smack. She sold the car for drug cash and, instead of living in daddy's big house, she lives in a shithole, shagging some scumbag dealer on a piss-stained mattress."

"A fair point," conceded Quist. "Eloquently argued."

The contrast in personalities puzzled people on meeting these two, but the consultant detective had purposely chosen his employee because of it. Bernard Quist had lived alone for decades, changing identities at regular intervals and moving around to protect his supernatural secret. Lengthy friendships were awkward for a man who never aged, and constantly striving to remain beneath the radar had left him feeling lost and isolated from society. He'd needed someone to reconnect him to the modern world and this streetwise youth had turned out to be the perfect choice.

Watson remembered how terrified he'd been on discovering the secret of Quist's furry alter ego, but soon realised there was no need for concern. *Ever since his mauling in 1790, the boss had managed to hang on to his humanity by never consuming meat and, more importantly, by never taking a life. The moment a werewolf killed a human, the blood lust and the evil, bestial side took over the personality. According to the Guv, there was no coming back from the darkness.*

The youth gave Quist a worried look. "I know her dad hired us to find her," he said. "But the thing is, she's seventeen and that kind of makes her an adult. We took her from that drug den without asking her permission, so you realise this is technically a kidnap."

"Where are we?" slurred a voice from the rear seat. "Where's Kareem? Who the fuck are you?"

"Yeah." Watson sighed. "See what I mean?"

Quist pulled over on the empty country lane and hunched forward over the steering wheel, his facial bones crackling as he partially transformed. An icy cold filled the vehicle as wolf ears sprouted and his features extended into a lengthy animal snout. The broad muzzle was unmistakably lupine, yet it always reminded Watson of an alligator, a furry alligator that wasn't particularly friendly.

"Where *are* we?" repeated the detective, his voice a rumbling, angry growl. He turned to Jocasta, exposing his razor-sharp teeth. "We're on our way to visit the three little pigs before dinner. I have to make a building inspection on three houses before I feast upon your delicious flesh."

The girl let out a choked whine and fainted again.

"I hope she hasn't pissed your car seat," said Watson, glancing back. "Sweet dreams, luv. It's scary shit, I know, but believe it or not, you sort of get used to it."

* * * *

27

Chapter 4

The city of York has a quirky description of itself, almost certainly created by the local tourism industry – *a place where the streets are gates, the gates are bars, and the bars are pubs*. To translate this, the Vikings lived here for over a century and surrounded their home with defensive walls. Their thoroughfares were named *gates*, the fortified entrances through the walls are named *barbicans*, or *bars*, and the *pub* part of the narrative requires no explanation.

Standing on a wide plain between the Howardian Hills, the North York Moors and the chalk Wolds, this is a truly beautiful city. But just as Hull has its Fenbrook, and in the same way you might find a grubby mark on a work of fine art, York has the Grimpen housing estate in the western suburb of Acomb. This ancient city overflows with exquisite architecture – Elizabethan, Georgian, Victorian and Tudor – but the post-war designers of Grimpen decided to introduce another building style into the mix: grey prefab concrete.

The dark red Range Rover cruised along Grimpen's main street, Oliver Tarrant slaloming around half-feral dog packs, discarded bottles and the occasional shopping trolley. It was a little after eight in the morning and the estate was fairly quiet this freezing Thursday, with the majority of the residents still tucked up in their beds. Many would remain warmly tucked up until after twelve noon. Some until after five o'clock when the evening television began.

"What do you suppose happened to the transponder?" asked Tarrant. "You fixed it under Quist's car outside his office and it was fine all the way to Hull. Why would it suddenly stop working like that?"

"God knows." Richard Brunton shrugged as he consulted a street map. "I suppose it could have been dislodged as he went over a speed hump or whatever, but it should still have continued to transmit even if it were lying in a gutter. Anyway, it doesn't matter. We have Quist's address in case anything should go wrong here."

Tarrant peered at the graffiti, the ubiquitous satellite dishes and torn trampolines. Someone had left a broken fridge in the middle of the pavement, unusual, as the majority of folk here seemed to dump their broken fridges in their own gardens beside their broken cookers. On a Monopoly Board, it was safe to say that *Grimpen* wouldn't cost the players as much as *Mayfair* or *Park Lane*. Tarrant turned into Bruce Crescent, one of the nicer streets on the estate.

"Just here," said Brunton, looking up from his map and pointing. "Number 22."

"This is the Watson kid's place?" asked Tarrant, pulling up.

"No." His colleague sighed irritably as he checked his watch. "I thought I'd have you park outside some random house. It's pretty early so he shouldn't have left for work yet. Come on, let's do this."

The two men climbed from the warmth of the vehicle interior, both tugging on black leather jackets and zipping them up against the biting December cold.

"Be friendly." Brunton sported a false smile. "Remember, we're new clients that he hasn't met and his boss has sent us here to collect him."

"Yes, I know the plan." Tarrant nodded, stunned that Brunton should have the sheer audacity to speak of *friendliness*. "We're supposed to give this Watson a lift to Quist's location, but it still sounds too contrived. What if the kid wants to confirm it by ringing his boss?"

The big man's smile grew tighter with exasperation. "Then we say we're running late and that he can ring him in the car. As soon as we get him in there, you zap him with the stun gun and away we go."

"That won't be a problem." Tarrant opened the garden gate and frowned to see the weird collection of resin gnomes on either side of the path. An advertising sign, erected on the grass, directed potential customers to a website. "Wow, just look at these things?"

"Never mind this shit." His colleague pushed him through the gateway. "We need to get it done quickly."

These knee-high figurines were very different to the *normal* gnomes found in garden centres and shops. Walking to the house, the two men passed a gnome injecting heroin, another buggering a squirrel, an escaped prisoner with a spade tunnelling out of the frozen lawn, and a mad cat lady surrounded by several miniature felines. Food delivery gnomes on pushbikes stood on the grass, a homeless gnome wrapped in a sleeping bag sat in a cardboard box, and a drowned gnome with swollen features floated in the pond.

Tarrant gripped the Taser stun gun in his jacket pocket and watched nervously as Brunton rang the bell. An attractive black woman in a white towelling robe opened the door, smiling sexily at her visitors. The belted dressing gown was short, showing off her shapely dark legs.

"Merry Christmas." She looked Brunton up and down. "Well, you're a big boy, aren't you?"

"Hi." He gave her his best friendly grin, something similar to a startled chimp. "Mrs Watson?"

"That's right." She noticed Tarrant gaping at the military gnomes abseiling down the wall, and the suicidal gnome dangling in its noose from a nearby bush. "Yes, they're all my own work. Are you here to buy one?"

"I'm afraid not," said Tarrant. "No, we're looking for a young man named John Watson."

"My son?" A fat ginger cat strolled by the woman's leg and she stooped to scoop it up, cradling the indignant animal on its back like a scowling baby. "So what's it about? You're not cops, are you? Is he in some sort of trouble?"

"No, it's a private matter," said Brunton. "As you know, he

works for a detective agency. We can't tell you much, but suffice to say our visit is work-related."

"Whatever it's related to, he isn't in." She stroked the cat's neck. "He spent the night at some girl's house. I don't know who and I don't know where."

"I see." Tarrant sighed. "When are you expecting him back?"

"God knows, luv. He comes and goes as he pleases." Mrs Watson tickled the ginger fur on the purring cat's head. "Just like Hucknall here."

"Okay, thanks." Brunton checked his watch. "I'm sure we'll catch up with him later. Merry Christmas."

Mrs Watson watched them head back to their car. "Hey, who shall I say called?"

Ignoring the question, Brunton jumped into the Range Rover and grabbed the map. "So it looks like we're going for Plan B," he said.

"Yeah, the far more dangerous option." Tarrant climbed back behind the wheel, switched off the Taser in his pocket and took out his hip flask. "Listen, why don't we just wait here until the kid shows up? We can park further along the street there and…"

"And what if he doesn't show up?" snarled Brunton. "You know we don't have the time to wait and see if…" Angrily snatching the flask from his colleague, he opened the glove compartment and shoved it inside. "I've told you to stop drinking that. There won't be any left if we should need it."

* * * *

Chapter 5

Askham Richard gets a mention in the celebrated Domesday Book of 1086, although visitors could be forgiven for wondering why. The small village lies in open countryside a few miles to the west of York, a pretty collection of limestone cottages clustered around a 12th century church, an old inn and a traditional green complete with a duck pond.

Bernard Quist's home, the ivy-clad Briar Cottage, stood isolated on the village outskirts set back from the rural lane. With a tangle of rambling roses draped over the front porch and a thick growth of wisteria covering the east gable, this was the sort of picturesque house that photographers often chose for jigsaw puzzles. Today it would be a Christmassy jigsaw, as the weak morning sun had yet to thaw the white coating of frost on the foliage and roof tiles. Quist's blue Ford car was parked in front of the cottage and, one-hundred yards away, partly concealed in a field gateway on the quiet lane, Brunton and Tarrant watched from their Range Rover.

Sitting behind the wheel, Tarrant broke the lengthy silence. "We've been away for far too long." He flexed his fingers nervously and massaged the skin on his hand. "How do *you* feel?"

"I'm fine," grunted Brunton. "If you feel any different it's just nerves combined with your frightened imagination and..." He glared as Tarrant reached into the glove compartment. "No! Leave the water where it is. You don't need it and there's hardly any left."

"But you know we're cutting it really close." Tarrant grudgingly took his hand from the hip flask. "Our time here in Yorkshire is almost up. Snatching his assistant would have been so much simpler."

"I fully agree," sighed Brunton. "But we couldn't just sit around on that estate hoping he'd turn up. I suppose you're right - we *have* been away from the Fountain for too long. I can't see how this could fail, but if it *does*, we'll head straight back there and leave the other team to handle things."

"Their approach is probably the best idea anyway." Tarrant peered anxiously at the cottage. "Crane warned us. She said that attempting to use force like this would be a bad move."

"It's broad daylight," snorted Brunton. "What can he do?"

"He'll still be fast and strong, even during the day."

The big man laughed. "I'm pretty fast and strong myself. Also, I've no intention of tackling him in the open,"

"She said there was no need for any of this. Quist would probably agree to visit us if we just asked him."

"But he might *not*," snapped Brunton. "The 21st is only two days away, so we need him right *now*. I know what Crane said, but we don't have the luxury of time and snatching him like this is the easiest way."

"Hey!" Tarrant sat up straight. "There he is."

Quist appeared from the front door wearing a black leather trenchcoat. They waited as he locked the cottage and scraped the ice from his car windscreen. Brunton smiled at Tarrant, then switched on his Taser stun gun, blue electricity crackling between the twin prongs.

"Right, here we go," he said, watching as the detective climbed into the car and drove away. "Get after him right now."

Quickly starting the engine, Tarrant pulled out of the field gateway to follow. The hedgerows and overgrown verges on either side looked to have been painted white and the multitude of spider webs sprinkled with diamonds. Under different circumstances, he'd have found it all quite pretty.

"Okay," said Brunton, gripping the stun gun. "You need to put your foot down, get in front and force him to stop. I'll go to the window to talk and then hit him with *this*. Like you say, he's fast and strong, but he can't do much if he's sitting in the car and tethered by a seat belt."

Cruising along the winding lane, Quist glanced in the mirror and smiled thinly to see the familiar red Range Rover coming up behind him fast. It pulled out to overtake, but he accelerated to prevent this and the two cars began racing side-by-side. Quist grimaced, acutely aware that, at any second, a vehicle travelling in the opposite direction could disastrously appear around the bend in front of them.

"Come on, floor it," shouted Brunton. "Do it. Get by him *now.*"

The detective was well acquainted with this quiet lane and the black ice that formed overnight in sub-zero temperatures. The patches were always in the same shaded areas and one particularly treacherous spot lay around the curve ahead, just before the T junction. Quist braked suddenly as the intersection came into view, his car slewing sickeningly on the frozen tarmac. The Range Rover flew on by at high speed before Tarrant braked too and then let out a strangled whimper as nothing happened. Skidding straight across the icy junction, he heard the deafening bang, but didn't see the collision – his eyes were screwed shut and his face was buried in an exploding airbag.

"What the *fuck...*" shouted Brunton. "What..."

He'd been looking back over his shoulder, watching Quist's car. Momentarily stunned, he pushed aside his own deployed airbag and peered at the roadside tree through the cracked windscreen and hissing radiator steam. With steel cage bodywork and more airbags than you could count on fingers and toes, these motors were built to withstand impacts, but apparently not impacts of over fifty mph into oak trees with diameters of four feet.

"I don't believe this," he seethed.

"I'm hurt," moaned Tarrant, realising both his legs were trapped beneath the crumpled dashboard. "One of my thighs... I think one is broken. You have to help me get out of this."

"Shut up," hissed Brunton. "You need to wait here." He tried

34

the passenger door, but the bent chassis had jammed it. "This car is finished, but we can take Quist's."

The electric window was still operational and, lowering it, he squeezed through and dropped in a heap onto the grass verge.

"Good morning," said Quist, appearing by his side and stooping to take his arm. "Please, allow me to assist you."

Feigning wooziness, Brunton let him help, climbing unsteadily to his feet and concealing the stun gun with his muscular bulk.

"These rural lanes can be quite icy on winter mornings," said Quist. "Perhaps you shouldn't have been driving so fast and attempting to run me off the…"

The big man wheeled around to stab the Taser into the detective's midriff, Fast as he was, he was still too slow. His wrist was caught in Quist's grip and painfully twisted until he released the weapon.

"That was rather rude," muttered Quist.

Brunton threw a punch with his free fist, but Quist blocked it, slammed him against the wrecked car and slapped him hard across the face, snapping his nose sideways. Brunton let out a yelp of pain and sheer surprise – he was used to hurting people, but couldn't recall the last time anyone had hurt *him*.

"Alright, that's enough foolishness," said Quist. "Who are you people? You've been following me since yesterday and now you try to run me off the road. I'd say you have some explaining to do."

The big man answered with a sarcastic laugh, blood pouring from his broken nose.

"This vehicle is registered to Oliver Tarrant." Quist stooped to peer in at the injured, groaning driver. "Would that be one of you two gentlemen?

The pair remained silent and the detective nodded resignedly.

"Very well…" Pinning Brunton against the car, he rummaged

through the pockets of his leather jacket, searching for identification. "Why don't we take a look here and see..." He pulled out a pair of handcuffs and immediately dropped them, wincing with pain as his fingers sizzled.

"Oops!" Brunton grinned. "Did that hurt?"

"I'll ask again," snapped Quist, shaking him roughly. "Who *are* you and what's going on? This was clearly some attempt at abduction. Your dangerous driving, the stun gun and those handcuffs all point to that, but why? More to the point, why did you bring handcuffs that are made from silver?"

A police car sped by them and vanished around the bend. It was travelling fast, but not so fast that the female officer didn't notice the crashed car and the two men standing beside it, one of whom clearly appeared to be assaulting the other.

"Damn!" muttered Quist, hearing the patrol car brake and fully aware that she was about to return. He didn't want any involvement with the authorities. "Goodbye for now," he said. "I've no doubt we'll be continuing this conversation in the near future."

Jumping into his car, the detective drove away in the opposite direction to the police vehicle.

"Get me out of here," shouted Tarrant from the wreck.

"Without tools? How the hell am I supposed to do that?" Leaning through the window, Brunton opened the glove compartment and grabbed the hip flask. "I'll take that."

"Give it to me," stammered Tarrant. "Didn't you hear what I said? My leg is broken and..."

"And my nose hurts like hell. Thanks to you guzzling this, there isn't enough left for broken bones." Brunton vanished through a gap in the hedge as the police car reappeared and pulled up by the accident. "I need to find a car rental firm," he laughed. "You're on your own, pal. Good luck."

* * * *

36

Chapter 6

"Ah, here he is – Sex on Legs." Watson's mother opened the kitchen door to Quist in her white dressing gown, her dark eyes twinkling as she slowly looked him up and down. "Merry Christmas. You're the third good-looking guy to call on my Johnny boy this morning."

"Really?" The detective gave an awkward laugh as he entered. "Well, how about that?"

He followed her into the dining area, his lengthy leather overcoat flapping about him like a vampire's black cloak. A loud musical programme played on the kitchen counter-top television, with the same show blaring from the lounge screen and at least one of the bedrooms upstairs. Like most of the Grimpen estate houses, every television in the Watson homestead was permanently switched on.

"Yeah." Mrs Watson eyed him sexily. "I reckon it must be *Hunk Thursday*. Two guys in a Range Rover were here earlier looking for my lad and one of them was huge. When I say *huge*, I mean tall and muscular, not..."

"Yes, I got that," said Quist, quickly. "Who were they?"

"Dunno." She shrugged. "They said it was something about work, but they didn't give their names. I asked too."

"I see." The detective knew exactly who this must have been and wondered why they would call upon his assistant. "I'd hazard a guess that their vehicle was dark red?"

"Actually it *was*; ooh, you must be psychic." She ran her eyes over him again, pursing her lips. "So what am *I* thinking right now?"

He cleared his throat. "You're probably thinking: is he here to give my son a lift, and indeed I am. It would be pointless him taking his usual bus to the office. We have to visit a client on Blossom Street."

Watson appeared from the lounge eating a slice of toast and

noticed Quist's pensive expression. "Happy birthday, Guv." He licked a lump of marmalade from his thumb. "Hey, is everything okay?"

"Everything is fine." Quist laughed dryly. "But it's been something of a curious morning so far. I had a little excitement on my way here..."

"It's your birthday?" Watson's mum raced forward, "Well, come here for a little *more* excitement."

She planted a huge wet kiss on his mouth, the detective tensing as her tongue unexpectedly massaged his tonsils. Watson turned away, cringing with embarrassment. His mum had always been attracted to Quist, but he knew this was partly due to the supernatural aura his boss emitted. Women were unconsciously drawn to his dark lupine side, but it didn't make it any easier or less mortifying.

"I'm thirty-eight," said Mrs Watson, huskily. "I'm guessing you're a little more mature. So which birthday is this one then?"

"Um..." The detective politely disentangled himself from her embrace. "To be honest, I lost count after my thirtieth."

"Speaking of exciting," she said. "You're a man..."

"Guilty as charged," he agreed, warily.

"So tell me, what do you think of *these*?" She opened her towelling robe wide and Quist's eyes widened too to see the lacy white underwear beneath. "They're brand new. I got them from Skanxxx, that new designer underwear shop on Coney Street."

Watson choked. "Bloody hell, mum," he stammered, spitting toast.

"I like them," she said, "but I could do with a man's opinion. After all, they're not really for *me*."

"*I'm* a man," pointed out her son. "You could have asked me."

"Well..." She gave Quist a suggestive smile. "You're not really the target audience."

The awkward atmosphere was broken by a frightened feline

squawk. Hucknall the fat ginger cat saw Quist and bolted for the kitchen door. Most animals panicked and vanished on sensing the detective's aura, but Hucknall slammed into the cat flap and fell back stunned.

"Weird," said Mrs Watson, bemused. "He always does that when you call here, but that cat flap is sticking again." She picked up the half-conscious animal and turned to Quist with a mischievous wink. "Here you go. How would you like to stroke my..."

"Right, that's it," blurted Watson, pushing his boss towards the door. "Off we go. See you later, Mum."

* * * *

"Silver handcuffs?" gasped Watson. "Wow! So if they came after you with *those*, then these twats must know all about the big bad wolf shit?"

"Indeed." Quist drove along Acomb Lane, heading from the Grimpen estate towards central York. "That would certainly appear to be the case."

"So the question is: *how* do they know? Who do you suppose they are?"

"Unfortunately, the police arrived and I didn't have time to question them. I presume one was called Oliver Tarrant. As I told you last night, your friend Lestrade checked the Range Rover license plate for me and it's registered to someone of that name."

"Yeah, in Northumberland." Watson nodded. "You told me, but remember, if they were trying to kidnap you, then the car could be stolen, or the number plate could be fake."

The youth peered thoughtfully through the windscreen at the distant York Minster, wondering what on earth these two men could be doing calling at his house earlier.

Bright white, and resembling a gigantic iced wedding cake, the Minster was the largest Gothic cathedral in Europe and there were few areas of the city, or indeed the surrounding countryside, where it *wasn't* possible to see the 13th century towers soaring hundreds of feet above the rooftops. Watson had heard how this gigantic building could be viewed from both Leeds and Sheffield, the latter city being forty miles away, although he suspected the viewer would require exceptional vision, a *very* clear day, and they'd probably have to stand on a tower block... on their tiptoes.

The youth smirked. *Quist was always rambling on about this "amazing" cathedral and what an "incredible" city this was. It was probably because he was still something of a newcomer.*

Over the decades, his boss had needed to move around and he'd lived in many places before settling in the village on the outskirts of York. Quist had immediately fallen in love with the city, the narrow cobbled streets and snickleways, and he constantly talked of the rich history. The Romans founded the original settlement and called it Eboracum. After they left, the Angles renamed it Eoforwic, meaning the place of many wild boar – a pretty silly idea, decided Watson, as Britain teemed with these animals back then and *any* woodland could have been given the same name. Later, under the Viking rule, it became known as Jorvik, which eventually changed to York.

Quist lit a cigarette and cracked the side window to draw out the smoke. "I don't like it," he said, angrily. "Before they turned up at my cottage, those two men visited *your* house. That concerns me greatly. Did they intend to abduct you too?"

"I've just been thinking about that," admitted Watson. "I'm glad I was still over at Donni's place. Apart from silver, fire and getting your head chopped off, there isn't much that can hurt *you*. You can handle yourself too, but I don't reckon I'd be much good against a stun gun, and definitely not against the big muscly twat you described."

Thinking about the Guv *handling himself*, Watson wondered what would happen if he ever hit someone too hard in such a situation and accidentally killed them. *He still wasn't sure how all this lycanthropy shit worked. If the Guv killed someone in his wolf form using teeth or claws, he'd lose his human side and the lupine darkness would take over. But what about if someone fell and banged their head after a punch? Or what if the boss shot someone? Or ran over them in his car? Have supernatural rules, by all means, but surely there should be some sort of explanatory handbook?*

"Silver handcuffs?" he murmured. "Complete strangers knowing about your shapeshifting shit? We need to have a good think about this together and work out what's going on. Remember, two heads are better than one." He winked. "Especially if those two heads belong to girls."

Quist tutted. "Yes, *I'm* glad you were out," he said. "It's safe to say they came looking for you because you work for me, and that would have made me responsible for any harm that befell you."

"Ah, you worry too much. I'm a big boy." He grinned. "Or so Donni tells me."

The detective smiled. "Speaking of which, how did the *hot date* go?"

"Yeah, great." Watson nodded. "I took Donni for a few lagers and an Indian and then spent the night at her place. Mind you, I regretted having the vindaloo this morning. Honestly, that curry came out of me like a flock of starlings."

Quist's eyes widened as he tried not to picture this... and failed. His phone buzzed and, tugging it from his jacket, he saw Gareth Lestrade's name and passed it to his assistant.

"Gazza, my mate." Watson switched it to the speaker. "How's it going?"

"Things are good, as usual," said Lestrade. "Your boss rang me last night and asked if I could trace the serial number on some transponder. It's a KT."

"Hey." Watson turned to Quist. "I once dated a girl called

41

Katie."

"The unit was bought three days ago on Monday, along with some other tracking devices, by someone paying cash. The store was Goodhall's Electrical in Newcastle."

"Newcastle?" The detective nodded. "And your DVLA check showed the Range Rover is registered to someone living in a village north of there."

"Yeah, Oliver Tarrant," confirmed Lestrade. "I looked into this guy like you asked, but there isn't anything about him on the internet. I checked with the cops to see if he has a criminal record, which he doesn't…"

"I wonder if you could check the York Hospital computer?" interrupted Quist. "He had a collision this morning which…"

"Which, if you'll let me finish, appeared on the police website literally minutes ago and it's the main reason I'm ringing you. An accident report was logged about his car hitting a tree outside Askham Richard village. Tarrant was driving and he's been taken to the hospital with two fractured femurs. The officer noticed two other men, who both vanished, and another vehicle parked at the scene."

"Do they have a registration for this other car?" asked Quist, hoping the answer was *no*.

"Afraid not."

"I see," said the detective, relieved. "Now I'm aware this must be a long shot, but is it possible to track in reverse, so to speak? I mean, is there any way you could use the serial number on the transponder to trace the people with the receiver?"

"Sorry," laughed Lestrade. "Not a chance, mate. Transponder equipment has come a long way in this digital age. With KT, you simply download their app onto any phone, pop in the serial number of the tracking device and away you go. I'm afraid it doesn't work the other way around."

"Understood," sighed Quist. "Well, thank you for that,

Gareth. I'll be seeing you in the near future with your usual fee."

Anyone eavesdropping on the conversation could be forgiven for wondering how Watson's friend could possibly view encrypted police records and other highly secure websites, but there was seemingly nothing that Gareth Lestrade couldn't illegally hack. His regular profession involved troubleshooting computer problems for wealthy companies, but his income was occasionally boosted by payments from Quist for these no-questions-asked jobs.

"Broken legs, eh?" said Watson, thumbing off the phone. "It looks like we're in for a trip to the hospital. I suppose we'd better buy a bag of grapes."

"Broken femurs are quite serious," said Quist. "Depending on the damage, they can be life-threatening. We need to give them time to work on the injuries and stabilise him before we visit."

"So later today? He isn't going to be signing himself out and vanishing with that kind of damage to the undercarriage, is he?"

The detective nodded. "I'm looking forward to an enlightening chat with Mister Tarrant. During our brief encounter this morning we were never formally introduced."

* * * *

Chapter 7

Constructed upon Roman foundations and rising high upon their grassy embankments, the limestone walls of York date back to the thirteenth century and encircle the city centre. Resembling small white castles, several fortified entrances punctuate the two-mile elliptical course of the ramparts, Bootham, Walmgate, Monkgate and Micklegate being the largest of these barbican towers. Built in the twelfth century, Micklegate Bar stands an imposing four storeys tall and has always been the traditional access for any visiting monarch.

Tourists love to photograph these ancient gateways, but they probably wouldn't have been so keen in the old days when the towers regularly sported human heads. Henry Hotspur Percy and Richard Plantagenet were two of the more famous celebrities to adorn Micklegate. The rotting heads would often be joined by arms, legs and other bits of traitors, hacked off during the *quartering* part of that ever-popular execution method known as 'hanging, drawing and quartering'. Such gory and, to be quite honest, *politically incorrect* decorations were now fortunately consigned to history books and, instead of stinking body parts, a sparkling curtain of Christmas lights had been draped over the barbican stonework.

Watson smiled warmly to see the twinkling festive scene as his boss drove along Blossom Street.

"Exquisite, isn't it?" said the detective, gesturing. "This city really *is* filled with splendour."

"Yeah," agreed Watson, proudly. "It's like the famous old saying: *if it's not Yorkshire, it's shite.*"

"I wonder who coined *that* expression?" Quist raised his eyebrows. "One of the Bronte sisters, I would imagine." Before reaching the barbican tower, he pulled across the wide road in a U-turn to park on a cobbled area outside the Bar Convent. "I'll just finish this before we call on our legal friend," he said, smoking his cigarette.

"Marvellous," grunted his assistant, scowling at the dashboard hi-fi. "We can listen to more of this classical shit of yours as we wait. Don't you have *any* modern stuff?"

"Modern?" Quist blew smoke through the open window. "You mean like Abba or the Beatles?"

"Bloody hell, Guv." Watson laughed. "You're so old, aren't you? Abba *sang* about Waterloo, but you were probably *there*."

"Actually I wasn't," said Quist. "But I did once meet Wellington and, I have to say, I didn't much care for the fellow."

"Wellington?" The youth smirked. "Hey, didn't he have something named after him?"

"Yes, the sandwich."

"Hey there you go." Watson clapped his hands in a short round of applause. "You used to be like a dreary wet rag when I first met you and just look at you now – you're cracking semi-funny jokes. You hired me to draw you out of your shell and this is kind of like the ending of *Mary Poppins*. I reckon my work here is done."

"Dreary, but now semi-funny?" Quist nodded slowly. "Good to know." Taking one final puff on his cigarette, he tossed the stub into the gutter and raised the window. "Well, don't go resigning and flying away on your umbrella just yet. You have a multitude of other practical uses than just keeping me grounded in the modern world."

"I've got to say…" Watson shook his head in puzzlement. "You're pretty calm about everything, Guv. You don't seem too bothered about those guys trying to grab you earlier. Two guys who obviously know all about your um, furry *other* self."

"On the contrary," said Quist, climbing out of the car, "I'm extremely concerned, but I don't intend to show it."

"Cool and composed, eh?" The young man grinned. "Yeah, I suppose it's pointless you biting your fingernails. They'd instantly grow back."

The detective smiled too. "Believe me, as soon as we're finished here, we'll be devoting our full attention to the matter."

Watson jumped out and peered up at the ornate frontage of the convent. Catholicism had been illegal when this place was secretly opened in 1686 so someone back then had clearly been extremely brave or very stupid. He'd occasionally seen the nuns from here in town and wondered why *anyone* would want to become a 'Bride of Christ' in the twenty-first century, turning their back upon the modern *real* world and devoting their entire life to God.

The youth nodded thoughtfully. *Given the chance, he'd soon cure them of such silliness. Not all of them, of course, just the younger, sexy ones who looked like Julie Andrews in the Sound of Music.*

They walked along to the neighbouring terrace where Laine's Solicitors stood halfway along the row, a three-storey Regency building with a smart white door and window shutters.

"I haven't seen Junkie Jocasta's dad since he called at the office," said Watson. "So this is his legal firm, is it?"

"Correct." Quist pushed open the door, lowering his voice as they entered the reception area. "By the way, it would probably be prudent if you didn't refer to this gentleman's pride and joy as *Junkie Jocasta.*"

"Whoops!" He gave a sheepish grin. "Understood."

"Good morning." The detective smiled at the Indian girl behind the front desk. "And a very merry Christmas to you. Quist is the name. I telephoned earlier and we have an appointment with Mister Laine," He gestured to the open office door at the end of the room where the solicitor could be seen talking to a young man. "I can see he's busy, but how long do you suppose he'll be?"

"Yes, Peter's with a client." She climbed to her feet. "But he said I should let him know when you arrived."

Watson followed the girl across the reception, listening to the solicitor's legal conversation with the burly youth.

"So let's be clear…" said Laine, "the police discovered the knife in your pocket, but I don't imagine it was ever *your* knife. I imagine you probably found it that evening. Would you say that was correct?"

"Eh?" The heavily-tattooed client sported that classical thick-as-pigshit expression – the semi-permanent frown and slack-jawed mouth that rarely closed. "What are you talking about. That knife was…"

"Yes, you probably found it," broke in Laine, "It was lying on the pavement and you conscientiously picked it up before someone else came across it and potentially hurt themselves. You were probably thinking of children."

"Children?" The man's eyes flared angrily. "Are you saying I'm a nonce?"

"I'm saying your judgement was impaired by inebriation when you *found* it." He gave the dense thug a pointed look, maintaining the stare until realisation finally began to dawn. "You now appreciate that you should have left the weapon alone and not picked it up out of some misguided sense of civic duty. Is that correct?"

"Ah!" The client smirked. "Well, yeah, that's right."

Watson listened, his eyes widening in sheer amazement. His knowledge of the legal profession had been shaped by television shows, where every crime drama depicts only *two* types of solicitor in the police interviews. One is almost like a shop mannequin, sitting in silence and writing quietly on a pad. They never speak, not even when their client is asked the most ludicrously leading of questions – "Did you kill him?". The *other* solicitor is a smarmy bastard who virtually runs the interview. They constantly snap: "Don't answer that", and "no comment", or "if you're not going to charge my client, we're leaving right now". Watson wasn't a betting person, but would have put money on Peter Laine being the latter type.

"Mister Laine?" The receptionist tapped politely on the door frame. "Mister Quist is here."

"One moment, please." Laine held up a hand, turning back to the leering man. "Thinking back to that night, would you say that you were holding the knife after picking it up and the other gentleman came walking towards you? Perhaps he wasn't watching where he was going?"

The thug nodded. "Yeah, I'd say exactly that."

"And as you were holding this knife in front of you, debating where you might find a bin to safely dispose of the dangerous weapon, would you say it was extremely possible that he might have clumsily lunged forward and, before you could prevent it, this man accidentally walked onto the blade?"

Watson shot Quist a disbelieving look. *It was little wonder these people charged so much cash. Very few normal folk would be able to talk such shit with a straight face.*

Laine patted his client's back, leading him out into the reception area. "Well, I'll leave you with those thoughts. You go and grab yourself a coffee in the lounge and have a good think about what *really* happened that night before we prepare your statement for the court. Now, if you'll excuse me for a few minutes, I need to speak with these people."

The thug noticed Watson as he walked past and, more to the point, noticed the dark shade of his skin. Racial hatred momentarily flared, along with regret that the authorities had taken his favourite stabbing knife and labelled it: *Court Exhibit A.*

Laine waited until he was alone with the two men. "Okay, so how did it go?" he quizzed. "Tell me you managed to find Jocasta?"

"We found her," confirmed Quist. "As you suspected, she was living in Hull with the heroin dealer you told us about. We tracked down his address and last night we managed to extricate her

48

from the, um, disagreeable situation. I've checked her into a private clinic where she…"

"Clinic?" Laine shook his head. "We never discussed anything about clinics."

"No, I made an impromptu decision," explained Quist. "It's a secure unit and also quite expensive, but I was sure you wouldn't mind that. Trust me. Mister Fadel isn't the nicest of people, but without professional help, Jocasta would definitely return to him at the first opportunity."

"She's got herself into a bit of a state with the smack," said Watson, nodding his agreement. "She was talking about seeing big scary monsters and shit. Werewolves, wasn't it, Guv?"

Quist glanced through the office window as his assistant spoke, stiffening slightly as he noticed a black car parked outside the front of the building. Weak sunlight reflected on the tinted glass of the BMW, making it virtually impossible to see who was inside, but the passenger window had been partially lowered and someone was pointing a telephoto camera lens at him.

"Excuse me," said the detective, rushing across the reception. "I won't be a moment."

He was, in fact, a moment too late. The camera lens vanished as the solicitor's door opened and the BMW pulled out into the traffic stream. Quist ran onto the pavement and sighed with exasperation to see the black car cruising away down the road, with a large van behind it obscuring the registration.

They'd definitely been watching him and attempting to take pictures. Oliver Tarrant was in the hospital, but the BMW had a driver and a photographer in the passenger seat. One of them could have been his big friend from earlier. The Range Rover was currently wrapped around a tree, so whoever these people were, they appeared to have access to a fleet of quality vehicles.

* * * *

Chapter 8

Bernard Quist's detective agency on Fishergate faced the medieval perimeter wall of York, standing just sixty feet across the main road from the grass banking and white limestone ramparts. Quist had discovered that office rental was much cheaper here than in the city centre on the other side of these limestone fortifications. Named after the busy thoroughfare that runs through it, the pleasant neighbourhood of Fishergate is filled with Victorian inns, artisan bakers, barbers, restaurants and independent shops.

Jehovah's Fitness – advertising itself as *York's Only Evangelist Fitness Studio* – stood on the corner of Baker Avenue, with Quist's office and a debt collection firm occupying the upper floors of the redbrick building. A poster on the gymnasium door depicted the bizarre image of Jesus, muscular and determined-looking, performing pull-ups on the side bar of a wooden cross. Watson leant out of the open window above it, gazing at the people strolling below and the food delivery cyclists weaving through the stream of cars and sightseeing busses.

York has always been filled with bicycles and, over the years, many careless pedestrians have been knocked down by them rushing along silently. Watson smiled to himself. *These days, if you had an accident with a cyclist, you ended up covered in chicken Madras.*

The Novotel stood just south of the detective agency and a crowd of young women in stilettos tottered into view, almost certainly originating from this large hotel. Hen parties like this were a common weekend sight, with around a dozen every day during the summer months. Despite the freezing temperature, they wore very little in the way of clothing, but sported pink sashes bearing the name *Kelli* and each carried a huge penis-shaped balloon. Watson spotted the blushing bride wearing a white veil and L plates.

"Hey, Kelli," he shouted down. "If he stands you up at the

altar, luv, give me a ring."

"Piss off," she squawked, glancing up from her phone.

The youth laughed. A corresponding stag party would doubtless be roaming another city, where the groom would eventually be stripped naked and handcuffed to a lamppost. There he'd sink into the darkness of alcohol poisoning from the pint of shorts he'd been made to drink. Meanwhile, his betrothed would be spit-roasted behind a late-night kebab shop by two Asian lads who'd film it on their phones for the internet. Watson felt like a misty-eyed romantic – he had a soft spot for all these quaint British traditions that accompanied the institution of marriage.

The young man strolled to the office desk to open a bag of crisps. Quist had been thoughtfully pacing the room since they arrived at the agency and paused to take his place at the window. Several starlings sensed him and took off in a squawking panic from the gutter above.

"Typical," he muttered, seeing the departing hen party and shaking his head with irritation. "Everyone that passes here has a phone in their hand. The majority are staring at one, but all of them are *holding* one, almost as if their lives depend upon it. I'm all for technological advancement, but why on earth can't they pop them away in a pocket for just two minutes? Honestly, they ought to change the name of Fishergate to *Phonergate*." He chuckled at his poor joke. "What do you think?"

The question was met with silence and, turning, he sighed to see Watson staring at his phone.

"You want one, Guv?" The youth glanced up from his social media to offer his crisps. "You're walking up and down thinking about those blokes who attacked you and, as we all know, food helps you think. They're ready salted, not beef, smoky bacon, or anything like that."

"No, thank you," said Quist, frowning as his assistant jumped up to sit on the desk; Watson constantly ate junk, yet somehow remained wiry and healthy. "I have a salad sandwich and a couple of apples in my coat pocket."

"Wow," mumbled the youth. "Lucky old you. I bet you can't wait."

His boss used yoga meditation to remain in control of his lupine side, but for the same reason, he wasn't able to eat meat, nor any animal product. Watson recalled how his boring geography teacher, had been a vegan too – Mister Horne, or *Mister Yawn*, as he was known to the kids. *Weirdly, the Guv wore a very similar bland jacket and trousers.*

"A girlfriend of mine is into all that vegetarian crap," he said, chomping a crisp. "She's also started attending church and she now calls herself a *Quorn-again Christian.*"

"Oh, that's quite good," admitted Quist, lighting a cigarette. "For you."

"What do you mean – for *me*?"

Smiling, the detective turned to stare again through the window. "If only I'd managed to see their registration."

"The BMW outside the solicitor's?" Watson stowed his phone in his jeans and rubbed his hands together briskly. "So we have mysterious people tailing us and taking pictures. Yeah, it's nice to have the excitement back, eh?"

"I'd say that strangers knowing about my *condition* is rather more perturbing than exciting." Quist blew cigarette smoke. "Besides, many of the cases we investigate *are* exciting."

"*Some* of the cases. Since I started working here, we've been involved in thirteen divorces. Can you believe that?" Watson let out a dry laugh. "Thirteen."

Quist smiled thinly. "I seem to recall you being terrified of the *exciting* cases."

"Hey, that was back then. As the time's gone by, I've grown

used to all the weird, supernatural shit."

Quist nodded. "Fortunately, you've also grown used to answering doors. Get that, would you?"

"Get what?" Watson gave a baffled frowned, then sighed as a knock sounded in the outer office. "Yeah, you get me with that shit every time – hearing people coming quietly along the corridor when us humans can't." He strolled through the empty reception area and opened the door to find a strikingly beautiful young woman. "Well, hello there. Hey, this is weird; I don't recall ordering a supermodel."

"Hello yourself." The caller was elegantly dressed, with lengthy red hair, green eyes and a self-assured smile. "I'm guessing you must be Watson?"

"Oh, I must," he said, grinning. He guessed her age to be mid-twenties. "Er, I mean, *yes*. Hey, listen, why don't you come on in?"

"Good morning." Quist ran an eye over the girl as she appeared in the main office and held up his cigarette. "I really must apologise for this. Would it be best if I got rid of it?"

"Absolutely not." She took out her own cigarettes. "I've been a smoker myself for many years."

"*Many?*" echoed Watson. "Your school playground must have had very relaxed rules."

"I overheard the exchange out there," said Quist. "I'm curious – how did you know my assistant's name?"

"Watson?" She unbuttoned her expensive black coat to reveal an even more expensive white suit. "I saw it on your website."

"I set up that site," said Watson, proudly. "I've made a few recent tweaks to it, Guv. I popped my name on there, and added the *private eyes* on the title page that look from side to side when you hover your cursor over them."

"Yes, I've noticed those," drawled Quist. "I keep meaning to tell you to get rid of them. So how can we help you, Miss…"

"*Mrs* Penrose," she corrected him, lighting a cigarette.

"Rachel Penrose. I have an awful suspicion that my husband is seeing someone else."

Watson rolled his eyes. *"Fourteen,"* he mumbled to himself. He wasn't keen on girls who smoked, but if *this* particular one twisted his arm, he'd still be prepared to have sex with her.

"I'm sorry to hear that." Quist sat behind his desk and gestured to one of the chairs. "Would you like a coffee?"

"Sure. No milk or sugar." Sitting opposite the detective, she crossed her legs and watched Watson head for the kettle. "Just black and hot."

Hey, he's asking about coffee." The youth laughed. "He doesn't want your description of me."

Quist visibly winced.

"My husband is Reece Penrose." Smiling at the joke, Rachel drew on her cigarette. "We live in York and he's attending a conference up in Newcastle on the 20th tomorrow. He told me he was staying overnight in the city, but I checked his phone when he was showering and found he's booked into a village hotel miles away from Newcastle. It's in the middle of nowhere."

Watson nodded resignedly. "Ah, so many folk are caught that way," he said, spooning coffee into three mugs. "I blame the phone manufacturers. It's time they made them fully waterproof so we could take them in the shower with us."

"An isolated hotel?" Quist nodded slowly. "I presume you believe he may be meeting someone there? Have you confronted him with your suspicions?"

"No, I haven't." Rachel lazily blew smoke. "I want to be sure of my facts before I mention anything."

"I have to say…" grinned Watson. "If *I* was your hubby I wouldn't be booking into hotels with anyone else."

"Flirting with the clientele?" His boss sighed. "How very professional." He turned back to the girl. "Where is this hotel your husband has booked?"

"The Fountain Hotel," said Rachel. "It's north of Newcastle in a coastal village named Ravenspoint."

"I see." Quist stroked his large nose to conceal a faint smile. "Northumberland tomorrow? You must of course appreciate how we have other cases and this is rather short notice."

The girl nodded. "I'm fully aware of that, which is why I'm willing to pay double your usual fee."

"Where do you live?" asked Quist.

"Like I said, York." Rachel hesitated. "Bishopthorpe Road."

"Very well." He slid a pad and pen across the desk. "If you'd be good enough to jot your full address down on there, along with a contact telephone number, I'll ring you before the end of the day and we'll arrange something."

"I wonder…" The girl finished her scribbling and rose to her feet. "Could I possibly use your bathroom?"

"But of course." Quist waved a hand to the outer office. "It's the door to the right of the reception desk."

"You know what?" whispered Watson, as she left the room. "I've always wanted to ask if I could use someone's bathroom and, later, when they come to check I'm okay, they find me bathing in the tub." His eyes narrowed as he pictured a bubble bath containing this lovely redhead and himself standing by her with a sponge.

"Well…" Quist pulled slowly on his cigarette. "This is rather intriguing."

"A girl taking a piss, or another cheating hubby?" Watson frowned. "Surely we don't have time for this divorce crap right now when we're looking for whoever tried to…"

"As you're aware, Oliver Tarrant's Range Rover is registered to an address in a Northumbrian village. Can you hazard a guess as to *which* village?"

"What?" The youth's eyes widened. "You don't mean…"

"Yes, Ravenspoint. Who would have guessed?" Quist smiled politely as Rachel reappeared. "Ah, there you are, Mrs Penrose. As I was saying, I'll ring you later today and..."

"I'm sorry." She held up her phone. "Yes, I'm afraid it *will* have to be later. I've just had an urgent text and I need to leave immediately. We'll speak when you ring."

"Very well." Quist jumped up as she hurried out. "Do take care, Mrs Penrose."

"I wonder why she..." began Watson.

"I need you to follow her." The detective pointed to the door and rushed to the window. "Quickly. See where she goes and, more importantly, see if she's with anyone. Be discreet."

"Are you kidding?" His assistant darted out. "Discretion's my middle name."

"Really?" mumbled Quist. "I seem to recall you telling people your middle name is *love machine*."

Watson ran down the stairs to find his way blocked by two young men from the gymnasium below the agency. They sported track suits and the sort of odd smiles that were only ever seen on the very religious and the mentally unwell. The evangelical staff at *Jehovah's Fitness* were constantly on the lookout for new members and they tried to persuade Watson to join whenever they spotted him.

"Hello again," beamed one. "Say, you're looking pretty good, but you could look even better by pumping weights to shame the Devil. The last time we spoke I asked you how often you read the Bible..."

"I remember." Watson attempted to push past the pair. "To be honest, I'm more into *Star Trek* than Jesus and I don't have any time for this."

"That's okay," said his friend. "Because the Lord has time for you, and if you allow us, we could soon teach..."

Ignoring him, the youth squeezed by and rushed out onto the

busy Fishergate pavement. There was no sign of Rachel, but checking around the corner, he spotted her heading down Baker Avenue. The cul-de-sac of terraced houses terminated at the River Foss and the confluence where this waterway flowed into its much grander cousin, the Ouse. Boasting a few public parking spaces – something of a rarity in York – this was where Quist always left his car when at the office.

"Oh, hello." Watson smiled knowingly as the girl jumped into a sleek car and pulled away from the kerb. "So you have a black BMW."

He stepped back into the doorway of *Jehovah's Fitness*, attempting to appear inconspicuous as Rachel cruised up the street towards him. The passenger side window lowered, a silver-haired man with a camera appeared, and Watson heard the whirr of his motor drive as several digital photographs were taken.

"Well, I'm pretty good-looking," murmured the youth, watching the car turn onto Fishergate. "But I've never had strangers taking pictures before."

* * * *

Chapter 9

Six bridges span the River Ouse as it winds its way through York. Four are Victorian structures, carrying three busy roads and a railway, the suburb of Clifton has a further road bridge dating from the 1960s, and the most recent Millennium Bridge, is purely for pedestrian and cycle traffic. Quist drove over Skeldergate Bridge, arguably the most ornate of these river crossings, to leave the bustling city centre behind and enter the more sedate neighbourhood of Clementhorpe. He turned onto Bishopthorpe Road, the main route through this vibrant little community, lined with inns, shops and restaurants.

"Yeah, Rachel Penrose was driving a BMW," said Watson, peering out of the car at a group of pretty girls leaving the Swan public house. "It was a black BMW saloon, just like the one you saw hanging around outside the solicitor's office, and the guy in the passenger seat was taking snaps of me. I wonder what could be going on."

Quist nodded. "You mentioned it had a private registration plate?"

"That's right. AC 666."

"So we have someone with a sense of humour." The detective gave him a lopsided smile. "Wouldn't you say?"

"I dunno." Watson frowned. "Isn't 666 the Devil's phone number, or some such shit?"

"I'm referring to the combination of the letters AC and the numbers 666. Aleister Crowley always referred to himself as the Great Beast, 666."

"Aleister who?"

"I've mentioned him to you before. He was an occultist, but it isn't important." Quist cruised along the road looking for the numbers on the surrounding shops and houses wherever they were displayed.

"As you know, I have an aversion to private plates, or rather the kind of individuals – usually men – who find it necessary to spend huge amounts to acquire them. If they really need to announce they own the vehicle, surely painting their name on the bonnet and boot would be far cheaper? *And* the letters would be larger."

"But not as cool," laughed Watson. "I really love private plates."

"Why am I not surprised?"

"I'd have WAT50N on my Ferrari, or maybe…"

"Or maybe you could describe the photographer in the BMW?" broke in Quist. "That might be useful."

"Some older white guy with grey hair." Watson shrugged. "That's about all I can tell you."

"Was he, by any chance, smoking a pipe?"

The youth looked puzzled. "A pipe?"

"Mrs Penrose had a slight scent of pipe tobacco on her clothing," explained Quist. "A strong, sweet blend."

"Really? I didn't notice."

"Understandable, I suppose," conceded the detective. "You don't have my enhanced senses. My nasal capabilities are somewhat remarkable and far superior to humans."

"Now there's a boast you don't hear every day. Yeah, that's a pretty good nose you have there, Guv." Watson smirked at his employer's outsized facial feature. "Anyway, why would they want pictures of *me*?"

"I honestly don't know, but I *do* know that everything about our Mrs Penrose felt wrong. I want to see the address she gave us and here it is on the left." Quist gestured to the Victorian terrace as he drove past and then turned into the next street to park. "I don't expect to find her living here."

"You think she gave us a false address?" asked Watson, jumping out of the car.

"Oh, I'm fairly certain of it, but let's make sure."

The youth followed him into a narrow alleyway that ran between the rear of the terrace and a parallel row of houses. Private yards backed onto this cobbled passage and, locating the correct back gate, Quist strode up the path to rap on the door. He waited, peering through a gap in the kitchen window blinds at the washing up left to drain by the sink.

"No one home," said Watson, eventually.

"Apparently not." Quist glanced left and right, checking the surrounding windows for unwanted observers. "I need you to wait out there in the alley and keep watch for a moment. I'm going to take a closer look at the place."

Heading back to the gate, Watson watched in amazement as his boss sprang onto a drainpipe and used his powerful grip to scuttle effortlessly up it like an ape. The detective arrived at one of the bedroom windows and leant across, cupping his free hand to the glass and gazing through for several seconds. Satisfied, he jumped back down, nimbly dropping the twelve feet into the yard and landing in a crouch.

"I was right," said Quist, returning to his assistant in the alleyway. "A plate and mug are draining on the kitchen sink, clearly the crockery of just *one* person. The bedroom cabinets up there are covered in male items, and the bedroom door is open, allowing me to see through into the spare room where a model train set is laid out. This is definitely *not* a girl's house."

"No," agreed Watson. "More like a single bloke called Matt."

The detective peered blankly at him.

"You can sometimes get information without doing a Tarzan impression," explained the youth. "I spoke to a neighbour in the yard over there when she came out to pop something in their dustbin. Matt's lived alone here for about two years. No young birds living with him, or visiting either."

"Well, as I mentioned, he *does* have a train set." Quist smiled. "Train sets and an active sex life aren't exactly renowned for going hand-in-hand. So, just as I thought, Mrs Rachel Penrose, if that is in fact her *real* name, gave us a fabricated address."

"So you won't be taking her cheating hubby case?"

"Well, of *course* I'll be taking it," laughed the detective. "For some reason, this girl wants us to go to Ravenspoint, the village where at least one of my would-be kidnappers lives. Those silver handcuffs mean that someone there either knows or strongly suspects my secret."

* * * *

Originally the site of the city market, the huge tree-lined square named Parliament Street is now York's largest pedestrianised shopping centre. Bizarrely, for York, the surrounding buildings are *only* two-hundred years old and are doubtless sneered at by the nearby medieval and Tudor structures. Many events take place here throughout the year, but the annual Christmas market, the St Nicholas Fair, is arguably the most popular. Every tree is festooned in flashing lights, non-stop festive music plays from speakers, and tourists flock to the countless wooden chalet shops that line the cobblestones.

Heading for Gareth Lestrade's apartment in Bedern, Quist and Watson walked alongside these rows of brightly-lit sheds, negotiating the warmly-wrapped crowds and the ubiquitous delivery bicycles. Watson gazed hungrily at their counters as he passed by, noticing the delicious cheeses, jams, gins, preserves and fudges. Richly inviting aromas drifted from the many food stalls and he licked his lips to smell mulled wine, hot chocolate, chestnuts and roasting German sausages.

"I've been meaning to ask," he said, pushing his hands deeper into the snug pockets of his canvas blouson. "Why did you say this Christmas fair reminded you of curried eggs?"

"*What?*" Quist had turned up the collar of his leather

trenchcoat against the freezing cold. He drew on his cigarette and frowned. "I didn't."

"Yeah, the other day when we walked through here."

The detective looked blank for a few seconds until realisation dawned. "Ah, no, I said the fair was like a curate's egg – good in parts."

"Oh, right," said Watson, bemused. "Hey, it's a bit nippy, isn't it?" He blew warmth into his hands, briskly rubbing them before returning them to his pockets. "Did I ever tell you about my Uncle Ray? He died from exposure a few years back."

"Really?" said Quist, slightly shocked. "You've never mentioned this before. How awful."

"Yeah," laughed Watson. "He was exposing himself to a kid in Rowntree Park one day when her father appeared and beat him to death."

Rolling his eyes, the detective took out his phone and paused by a tree to ring York Hospital. His assistant bought himself a hot Cornish pasty from a chalet stall as he waited, along with two coffees from the neighbouring outlet, one black and one white with extra sugar. He munched on the pasty, his face lighting up as he spotted a drunken hen party staggering past. The temperature was below zero, but from their scanty attire, the girls didn't appear to have noticed.

"Hey," laughed the youth, "if he stands you up at the altar, luv, give me a ring."

"Thank you," said Quist, finishing his brief telephone call and taking the black coffee from his assistant. "I can't help but notice how you say that to the bride in every hen party you see."

"It's a habit," grinned Watson. He nodded to the detective's cigarette. "I can think of much worse habits. So what did the hospital say?"

"I claimed to be Gerald, a family member," said Quist, sipping the hot drink. "Oliver Tarrant is out of surgery. He's somewhat groggy, so we can't see him right now, but the nurse said later today should be fine. With two broken legs, he certainly won't be released in the near future."

They left Parliament Street and turned right into Jubbergate and the equally crowded Shambles open-air market. Beautiful, half-timbered Elizabethan buildings stood on every side and a multitude of food vending vans were clustered around the stalls, filling the air with the heady fragrance of sizzling Asian spices. These culinary outlets were a permanent fixture all year round and Quist often called at one of the Thai vans. They knew his weird vegan requirements and the food was truly amazing. Spotting a vacant bench, Quist sat with his coffee and cigarette.

"Ravenspoint," said Watson, sitting beside him. "So one of the two guys who tried to grab you lives there and then the redhead comes to us with a story about a hotel in the same village. Her address was fake, so her cheating hubby stuff is probably crap too."

"Yes," agreed Quist. "She wants us there for some obscure reason, and I *have* to go. As I said, someone there clearly knows my secret and I need to know who."

"So where *is* this Ravenspoint? It has the same name as one of the houses at Harry Potter's school. It must be a shit one too, as they hardly mention it in the films."

"I looked it up on the map when Lestrade checked the Range Rover registration," said the detective. "The village stands on a Northumbrian promontory known as the Craggan Headland, about twenty miles south of Berwick-upon-Tweed. Coincidentally, there was an accident on that very headland that made the news last week. A young couple in a car left the clifftop road and crashed into the sea. Neither of them were found."

"Terrible." said Watson, through a mouthful of Cornish pasty. "Hey, Guv, you were once a doctor, weren't you? A medical doctor, right? Not a doctor of media studies, or the daft shit they all get

.

degrees in these days."

"That's right." His boss nodded. "Many moons ago I was a General Practitioner in Edinburgh. Why? What's wrong?"

"I don't really know." He rubbed his eyes. "What causes a fizzing inside your head? A weird feeling like you've been snorting lemonade?"

"Are you serious?" Quist took out his phone. "Wait a moment while I call Lestrade."

"I doubt *he'll* know," laughed Watson.

"I need to ensure he's home and let him know we're on our way." Quist keyed in the number. "Ah, Gareth," he said. "That Range Rover registration number you looked up for me..."

"Yes?" said Lestrade. "Which you've yet to pay me for."

"Which I'll be paying for shortly. I have another one for you. A BMW with the license plate AC 666. I wonder if you could check it with DVLA?"

"I'm at the computer right now, if you'll bear with me." Lestrade paused for several seconds. "Got it. Yeah, that one's registered to an Adrian Crowther."

The detective nodded. "Well, that would explain the letters AC."

"Hey, there's a coincidence," said Lestrade. "I'm just looking at his details. You remember how the Range Rover is registered to a guy in Ravenspoint? Well, this BMW is registered to an address in the same village. "

"Oh, what a surprise," murmured Quist. "Are there any mentions of this Adrian Crowther on the internet? Does he have a website, for example? Who is he?"

He waited, sipping his coffee and glancing at Watson. Weirdly, the young man sat quietly with a vacant expression.

"Yeah," said Lestrade. "He appears here and there on the web, mostly on dancing websites and he seems to have won trophies and awards for quite a few ballroom competitions. Ah, here he is again; he's an entrant in the televised *Dance Away* finals in Newcastle this Saturday night."

"Well..." Quist turned again to Watson. "That BMW is also from the village of Ravens..."

Save for a half-eaten pasty, the bench beside him was empty and his assistant had completely vanished.

* * * *

Chapter 10

Hurrying through the bustling Shambles market, Quist checked down the narrow side streets and snickleways for any sign of Watson.

Where the hell was he? Had someone snatched him?

He quickly contemplated the logistics of abducting someone in broad daylight, recalling the stun gun, the hand-held Taser, that his attacker had wielded this morning.

Using such a disabling weapon, it might be possible to silently grab someone, but surely not in a crowded market in daylight? The youth had been sitting right beside him and he would definitely have noticed. But then again, there was no reason whatsoever why Watson would have left by himself without saying something.

Cursing under his breath, Quist tried ringing the youth's phone again, but as with the previous three attempts, the call went straight to Voicemail.

"Hi there," chirped the recording. "If you genuinely need instructions on how to leave a message here, then you're far too thick to be a friend of mine. Over to you."

He waited impatiently for the bleep. "Where on earth did you disappear to?" he snapped. "Look, I'm quite concerned by this, so what exactly is going on? Why aren't you answering these messages?"

Switching off, the detective started slightly as the phone immediately buzzed in his hand. He checked the display, assuming it would be Watson, but saw it was his assistant's mother. After their initial meeting, over a year ago, Mrs Watson had bombarded him for a while with highly suggestive calls, but since she realised he wasn't interested, he hadn't heard much from her.

"Hello," he said, warily. "Um, how can I help?"

"Well, hello," she purred, sexily. "Hey, don't you be doing any heavy breathing on here and getting me all excited."

"I'll try not to," said Quist.

"Yes, you'd better behave yourself, or you'll be in for a spanking." Mrs Watson laughed. "So what's my lad up to?"

"Um, I don't know," said the detective, puzzled. "What *is* your lad up to?"

"I just rang him about his cousin's Christmas party and he said he was..."

"He answered his phone?" broke in Quist. "*I* keep ringing him and he isn't picking up."

"Well, he said he was on his way to the station."

"*Station?*" The detective shook his head, confused. "The police station or..."

"No, the railway station. He says he's going to a place called Ravenspoint and..."

"*What?*" gasped Quist.

"Then he rang off," continued Mrs Watson. "I tried calling him back, but he isn't answering now, just like you said. So what's he up to?"

* * * *

The majority of York's buildings are listed and, along with its adjoining five-storey hotel, the city railway station is, unsurprisingly, no exception. Constructed from honey-coloured Scarborough brick, metal columns and masses of ornate ironwork and glass, the huge Victorian complex constantly bustles with travellers.

An icy shower of grey sleet had begun to splatter down as Quist raced through the Station Road taxi rank and into the entrance hall. He paused to quickly check one of the overhead television screens for details of the trains heading north. When this place opened in 1837 it was the largest railway station in the world and boasted fifteen platforms. Unfortunately for the anxious detective, it still had

67

eleven of them and he quietly cursed to see that the northern-bound trains were departing from Platform Nine at the far side of the building. He ran into the main hall and bounded up the steps to reach the lengthy internal footbridge which crossed the various sets of tracks.

"What on earth can he be *doing*?" he muttered to himself.

Eight carriages in length, the sleek Newcastle train stood purring and ready to leave Platform Nine and Quist hurried along beside it looking through the windows. Spotting Watson sitting in the third carriage, he angrily tugged open the door and jumped on board. His assistant sat playing a game on his phone.

"What's going on?" snapped Quist, angrily.

"Oh, hi, Guv." The youth looked up, smiling politely. "Going on? What do you mean?"

"What do I mean?" laughed the detective. "Well, let's try the obvious questions – why aren't you answering your phone and what the hell are you doing sitting on a train?"

Watson frowned. "Well, I'm not answering because I'm playing the *Shoot Em Up* game and I've got the ringtone switched off," he explained, as if everything was perfectly normal. "I'm sitting on a train because I'm on my way to Ravenspoint."

Quist shook his head, astonished. "Do you even know where it is?"

"Er, near Newcastle, isn't it? This train is going to Newcastle and then I'm going to get a… er, I'll get a…"

"Ah, I see." Quist's eyes narrowed suspiciously as realisation dawned. "And why, pray tell, are you trying to reach the village of Ravenspoint?"

"Um…" His assistant grew confused at the question. "I don't really know."

"Of course you don't." The detective smiled grimly. "But fortunately I have a damn good idea. I don't suppose you have a ticket?"

"No."

"I didn't think so." Snatching his arm, Quist jerked the young man to his feet. "Come on. I just heard a whistle and we need to get off quickly."

"No, I can't." Watson wrenched himself free as the train began to slowly move forward. "No, I have to go to Rav…"

"Now." Quist grabbed him again, dragging the struggling, kicking youth through the carriage as the passengers eyed them suspiciously. "Nothing to see here," he announced, breezily. "Have a nice journey, everyone. Merry Christmas."

The departing train was picking up speed as the detective reached the door and pulled his assistant through, the pair falling in an untidy heap onto the end of the platform with onlookers watching and tutting their disapproval. Watson yelped in pain and jumped to his feet.

"Are you alright?" asked Quist, dusting himself down and straightening his overcoat.

"I think I've broken my wrist." Cradling his arm, the youth looked around, confused. "Er, sorry, but what just happened? I really don't understand. What the fuck was I doing on a train to Newcastle?"

"That's a very good question." The detective led him to a platform bench. "Sit down and let me take a look at that."

Watson held the hand out hesitantly. "Careful, Guv."

"This is a little easier to examine than the fizzing sensation inside your head that you mentioned in the Shambles Market." Quist gave it a swift inspection. "No, don't worry; it's only a bad sprain. You'll be fine."

"Absolutely," grinned Watson, winking. "It's my *left* wrist."

"Ah." Quist rolled his eyes. "Yes, it would appear you're clearly back to normal."

"Well, my head feels kind of woozy," he murmured. "Like I

say, I don't understand. I *knew* I was sitting on the train and I *knew* where I was going, but I've no idea *why*. It was really weird; a bit like a dream."

"More like a nightmare," corrected Quist. "We've encountered this sort of thing before."

"What sort of thing?"

"My dear Watson," said Quist. "I'm fairly certain you've been… How should I put this? You've been bewitched."

* * * *

Chapter 11

The area of York known as Bedern lies inside the city wall to the east of Goodramgate. The Anglo-Saxon name means 'house of prayer' but, from the 1800s to the 1960s, Bedern was a slum of grim tenements and there was very little praying going on. Back then, this was *the* place to visit if you fancied meeting a cheap prostitute, fencing your stolen goods, or getting yourself stabbed. Apart from a handful of ancient chapels and medieval halls, the quiet neighbourhood is now filled with relatively new dwellings, although in a city where the majority of the architecture is medieval, even the Victorian and Edwardian buildings could easily be classed as *new*.

St Andrewgate runs through Bedern and Watson's friend Gareth Lestrade lived just off this narrow thoroughfare in an old converted granary. His top-floor apartment would originally have been quite spacious, but an array of computer equipment, and a vast collection of science fiction memorabilia and comic books now took up a great deal of the room.

"So you're sure about this?" whispered Watson, ringing the bell. "I was actually *bewitched* by someone using an occult ritual?"

"Yes, bewitched," confirmed Quist, waiting. "Enchanted, entranced, mesmerised, whatever you wish to call it. Basically, you were remotely hypnotised by an adept of the occult. They commanded you to board that train and you had no choice, but to obey."

"It sounds crazy." The young man shook his head, astounded. "But we've come across occultists in the past. I'll be honest, if I hadn't seen this kind of magick shit before, I'd think you were some thirty-two-cat loony."

"You grade the severity of mental health issues by the number of cats a person owns? That's interesting." The detective frowned. "Yes, remote hypnotism is far from easy. An accomplished magician is needed to perform the ritual and they'd require a sample of your blood, hair, or semen. Magick is the only explanation for what happened earlier. Either that, or you've recently taken ownership of thirty-three cats."

The conversation ended as Lestrade opened the door and stepped back to allow the pair to enter.

"It's good of you to see us at short notice," said Quist, peering curiously at the full-size metal skeleton of a Terminator standing threateningly in the hall corner. "As I mentioned on the phone, I'm hoping you can assist us in your usual inimitable fashion."

"No problem." Lestrade closed the door and waved a hand towards the lounge. "You know the way to the Cyber-cave."

Pale-skinned and fair-haired, this bespectacled young man would be the first to admit he wasn't much of a dynamic outdoors person, but spending his time hunched over computer screens clearly paid well. The cash-in-hand supplements from people like Quist were nothing compared to the *real* money he received from British companies for troubleshooting their systems. His income allowed him to indulge his interests, something which was evident to anyone seeing his cabinets of science fiction models and the autographed movie posters on his walls.

Quist looked around the lounge, smiling tightly at the expensive framed comics. He couldn't help, but feel a slight twinge of guilt. Hacking encrypted computer systems, including the police and the DVLA, was highly illegal, but Lestrade only supplied information that would be used for good and he never did anything *too* wrong. He might provide details of a car owner, or a police post mortem report, but he'd never dream of emptying someone's bank account to spend the cash on white powder.

"Hey, what's been happening here, Watty?" Lestrade nodded to his friend's hand. Quist had called in a pharmacy and Watson's left wrist was now enclosed in a compression bandage. "Are you okay?"

"Ah, it's not too bad." The youth held it aloft. "I've taken up falconry and the bird squeezed it's claws a bit tight."

Laughing, he painfully flexed his fingers, but the injury wasn't his primary concern. *The boss claimed he'd been the victim of an occult spell – remote hypnotism forcing him to get on the train. What if these bastards had forced him to jump UNDER a train?*

Like most people, Watson had always believed such things were nonsense, but that was before the weird cases he'd investigated with Quist. Since discovering his boss was a werewolf, his scepticism had diminished somewhat and he was slightly more open-minded. It was almost as if the boss had read his mind. Lestrade headed to a bureau and Quist took the opportunity to lean close to Watson's ear.

"Don't go wandering off again, will you?" he whispered, smiling. "I'm hoping I don't need to invest in a set of those reins that parents use to restrain their toddlers."

"Yeah, yeah," muttered the youth, sarcastically.

"You'll love this," said Lestrade. Opening a drawer, he passed Watson a small metal starship around six inches in length. "I spotted five of these at a sci-fi convention and bought the lot. Only two were in their original boxes, I'm afraid, but these are the actual toys from 1968. You put so much business my way by bringing your boss here with his oddball requests, you can have one for free."

"The USS Enterprise?" Grinning widely, Watson showed Quist the model with its saucer and long engine nacelles. "Hey, just feel the weight of this. It's your proper die-cast metal instead of the plastic crap we get today. This is brilliant. Hey, thanks a million."

Lestrade nodded. "The ideal gift for an injured friend."

"A bag of frozen peas for his wrist would be a more useful gift," suggested Quist.

"Sorry, I only have pizza in the freezer." Lestrade walked to the lengthy desk beneath the lounge window with its extensive arrangement of computer equipment. He sat in the leather swivel chair in front of the massive screen. "So what can I do for you this time?"

"You found the driver of the BMW." Quist sat on a stool beside him. "Adrian Crowther, I believe you said? I need his details and I'd like to see photographs of him."

"No problem." Lestrade flexed his slender fingers and typed fast on the keyboard. "I found a few photos earlier on various websites devoted to dancing. Ah, here we go. As you can see, this one was taken at a ballroom competition in Manchester last year and he won the trophy."

"Hey, that's him." Watson perched on a stool beside Quist and pointed. "I'm sure that was the guy in the car with the camera."

"The caption says *Adrian Crowther*." Quist nodded slowly. "I've never heard that name before today, but his face is so familiar."

"There are more." Lestrade tapped at the keyboard and brought them up. "But to be honest, they're all pretty much the same. Shots taken over the past few years at various dance contests around Britain."

"These pictures all appeared when you entered Crowther's name," said Quist, thoughtfully. "I wonder if we could try searching with his image instead? I understand it's possible to find photographs of people on the internet by using their face?"

"Facial recognition?" Lestrade nodded. "Yeah, with the right software you simply scan in a picture of someone and it searches the entire web for other images of that face. The cops and security services use it when they're looking for suspects. There are various programmes out there, but I tap into VIZION on the North Yorkshire Police computer. It's really good."

"*And* really unlawful, I presume?" The detective shot him a deadpan look. "Nevertheless, could we perhaps try the process using one of these photographs of Adrian Crowther?"

Lestrade winked. "It shouldn't take me long," he said, cropping and copying the clearest of the ballroom shots.

Watson and Quist watched with interest as he entered the

police website through the trusty, and highly illegal, backdoor that he'd created three years ago. He navigated several menus to arrive at their VIZION resource, pasting in Crowther's face and clicking *Search*. Over a minute ticked by.

"As you know, I leave no traces," said Lestrade, waiting. "They've no idea I've ever been in here, and they can't tell that I've used their facial recognition..." He paused as the screen changed. "Ah, here we go, although these new pictures we've found don't seem to be much different. Just lots more dance shots..." He peered closer at various black-and-white images mixed in with the ballroom photographs. "Oh, and a few that are obviously wrong."

"Wrong?" echoed Quist.

"Yeah, this happens sometimes. The programme finds photos with a similar looking face." Lestrade read the captions beneath the older pictures. "VIZION has incorrectly identified our Adrian guy as someone from way back called Aleister Crowley."

"Oh, of course." The detective peered closely at the screen. "I thought I recognised Crowther, but I was mistaken. I must have been recalling these old pictures of Crowley that I've seen before in books."

"You mentioned the name Aleister Crowley earlier," said Watson. "When we were talking about number plates."

"Yes, he was a famous occultist," said Quist. "He died back in the 1940s."

"These facial recognition programmes aren't perfect," pointed out Watson. "If you scanned in *my* photo, it'd probably find a few pictures of the young Will Smith and mistake them for me." He shrugged. "Although, let's face it, Will was never *this* good-looking."

"I have to admit," said Quist, thoughtfully, "Crowther and Crowley *do* look the same. Not alike, but exactly the same."

"A family connection?" suggested Watson. "Maybe the dancing guy is a grandson with incredibly similar looks?"

"Possibly," said Quist. "After all, Crowther *does* drive a car with 666 on the plate, indicating that he's fully aware of Crowley. Speaking of the plate, I presume his address is in the DVLA records?"

"Yeah, and it's a pretty cool one." Lestrade brought up a website with a colourful coat of arms on the home page. "He lives in Ravenspoint Castle. The place is owned by the Mulgrave family, who also own the village hotel, the Fountain."

"Could I see, please?" Quist sat forward and scrolled through the site. "Mmh, this is a typical business website where I can book rooms in the hotel and tables in their restaurant. A guided tour of the castle too, I see. Now I'm aware that this may sound somewhat shady, but is it possible to hack into this site and access the private records and accounts?"

"Shady? Ooh, not at all." Lestrade pulled the keyboard towards him and began typing. "It shouldn't be a problem."

"Why?" asked Watson. "What are you expecting to find?"

"Truthfully, I've no idea," admitted Quist. "But as you're aware, someone in Ravenspoint knows certain *things* about me and I'll try any avenue that may shed light upon it."

"Er, when I said it shouldn't be a problem..." Lestrade grimaced. "Actually it *is* a problem. I can't seem to get in here."

"What do you mean?" Watson laughed. "You can hack *any* system."

"Given time, I'm sure I could." The young man shook his head. "But this site has triple-lock encryption. I don't get it. It's some small hotel business, yet it has Pentagon-style protection."

"Intriguing," murmured Quist. "Alright, Gareth, one final task for you. I'd like to know where Crowther is staying in York. To leave his BMW in a hotel car park, he needs to provide the registration, so AC 666 will be on the computer of whichever establishment he's chosen."

"There are dozens of hotels," pointed out Lestrade. "You

76

realise I'd need to hack each system to read their guest bookings?"

"That may be unnecessary. Firstly try Middlethorpe Hall and Spa."

"The posh place by the racecourse?" said Watson. "Why there?"

"Elementary deduction." The detective shrugged. "I asked Mrs Penrose for her address and she told us Bishopthorpe Road, but remember how she stiffened and said it quickly. I don't believe she expected the question at that moment and she hadn't prepared. I'm assuming it was the only York street name she could immediately recall. She'll have seen the sign displayed on the wall opposite the hotel driveway exit."

"And the house number she gave us?"

"Oh, come now. Plucking a random number from thin air isn't difficult." Quist gave a lopsided smile. "I'm willing to bet even *you* could do it."

"It looks like you're right," said Lestrade, completing his hack and bringing up the guest list.

"There's a surprise," muttered Watson.

"Yeah, here he is." Lestrade gestured to his screen. "Adrian Crowther and a companion booked into the Middlethorpe Hall Hotel yesterday for one night. They were staying in the Knavesmire Suite, but according to this, they've recently checked out."

"The companion was Rachel Penrose," said Quist. "I'd like to call there and take a look at this suite. Do we have a plan of the building on there? Something that shows us exactly where the room is situated?"

Lestrade swiftly navigated through menus and brought up a floorplan.

"Ah, that could be useful." The detective studied the layout. "The suite is on the eastern side of the hotel, at the rear and close to the external fire escape. I assume the doors onto the exterior staircase are alarmed?"

"At the moment, yes," said Lestrade. "If I enter the system, I can change that and add the fee to my ever-growing bill."

"Actually, I'll settle that debt right now." Smiling, Quist took out his wallet. "Don't switch off the alarms just yet. I'll give you a ring when we're in position and ready." He turned to Watson. "Are *you* ready?"

Watson grinned. "The boss is asking his attractive assistant to accompany him to a country hotel? Hey, just what sort of boy do you think I am?"

* * * *

Chapter 12

The vast expanse of grassland known as the Knavesmire lies on the southern outskirts of York. Before it was moved to the castle prison in 1801, a gallows stood here beside the road and hundreds of people were publicly executed, their bodies left dangling for days; on display to anyone travelling in or out of the city. Just as visitors to New York are welcomed by the Statue of Liberty, visitors to York were welcomed by rotting corpses. Attending the hangings was a popular pastime and, after the Knavesmire acquired a racecourse in 1731, the crowds would enjoy the fun of the executions and then stroll across for the horse racing to complete their family day out.

Surrounded by twenty acres of lush parkland, Middlethorpe Hall stands just off Bishopthorpe Road on the eastern edge of the Knavesmire. Built in 1699, this lovely redbrick mansion has been through several transformations since the regal age of William and Mary, morphing from a private dwelling into a boarding school and even an upmarket nightclub, before finally being turned into a luxury hotel and spa.

Deep twilight had fallen, but Quist killed his headlights as he cruised past the main building and entered the woodland car park to pull up behind a dense stand of trees. This secluded parking area was situated away from the hotel and out of sight. It was unlikely that anyone would have noticed their arrival.

"Lights off and stealth mode, eh?" said Watson, climbing out. "We know this Crowther guy and Ginger Rachel have already left, so what are you hoping to find here?"

"Confirmation." The detective closed the car door and eyed the building through the wintry tree branches. "Confirmation to a few dark suspicions, but our visit needs to remain clandestine. We'll avoid the path to the front entrance and approach through this woodland in, as you say, *stealth mode*."

The earlier deluge of sleet had stopped and the rich scent of wet soil filled the freezing air. Quist glanced up as a tawny owl called from a nearby tree. Despite the flight being virtually silent, he'd heard it land and knew it had yet to pick up on his supernatural presence. Shakespeare mentioned this bird in *Love's Labour's Lost* – "Tu-whit; Tu-who, a merry note" – and he wondered which recreational narcotics the playwright must have been using to decide the melancholy warble was *merry*. Sensing him, the owl screeched in panic and fled.

"Sounds like the local wildlife has spotted you," murmured Watson, painfully flexing his fingers. "This wrist is still throbbing."

"You need an improvised sling" said Quist. "Unzip your blouson to your sternum."

"Speak English, Guv."

"Your breastbone. Then shove your hand inside the jacket to keep the arm elevated. That should alleviate the pain."

Watson secured his wrist as instructed, looking around warily as some other unseen creature cried out. Quist knew it was a peacock settling down to roost. These glamorous birds were introduced into Britain from India, but he now regarded their mournful mewing as synonymous with English stately homes and parkland.

The two men made their way through the trees to a small area of lawn and, ensuring they were hidden from windows and any CCTV cameras, they hurried across the grass to arrive at the side of the hotel. The youth peered up at the ornate fire escape, a spiral staircase of iron bolted to the western gable, and he noticed that the moon had risen over the woods to his left.

"Ah, your old pal has come out to say hello." Watson nodded to the eerily glowing orb. "It's the wrong time of the month, as they say. Are you sure you're okay with this, Guv?"

"It isn't quite full." Quist smiled reassuringly and lifted the leather folds of his long trenchcoat to begin climbing. "Even if it *were*, I'm fully capable of keeping my dark urges in check. I've had years of practise, so you don't need to worry about me giving you any, um, love bites."

They silently ascended the tightly winding metal steps and paused at the highest door, peering through the glass pane into the empty passage beyond. Quist glanced around the darkening grounds below before taking out his phone to ring Lestrade.

"Hello, Gareth," he murmured. "We're at the hotel. I wonder if you'd be good enough to switch off those fire exit alarms that we spoke about?"

"I have the system open and ready." Sprawled in his swivel chair, Lestrade leant forward to tap the keyboard. "They're disabled now. By the way, after you left, I noticed the room doors in there are controlled by electronic key cards. Housekeeping can unlock them via their computer and, seeing as I'm in the hotel system, so can I. You were interested in the Knavesmire Suite. Would you like me to open it?"

"Oh, I'd like that very much." Laughing quietly, Quist, pulled open the fire exit and entered the corridor followed by Watson. "We're outside now," he said, hurrying to the correct door. The lock buzzed, the light turned green and they slipped inside. "Thank you so much, Gareth. Once again, you've proved yourself indispensable."

Watson clicked on the lights as his boss finished the phone call. The king-size bed was unmade and he noticed discarded items in the waste basket.

"As I hoped," said Quist, looking around. "Someone came in to count the minibar items when the occupants checked out. They've left a clipboard on the bureau there with the list of rooms that require cleaning and restocking, but the Room Service team have yet to start on this one."

His assistant nodded. "Meaning?"

"Meaning the evidence will still be here."

81

"Evidence of what?"

Ignoring the question, the detective swiftly shrugged off his overcoat and jacket. "I need to do this properly."

Watson's eyebrows rose. "Surely you're not actually going to…" He nodded as his boss pulled down his trousers. "Yes, apparently you *are*."

Tugging off his shirt and clenching his teeth, Quist bent double, a mass of thick hair sprouting to cover his expanding back. He shook his head hard, pointed ears emerging and his unrecognisable face elongating into a large lupine muzzle. Watson winced to hear the horrific sound of bones snapping and crunching as they lengthened. Arms became front legs with taloned paws and a bushy tail sprouted from the base of the creature's spine. The room temperature plummeted alarmingly as his boss grew in furry bulk and height, until finally the human had vanished and a huge black wolf stood on two legs in his place.

"Shit," croaked the youth, his mouth dry and his breath clouding on the air. "Every time I see that, it always feels like the first time." He gaped at the enormous beast with its glowing amber eyes. "Tell me again about this weird cold thing. You say your change sucks up energy?"

The wolf nodded its head. "The transformation drains natural energy from the surrounding atmosphere. Corporeal energy is changed into esoteric, ethereal energy."

"Sounds simple enough." Watson grinned nervously. "Why did they never teach us that in school?"

"We don't know how much time we have," growled Quist, dropping onto all-fours and prowling the suite with tail thrashing from side to side. "I'm afraid the shapeshift was necessary. As you can doubtless imagine, my sense of smell is far keener in this form."

The young man watched whilst listening carefully at the door for anyone approaching. Even on four legs, his boss looked nothing at all like a *normal* wolf. The wolves on television resembled big scruffy dogs and Watson had seen much scarier animals trotting around his council estate. *This* wolf, however, was very different – it was far larger, far more muscular, and far more terrifying. Although Quist was a genuinely nice human being, his lupine features were inescapably fixed in a permanent ferocious glare. *This* huge black wolf belonged in a horror movie, a movie filmed by a director with an odd fetish for making the audience soil themselves.

"Yes, the Penrose girl was here," said Quist, sniffing the carpet as he criss-crossed the suite. "I recognise her natural smell and the perfume she wore at the office." He rose onto two legs to look in the drawers, the wardrobes and even the minibar fridge. "There's an obvious male scent everywhere too and this bed positively reeks with the smell of sex."

"Nice to know," muttered Watson, to himself. "Hey, what did you do at work today? Oh, you know, the usual stuff; sniffing beds where folk have been shagging."

"I'm detecting tobacco too," said the wolf. "A strong blend of pipe tobacco mixed with something dark and sweet. Mmmh, it's molasses. How extraordinary."

"*Really* extraordinary," agreed Watson. "To say that all hotels are non-smoking."

"That's why it's stronger *here*." Quist pulled back the curtain. "Yes, he's been sitting next to the open window, blowing out the smoke. It's faint, but traces have permeated this curtain fabric. Ah, there's another, more recent, scent beneath this window. This is what I was expecting to find, the smell of incense and burnt human hair."

"What?" Watson walked over. "Burnt hair?"

"A ritual was performed here earlier today," snarled the wolf. "Presumably, the ritual designed to draw you to Ravenspoint."

"So Ginger Rachel and this dancing guy are occultists?"

"One of them most certainly is. I told you, they'd require

certain items for such magick." Quist walked to the rubbish bin beneath the desk, his front paw crackling into furry fingers as he stooped to take out a crumpled sheet of paper. "For example, they'd need an image like *this*."

"Unbelievable," whispered the youth, staring at the close-up photograph of himself standing outside the Fishergate gym. Mystical symbols, in what appeared to be blood, had been drawn around his face. "They only took that a few hours ago."

"They must have connected their camera to the hotel printer to produce it." The wolf studied the picture. "I wrongly assumed they were trying to photograph *me* when I saw the camera outside the solicitor's office, but it was an image of *you* they wanted. Such magick wouldn't work on a supernatural creature such as myself; yet more proof that they're aware of my lycanthropy." He reached into the bin again. "Do you recognise this?"

"Hang on," gasped Watson. "That's one of my hairbrushes. It should be in the office bathroom."

"The same bathroom our Mrs Penrose asked to visit. This is why she left so quickly – she had what she wanted." Quist took a Coke can from the bin and sniffed it. "This tin is a different size to the ones I noticed in the minibar over there. It has your scent too, which means it's one of your empties, *also* from our bathroom bin."

"So why would she want *that*?"

"Your saliva, of course." The wolf tapped the drinking aperture with a huge finger talon. "Swabbed from here with a cotton bud."

"Right, you said they'd need blood, hair or semen." Watson grinned nervously. "I've been racking my brain to think where they could get hold of something like that. I thought about Donni last night, but I guess this lets *her* off the hook."

"Crowther or Penrose," said the wolf. "One of them is clearly an accomplished magician. Used in the ritual, your hair, saliva and photograph gave them a strong hold over you."

"We know this Crowther guy looks just like the dead occultist you told me about."

"Aleister Crowley?" Quist nodded. "Yes, the resemblance is uncanny. He could easily be a descendant and, if so, he would probably have the same magickal interests."

"I couldn't speak in front of Gazza," said Watson, "but could he actually *be* Crowley?"

Quist eyed him speculatively. "Around one-hundred and fifty years old?"

"*You* can talk," snorted his assistant. "You don't reckon he could be one of your lot, do you?"

"*My* lot?" The wolf smiled, something which, thanks to the lengthy fangs, always unnerved Watson. "I don't know. Believe it or not, we don't meet up at werewolf conventions and suchlike, or…"

The pair froze as the door suddenly opened and a young hotel cleaner walked in staring at her phone. Heading for the bureau, she picked up her Room Service clipboard, turned, and walked back out of the suite without looking up from the social media on her small screen. The door closed behind her and the wolf was finally able to release its breath in a relieved sigh.

"Incredible," whispered Watson, gulping. "Bloody hell, Guv, that was a bit *too* close."

"That's definitely the last time I complain about people staring at their phones," growled Quist. "Right, it's time we visited the hospital. Mister Tarrant will be able to tell us all about the person who took your photograph and performed the ritual."

"I'm guessing you're going to change first?" Watson held out the detective's clothes. "I don't think they allow smoking, or wolves in hospitals."

* * * *

Chapter 13

A sprawl of modern buildings in the suburb of Clifton, York Hospital stands one mile north of the city centre on Wigginton Road. Quist and Watson strode along one of the third floor corridors, the latter still cradling his wrist.

"Magick," whispered the youth, glancing about to ensure he wasn't overheard. "You've always said that magick is a science."

"That's true," confirmed Quist. "An incredibly ancient and well-guarded science that harnesses the natural ethereal energies and causes change to occur in conformity with human will. There are many occultists out there, the majority of whom loudly announce themselves on social media and even run occult websites. The genuine adepts, however, the powerful individuals that we've occasionally encountered, are very secretive about their abilities."

"Right," said Watson. "And one of these *genuine* occultists performed a magickal ritual in that hotel to remotely hypnotise me and force me to go to Ravenspoint. God knows why."

"*I* know why," said Quist, nodding grimly. "Whoever they are, I'm certain that it's *me* they actually want and, with you in their clutches, they assumed I'd come to this village looking for you."

Watson grinned. "And here's me thinking I was totally irresistible." He held up his bandaged hand. "Hey, seeing as we're here, I wonder if I should let someone take a look at this?"

"You could," said the detective. "But it's a sprain and they'll only give you the same advice I did. Rest it, apply a bag of frozen peas on the swelling and continue to use that compression bandage."

"I suppose." The young man looked around, wrinkling his nose. "I've never liked hospitals," he muttered. "They always remind me of disease and sick people."

"Really? Do you find libraries tend to remind you of books and people reading?"

"Yeah, that's really funny." He pulled a face. "But you know what I mean. Hospitals are always too warm and they have that *smell*. It's a smell all of their own; disinfectant, bleach and stuff. I honestly can't imagine what horrible scents you must be able to pick up with *that* nose."

His boss turned to him with an inquisitive expression.

"No, I meant the enhanced sense of smell," blurted Watson, quickly. "The supernatural thing, not the fact that you have a..."

"No need to dig that particular hole any deeper," said Quist, smirking. "This is the ward we're looking for."

They pushed through a pair of swing doors to find a work station manned by a slender male nurse. Watson ran an eye over the sculpted beard, hair bun, crowned white teeth and mahogany face, the latter courtesy of far too many sessions with a sun bed. On a dating website, the youth guessed this guy would probably list his interests as *gym, male grooming, gym and male grooming*.

"Hello there, Ryan." Quist read the nurse's name badge and gave him a warm smile. I wonder if you could help? We're looking for a patient named Oliver Tarrant. Your main reception informed us he was on this ward."

"The vehicle collision?" Returning the smile, the young man fluttered his eyes at the detective. "Mister Tarrant's been down in surgery, but I'm pleased to say he's conscious now. The thing is, ever since the anaesthetic wore off, he's been in a rather agitated state. Doctor Madden doesn't want him bothered by visitors."

"You come across as a caring soul, Ryan." Quist leant closer and lowered his voice to a sexy purr. "I can tell these things. I'm Gerald Tarrant and it's so reassuring to find my brother in such capable and, I really must say, such beautifully-manicured hands. I've travelled quite a way to see him and I'd be ever so grateful if you were to allow us just a couple of minutes together."

"Oh, my." The nurse grew flustered, his breathing speeding

up. Somewhere beneath the chocolate tan, his face turned a bashful shade of crimson. "Well, what can I say? You've twisted my arm, haven't you? Go on then, just for you. He's in one of the private rooms along the corridor there. Number four."

Those supernatural werewolf hormones could sometimes come in very useful, thought Watson, smirking. *Especially when combined with a little flirting.*

The youth followed Quist to the room where the patient lay half-asleep in a motorised bed. He wore a hospital gown, his upper body was raised into a semi-sitting position and the sheet over his broken legs was supported by a tubular frame.

"Hello again, Mister Tarrant." The detective closed the door behind them. "I'm afraid we didn't bring flowers, or..." He paused, peering curiously. He'd only glanced into the wrecked car this morning, but he knew that the person he'd seen at the wheel had curly blonde hair and he'd been much younger than this frail, white-haired character. "Um, you *are* Oliver Tarrant, aren't you?"

"Yes, I..." The elderly man roused himself from the doze and then stiffened. "Why do you ask that? How long was I asleep? How long have I been lying here in this place?"

"It's around nine hours since the accident." Quist walked to the foot of the bed and flicked through the clipboard notes. "They've neglected to record what time you were brought up to the ward from surgery. I take it you recognise me?"

"Of course I do," muttered Tarrant, examining the backs of his wrinkled hands and nervously fingering his facial lines. "No, this is wrong. This is happening far too fast."

"What's happening?" quizzed Watson.

"I can't stay here." Clearly scared, Tarrant threw back the bedsheet. "No, I have to leave. You have to help get me out of this place."

"I don't think you'll be going far, mate." Watson shrugged

apologetically. "Not with two broken legs."

"Why did you try to snatch me this morning?" asked Quist. "And why did you have those specialised handcuffs with you?"

"Be serious," snapped Tarrant. "You know perfectly well why they were silver."

The detective smiled tightly. "You called at Watson's house," he said. "I assume the idea was to abduct him too?"

"Look, I'll tell you everything," The old man began to tremble, his words a frightened stammer. "I swear it, but first you need to get me out of here."

"Surely the hospital food isn't *that* bad?" Watson grinned. "Listen, mate, you've got two broken legs and you..."

"It doesn't matter," whined Tarrant. "I can sign myself out and you can drive me, but it has to be *now*. I'll pay anything you ask – *anything*. Just drive me to a place named Ravenspoint. It's about three hours away in Northumberland."

"I know where it is," said Quist. "But before I agree to do anything, I want a few answers. An occult ritual was performed to draw my assistant to that village. Who do you have working as your magician?"

"Crowley," hissed Tarrant. "It's Crowley, but we don't have time for this. I have to get back to the Fountain."

"A descendant of Aleister Crowley?" asked Quist. "Are you talking about the man going by the name of Adrian Crowther?"

"No, Crowley – *the* Aleister Crowley."

The words were gargled, as if fluids were bubbling up to fill his wizened throat. Watson noticed how wisps of white hair had begun to drift away from the man's head, strangely reminiscent of a dandelion shedding its fluffy airborne seeds in a breeze.

"What do you mean by *we don't have time?*" The detective wrinkled his nose. "Why the urgency, and what on earth is that awful stink?"

Watson briefly wondered if there were any stinks that *weren't* awful, but he had to agree. A revolting stench had flooded the room, causing him to quickly clasp a hand over his mouth and gag. He'd never ventured down an Indian city sewer in a heatwave, but guessed the experience would probably be something like this.

"No," babbled Tarrant. "No, this is too soon. Not yet. Not..."

The words turned into a ghastly wet splutter as both eyes, followed by his whole face, sank inwards. The facial bones and skull collapsed, allowing his wrinkled head to horrifically deflate over the pillow like a punctured balloon.

"What the *fuck*?" Watson leapt back, pressing his spine hard against the wall and shaking uncontrollably. "What the fuck is *this*?"

The hideous transformation took only twelve seconds. Tarrant's ribcage crumbled beneath the hospital gown, his flesh swiftly putrefying and disintegrating, until the old man had disappeared completely and a gelatinous puddle of dark slime covered the bed in his place.

Five further seconds passed, silent save for Watson's terrified panting.

"Well..." murmured Quist. "I believe it's safe to say that neither of us were expecting *that*." He shot his assistant a concerned glance. "Are you alright?"

"Compared to *that* guy, I'd say I was doing really great." Nauseous and retching, Watson waved a shaking hand at the bed. Unspeakable goo had begun to drip from it and pool on the floor "What just happened, Guv? Right in front of our eyes, a guy turned into..." He groped for the correct word and came up with: "*Shit.*"

Quist nodded. "Loathe as I am to admit it, there is a certain resemblance."

"What do we do?" Gagging again, the youth turned away from the sickening sight. "What the hell do we do?"

"This smell is beyond belief." The detective gave him a

lopsided smile. "I think we should open a window."

"I meant…"

"I'm perfectly aware of what you meant." Quist grabbed his assistant's arm and pulled him to the door. "Come on, we're leaving."

"Are you crazy? We can't go anywhere without telling the doctors or someone about *this*."

"No, we're leaving right now, *fast*." Still gripping Watson's arm, his boss cracked open the door, checking both ways along the corridor, before hurrying out and turning right. "I noticed they have a camera covering Ryan's work station down there, so we need to go this way. We have to get away from here quickly before someone turns up."

"But why?" Watson glanced nervously over his shoulder. "We haven't done anything wrong."

"Very true," confirmed Quist. Spotting a door marked *Fire Exit*, he pushed it open, checking for cameras and pulling his assistant into a stairwell. "But the moment someone sees Tarrant, or rather what's left of him, the police will be called. God alone knows what they'll assume – dangerous chemicals, or some sort of acid attack – but we can't possibly explain what happened. A patient has somehow dissolved and the two men who were with him at the time falsely claimed to be his relatives. That will generate an entire night of questioning."

Watson raced down the steps behind the detective. "So what *did* happen to him?"

"I honestly don't know," admitted Quist. "But I can assure you it wasn't natural."

The youth laughed. "Hey, you don't say?"

"Tarrant had aged considerably since I saw him this morning, going from a blonde-haired man of around thirty to the white-haired geriatric we saw tonight. What we just witnessed seems to have been the fatal culmination of that accelerated aging process."

Quist arrived at the bottom of the flight and paused to ease open the exit door and peer into the hospital reception area. "He was desperate to get to Ravenspoint. That village is definitely where I'll find the answers. I'm going up there tomorrow to investigate Rachel Penrose's husband, if he even exists."

"*I'm* going?" Watson shot him a puzzled look. "What happened to *we're* going?"

"Follow me and act natural." The detective walked across the main lobby and out into the car park. "In answer to your question, you know how I feel responsible for your safety. This little mystery has intrigued me, but all of that just changed. We saw something back there which tells us this is going to be far more dangerous than I originally anticipated. Plus, you're injured…"

"I've twisted my wrist." The youth held up the bandaged hand as he hurried across the tarmac. "Bloody hell, Guv, it's not like I'm nine months pregnant. I'm fine and, if there's danger, you'll need me to watch your back."

"But you saw what happened to Tarrant." Arriving at the parked car, Quist jumped in. "I have no idea what caused that."

Watson grinned. "Hey, working with you, I've seen far worse shit. Isn't that what happens to Ubasteri when they die?"

"Yes, but this was very different." The detective stared pensively for a moment. "I'm not happy about you accompanying me, but if you're sure…"

"Of course I am." His assistant climbed into the passenger seat. "Hey, was he telling us the truth? Could this Ali Bongo magician guy somehow be alive?"

"Aleister Crowley? I really don't know." Quist started the car and pulled out of the hospital grounds. "It seemed to me that Tarrant would have said literally *anything* to get home to Ravenspoint. He realised he was aging fast, so I can only presume that getting back there would have somehow prevented the molecular decomposition."

Watson nodded. "If that's right, then I can see why he was so desperate. He mentioned a fountain. I wonder if he meant the village hotel?"

"Perhaps." Pulling into a pub car park, Quist lit a cigarette and dropped the window to vent the smoke. He took out his phone and a scrap of paper and keyed in a number. "Now that we're clear of the inevitable police circus that will soon be appearing back there, I can speak to our new client." Smiling thinly, he switched to speaker and waited.

"Hello there," said Rachel. "Mister Quist? It's good to hear from you. Before we go any further, I ought to apologise for leaving so abruptly earlier. I received an urgent text and..."

"Oh, that's fine," lied the detective. "Think nothing of it. This is just a quick call to let you know that we're heading up to Ravenspoint tomorrow. We'll be visiting this Fountain hotel you mentioned to investigate your husband's movements."

"That's great news," said the girl.

Quist smirked at his assistant. "As a matter of fact, Watson was so keen to begin the case, I had to actually restrain him from travelling up there today."

There was a pause. "Er... right."

"Anyway, let's hope this was all just a misunderstanding."

"I'm sorry?" Rachel sounded wary. "What do you mean?"

"Your husband, of course. Let's hope these fears you have are unfounded."

"Oh, yes," she said. "I see."

"Well, that's all for now, Mrs Penrose," said Quist, breezily. "I'll be in touch again as soon as I have anything to report."

"So she lied to us?" said Watson, watching him pocket the phone. "She lied, those people tried kidnapping both of us, and they put some sort of magickal spell on me. But despite all that, we're still taking her case?"

"We are indeed," confirmed Quist.

"This is almost certainly a trap, but we're still going to Ravenspoint?"

"We're still going." The detective blew a cloud of cigarette smoke through the window and gave him a lopsided smile. "Sometimes the best way to fully understand a trap is to simply walk into it."

"Er, yeah…" Watson frowned as he tried to make sense of this statement.. "Yeah, good point, Guv."

* * * *

Chapter 14

The bleak vastness of Northumberland extends from the northern moors of Yorkshire to the mountains of southern Scotland. Apart from Alnwick, Amble, and Berwick, none of which are exactly huge, there's very little habitation to be found between Newcastle and Edinburgh. The snow-covered Cheviot Hills were visible in the distance as Quist motored north through the county with Watson holding an open road atlas on his lap.

The youth had never understood how his boss could drive with the radio switched off like this. Watson didn't own a car, but his young friends found it impossible to be inside one without loud music constantly playing. Their radios burst into life with the ignition and only ended when the vehicle was vacated and locked. Passengers shouted over the noise, and if something of importance needed to be discussed, or if the car was part of a funeral procession, the music was turned down, but *never* off. He decided it was best not to voice his thoughts. *It might prompt the Guv into putting on some of his classical crap.*

Watson had heard enough of this last night to keep him going for an entire year. Concerned with his assistant's safety, following the house visit from Tarrant and his huge accomplice, Quist had insisted that Watson should pack a small bag and stay at his cottage. The evening had been spent with the detective browsing occult volumes from his extensive library and Watson browsing social media, all to the *wonderful* background strains of Mozart and Grieg.

"Hey, this is some weird shit," muttered the youth, staring once again at his phone.

"What have you found?" asked his boss. "Another one of those films you insisted upon showing me last night of cats doing handstands?"

"No, you remember the news the other day about the Mexican

drug cartel? Someone's posted pictures of the bodies."

"A little ghoulish," said Quist, turning from the wheel to glance. The shots were pixelated, but the digital camouflage couldn't disguise the fact that there was an awful lot of *red* in the photos.

"Some police expert's given his opinion," said Watson. "He reckons they looked as if they were torn apart by wild animals."

"I suppose we should be thankful that drug wars and massacres such as this occur on the other side of the world." The detective nodded. "For now, at least."

They'd passed by Durham and then Tyneside before noon this Friday morning, the pockets of civilisation noticeably diminishing the further north they travelled. Thorny hedgerows traced dark, straggly lines across a winter wilderness punctuated with rocky outcrops, lone blasted trees, and the occasional woodland clump nestled by isolated farmsteads. An icy breeze rippled the frosty grass, and skeletal bushes were twisted into grotesque weather-beaten shapes. Dotted with surly-looking gulls and crows, the snowy landscape to their right rolled away towards a choppy grey ocean.

Pocketing his phone, Watson spotted a hare racing across a white field and vaguely contemplated how it might taste with chips and beans. Quist had prepared breakfast before leaving, aware of how his assistant constantly grumbled about hunger, and then he'd stopped at an A1 service area for something extra to eat. That was sixty minutes ago, however, and Watson was already musing about his rucksack stowed in the boot. He'd packed the bag with a few overnight essentials: toothbrush, a change of underwear, phone charger and a tube of cheese Pringles. The young man pictured the crisps and sighed. *So close, yet so far away.*

"Are you alright?" asked the detective.

"Yeah, just a little peckish."

"Unbelievable," muttered Quist, shaking his head.

"Well, it's okay for you, but I'm a growing lad, aren't I?"

Watson shoved the road atlas back in the glove compartment, wondering if *anyone* over the past century had ever kept gloves in one of these. "I've never really thought about it, but do you actually *need* to eat? I mean, let's face it, you're not going to die of starvation if you don't."

"Quite true," admitted Quist. "All those years ago, when I came to terms with what had happened to me, I realised I'd no longer require food. I *also* knew that I'd never age and it was imperative that I should blend in with society. I went through the daily ritual of eating meals to appear like a *normal* person and, very quickly, I grew accustomed to it. I still enjoy the taste too."

"Seriously? All that vegan crap, like the porridge you made with almond milk this morning?" Watson laughed, before pausing for a long moment. "Speaking of porridge... Listen, Guv, I've seen some crazy paranormal shit with you, so watching a guy turn *into* porridge doesn't shock me the way it would have done once, but..."

"But it was still somewhat weird?" broke in the detective.

"You could say that." He laughed again. "Some might say *impossible*. What could have caused him to dissolve?"

"As you can probably imagine, I've thought about little else," admitted Quist.

The pair had checked the local news on the morning television channels before leaving. As expected, the police had arrived at the hospital shortly after they left and the ward was evacuated. The reporter explained how details of Oliver Tarrant's death remained confidential. Chemical specialists had been called in, however, along with germ warfare experts and a Hazmat team, the news of which must have quickly alleviated the problems of any patients suffering from constipation.

"I'm guessing they won't find much," said Watson. "You reckon the explanation is almost certain to be supernatural? I mean, we've seen something similar with the Ubasteri when they die"

"Supernatural molecular breakdown." Quist nodded. "Yes, but Tarrant wasn't connected to that cult and the disintegration was different. As you know, I poured through all those occult books last night searching for some sort of answer. After you'd retired to bed, I also read up on the magician Aleister Crowley. He was quite a character and famously coined the phrase: *Do what thou wilt shall be the whole of the law.* It became his personal motto. Basically do anything you want, no matter what the consequences and..."

"Er, no," said Watson. "I think you'll find *that* was coined by the rock group Thin Lizzy. They had a big hit with it."

His boss looked blank.

"Ah, no, my mistake. That was: *Do Anything You Want To.*"

"Crowley was born in 1875," continued Quist. "He was an artist, an author, a poet and a mountaineer, but mostly he was famous, or rather infamous, for his occult practises. He referred to himself as the Great Beast and he's the one who began the trend of spelling magick with a letter K to differentiate *real* magick from the stage magic of theatrical conjurers."

The youth nodded. "We've met occultists before."

"We have indeed," agreed Quist. "But Crowley has always been the most prominent name in that field and he's the glorious poster boy for all the occult wannabes, sometimes quite literally a poster boy. Most people are only aware of *one* picture of him, the staring photograph with the shaven head, and you can find it on posters, book covers and sometimes tattoos. The image even appears on a Beatles album cover."

"There must have been other magicians," pointed out Watson. "So why is this one so famous?"

"Crowley went out of his way to cultivate fame by shocking society with his outrageous and disreputable lifestyle. He conjured up the demon Choronzon in the Egyptian desert. He worked extensively with sex magick and..."

"Whoo!" The youth sat upright. "Shagging birds on altars?"

"There's a little more to it than that," sighed Quist. "It's telling, however, that you should be more interested in sex magick than the invocation of an actual demon. Crowley also devised his own religion which he named Thelema and he established an abbey to the cult on Sicily."

"Oliver Tarrant told us this guy was their magician," said Watson. "But like you pointed out, that would make him about 150."

Quist nodded. "He died in Hastings just after the war, or at least that's what everyone believes."

"But he could have survived somehow? Like I said yesterday, he might be one of your lot." Watson turned with a puzzled frown. "So how come you don't know anything about Ravenspoint? You seem to have been to most places over the years."

"I've travelled through this area many times," said Quist. "But it remains one of the few places where I've never stayed for any length of time. Northumberland has the lowest population of all the counties and it's always been prudent for me to live somewhere with more people, somewhere that allows me to more easily blend in with the crowds." He gestured across the snow-covered fields. "This is one of the wildest parts of Britain."

Watson shrugged. "Great, if you like everything deserted."

"I must admit I do love the openness." His boss nodded to the sea and the distant archipelago of dark rocks. "Look, those are the Farne Islands. That's where Grace Darling, the lighthouse keeper's daughter, made her famous boat trip to rescue the shipwrecked mariners."

"Another enthralling history lesson that I must have missed," drawled Watson.

They headed through the village of Longhoughton and past the picturesque fishing hamlet of Craster, following the meandering coastline of bays, dunes and rugged headlands. The ocean stretched to the horizon, scudding snow clouds transforming the water from sparkling blue to a gunmetal grey.

"Hey, look at that." The youth pointed to the imposing ruins of a castle ahead.

"That's Dunstanburgh," said Quist. "Warkworth, Alnwick, Ravenspoint, Bamburgh, Lindisfarne – there are more castles in Northumberland than any other county. This whole area was a buffer zone between England and Scotland, so you can imagine the violent past of these buildings. The Battle of Flodden took place just over the hill to our left."

"Never heard of it."

"Didn't you *ever* listen in history at school?"

"Excuse *me*," said Watson. "But I went to an *academy*, not a school. The government changed the names years ago to make them sound a bit more upmarket. I suppose it was to make us all academics rather than thick kids."

"*Thick?*" echoed Quist. "On the contrary, I've always maintained that you're far more intelligent and astute than you realise. Your mind is sharp and enquiring and what you lack in knowledge, you make up for in streetwise common sense."

"Ah, cheers, Guv, but I still won't sleep with you." Watson laughed. "Anyway, they did the same with the polytechnic colleges too and renamed them all universities. My mate went to one and came out as a Doctor of Welding. But, no, I don't suppose I listened much in the lessons. I hated science, in fact I think I might have been Newton Intolerant."

"You clearly listened in whichever lesson was devoted to terrible puns."

The youth grinned. "But getting down to detective business, what's the plan when we get to this place? Are we just sniffing around, or are we actually going to investigate this woman's hubby?"

Quist let out a dry laugh. "We both know this *husband*

doesn't exist. Rachel Penrose's story was a ruse to get us here, but if someone *has* checked into the village hotel claiming to be Reece Penrose, then yes, we'll keep a close watch on him."

"Why?"

"Because that's what she asked us to do. Everything so far has been engineered to get us to this village and I intend to allow this bizarre situation to play out and see what transpires. Someone in Ravenspoint is obviously aware of my secret. They desperately wants us here and we need to discover why."

"We're guessing they know about you because they had those silver handcuffs." Watson frowned. "What if they have *other* things made of silver? You know, the sort of things you fire out of a gun?"

"That doesn't make sense." Quist turned the car onto a narrow stretch of road that ran parallel with the coastline. "If killing me with silver bullets was their intention, they could shoot me in York with a long-range rifle. They wouldn't need to bring me all the way to Northumberland to do it."

The road led up onto the Craggan headland, a tapering mass of volcanic whinstone that thrust out into the North Sea. A village stood at the end of the promontory with a castle at the furthest point, its towers a dark golden stone that shone picturesquely in the bright December sunlight. Waves crashed in white explosions against the rocks below.

"There it is," said the detective. "That's Ravenspoint."

From a distance, like this, it was hard to distinguish where the bedrock ended and Ravenspoint began. A rampart wall ran along the edge of the low cliffs, surrounding the grey buildings and blending with the rugged terrain. Some ten feet in height, the wall cut straight across the short peninsula, completely separating the triangular-shaped community from outsiders.

"Impressive," said Quist. "There are plenty of British towns and cities with fortifications, but there can't be too many walled villages. Like I said, this was a volatile area. Their wall is lower and far less substantial than York, but it would have afforded them protection from the infamous Border Reivers and other marauding Scots back in the Jacobite days."

"Jacobites?" echoed his assistant, grinning. "Are they the ones that grow *down* from the roof of the cave?"

Flanked by thick gorse bushes, this road along the peninsula was the only way into the village and Watson noticed the yellow *no parking* lines that ran along either side of the tarmac starting a half-mile away. He guessed this was a mercenary way to make money. Like many tourist attractions, there would be a private car park within the walls where any visitors wishing to look around would have no option, but to pay an extortionate fee.

The road arrived at the perimeter wall where an entrance tower with rooftop crenulations housed an open gateway. Compared to the splendid York barbicans, this really *was* a poor relation, just a functional archway to admit traffic. Motor vehicles hadn't been dreamt of when this was constructed, but fortuitously it was large enough to accommodate ambulances and fire engines.

"This would appear to be the only way in," said Quist, driving through. The road tarmac ended beneath the tower and changed to cobblestones beyond. "Sturdy gates would have hung here in the past, to be closed when the Scots were raiding the…"

The detective convulsed as his car exited the archway and, stamping on the brake, he pulled up to the kerb.

"Guv?" quizzed Watson. "Hey, are you okay?"

"What the hell *was* that?" Quist twisted in his seat to look back at the barbican tower. "I just experienced a sharp jolt. A seizure, almost like an electric shock as we drove through there. Did you feel anything?"

"Who are you?"

"I'm sorry?" said the detective.

"Eh?" Watson looked puzzled. "Sorry for what? For braking so hard?"

"What do you mean?"

"What do you mean – *what do I mean*?"

Quist let out an exasperated sigh. "This conversation is beginning to resemble an old music hall comedy routine. You just said: *who are you*?"

"No I didn't."

"What?" He gave his assistant a curious look and then shook his head. "Very well. Let's forget about it."

Slightly shaken, the detective glanced again at the entrance arch in the rear view mirror as he pulled away to drive along the narrow street.

What the hell was all that about? wondered the bemused Watson.

* * * *

Chapter 15

The cobbled streets of Ravenspoint were tight and winding, and the buildings tall and huddled to utilise the limited space within the defensive boundary wall. Oriel windows with leaded glass were everywhere, along with the old bull's-eye sixteen-pane sashes. This place reminded Watson of a miniature version of York; most of these streets resembled the Shambles, but in place of a Minster, Ravenspoint Castle rose from the eastern end of the village to dominate the community.

"Mmh, how about that?" murmured the youth. "No signal."

Quist turned from marvelling at the architecture to see him fiddling with his phone. "Put it away," he snapped, irritably. "We have more important things to concern us than social media and whatever Bryony had for her lunch."

The detective was still pondering the bizarre electrical jolt he'd felt on passing through the village entrance. He had no idea what it could have been and, ever since, he'd felt a mild tingling sensation in his head.

"Weird though, don't you reckon?" Watson slid the phone back into his blouson pocket. "These days, the only time you *don't* get a signal is if you're a character in a horror movie."

"I'll tell you what *is* weird," said Quist. "This small village has sustained a fair amount of damage over the years."

"What do you mean?" The young man looked around.

"There." His boss gestured to a crack in a house wall, pointed with cement. "And there on that gable end. Look, there are cracks everywhere. Some are old, but the majority appear to be more recent."

"Whatever." Watson shrugged. "I thought we were here to see why they tried to kidnap us, and why that Tarrant guy melted into a pile of sludge, not to investigate cowboy builders."

Quist smiled, still wondering what could possibly be causing this bizarre buzzing inside his head. Being a werewolf certainly had its drawbacks, but ever since he was attacked and left for dead all those years ago, he'd never once been affected by headaches.

Watson realised he'd been wrong to expect a village car park with expensive payment machines to fleece the tourists. There were very few open areas within Ravenspoint and certainly nowhere whatsoever dedicated to parking. *No Parking* signs were displayed above any spots large enough for vehicles and yellow lines ran alongside the gutters of every thoroughfare. Some cars stood on the streets, but these almost certainly belonged to residents with permits.

He shook his head, baffled. *So where the hell were visitors supposed to leave their cars?*

"This is like something from a Hammer horror film," he said, peering up alleyways and snickets as they drove by. "One of those little Transylvanian villages filled with vampires." He glanced at his boss, smirking. "Or maybe werewolves. Have you seen the spooky mist down these alleys?"

"Yes." Quist glanced up a snicket. "It's a ground mist that seems to congregate in the back streets and yards. Some sort of meteorological phenomenon caused by this icy coastal weather, I presume."

Noticing more cracks and repair work, the detective continued along the short street to a crossroads with a solitary shop. Clearly the village store, its ornamental timber frames and cornices surrounded two Georgian bay windows filled with provisions. People walked the narrow pavements and Quist saw how some of them stopped to look as his car passed by, almost as if they knew who he was. He turned towards the castle and followed the meandering cobbled street of houses to one of the few open areas where the clifftop defensive ramparts came into view on their left. Another wall, again ten feet in height, abutted this and crossed the space in front of them, separating the castle and its courtyard from the village.

Ravenspoint Castle wasn't built of the grey granite used in the rest of the community, but a honey-coloured sandstone, leading Quist to guess that this building would have appeared first on the headland and the village then grew around it. It wasn't a medieval stronghold with a drawbridge, but a fortified manor with its mullioned windows set high and fitted with heavy shutters. Built on the very edge of the Craggan promontory, the wall protected the castle on the village side and the cliffs rendered it unassailable from the ocean. This place would never have impeded a real army with canon firepower, but during the volatile times here in the border country, the villagers would have retreated inside and it doubtless provided sufficient safety from marauding Scots.

"Have you seen all these *no parking* lines?" asked Watson, tetchily. "Whoever sells yellow paint around here must make a friggin' fortune. It's like they don't want anyone visiting."

"Yes, I've noticed." Quist narrowed his eyes. "Rather peculiar, isn't it?"

A small barbican gateway tower was built into the castle wall leading from this square into the private courtyard beyond. Even though such fortifications were no longer necessary, the row of stalactite-like spikes showing beneath the archway suggested it housed an actual portcullis. Ignoring the yellow lines, a minibus was parked beside this entrance and the passengers, a group of surly youths, were slouching through with hands stuffed in pockets. They were led by a smartly-dressed woman with a clipboard and a fraught expression.

"What's going on there?" asked Watson. "Is it a school daytrip, or something?"

"They look a little old for school," said Quist, turning the car into the street on his right. "Let's take a look along here. According to our supposed *client*, Mrs Penrose, they have a hotel in the village named the Fountain. This place isn't exactly large so we shouldn't have any difficulty finding it."

"Pain," muttered his assistant. "The pain is so bad."

"I'm sorry? Do you mean your wrist?"

"Eh?" The youth frowned. "I didn't say anything."

"Really?" Quist regarded him curiously. "My mistake."

* * * *

The only hotel in Ravenspoint, the Fountain was surprisingly large and upmarket, with white-painted stone walls, bay windows, and an arched tunnel leading through to a rear car park. Decorative iron mangers were fixed to the frontage and Watson thought how nice these would look filled with flowers, along with a few hanging baskets. He suddenly realised he hadn't seen a single flower, bush or tree anywhere in the village.

"Ah," said Quist, spotting a large *No Vacancies* sign by the front door. "It seems the establishment is full. Nevertheless, we'll call in for a drink and get a feel for this place."

"Look at that." The youth peered up at the swinging sign as his boss turned into the archway. The painted illustration showed what appeared to be a brown star with radiating lines of light. "What's it supposed to be?"

"I can't imagine," admitted Quist, driving through the tunnel. "It doesn't look much like a fountain, does it?"

"To be honest, it looks like someone's bumhole," laughed Watson.

The detective raised an inquisitive eyebrow as his assistant clamped a hand to his mouth to supress a fit of giggling.

"So is this *the* fountain?" asked the young man, wiping tears of laughter from his eyes. "The one that Oliver Tarrant was so keen to get to?"

"Perhaps," said Quist. "There doesn't appear to be an abundance of fountains in Ravenspoint, so this hotel would certainly be the most plausible explanation. However, *keen* is something of an understatement. Tarrant gave me the impression he would have literally killed to reach it."

He drove through the freezing mist that drifted across the cobbled rear yard and parked in one of the spaces, eyeing the other vehicles as he pulled on his jacket. Watson noticed them too and nodded approvingly at the Bentley, the two Porsches, the Range Rover and the Maserati.

"Nice motors," he muttered, following his boss to the rear porch. "I wonder if they've got a football team visiting?"

Quist led the way through an entrance hallway, with a large fake Christmas tree standing at the bottom of a tinsel-covered staircase. The two men walked into a luxurious lounge bar where several groups of people sat drinking and chatting. Oak ceiling beams were draped with festive decorations and a welcoming stone fireplace crackled with a pile of burning logs.

"Hey, who's that guy there?" whispered Watson. He nodded to a plump, middle-aged man who sat by the fire sipping a brandy and chatting with a long-legged girl. "I've seen him on television."

"You've probably seen him on the news," said Quist, heading for the bar. "That's the Tory politician Nigel Drummond."

A busty blonde woman appeared behind the counter, smiling at the visitors.

"Good afternoon," said Quist. "I saw the sign outside, but I was wondering if perhaps you had anything available for tonight?"

"Ah, the sign." She shook his head. "No, actually that's a mistake. We *do* have rooms."

And you haven't thought to take it down? thought Watson, bemused. *Yeah, that's great business sense. Why not stick up another wrong sign telling potential customers you have no beer?*

"Let's take a look now..." The woman brought out a laptop from beneath the counter. "A double room, is it?"

"A twin," corrected Quist. "We're together, but we're not

actually *together*."

"That's right, luv." Watson grinned. "I'm a good-looking guy, but believe me, if I were gay, I could do a lot better than *that*." He jerked a thumb at his boss and began to laugh again.

"Calm down," said Quist, handing over a credit card.

"Yeah, yeah." The youth took out his phone as the girl entered the booking details into her counter laptop. "I don't know why, but I just feel full of life and... Hey, there's a signal in here."

"Oh, the Lord be praised," muttered the detective, heading for the door. "Wait here, would you? I'll go and bring in our things."

"We're in lucky seven," said Watson, as his boss returned with his leather trenchcoat and the two small bags. "Willow here says it's at the top of the stairs on the right."

"Enjoy your stay with us," said Willow, returning to her bar work. "I'm sure you will."

"Yes, merry Christmas," said Quist, feeling once again the peculiar mild buzzing inside his head. The sensation was almost like something tickling the inside of his skull. *What the hell was it?*

Returning to the hallway, they climbed the staircase and walked along a plush corridor. Watson tapped the key card on the lock, pushed open the door and let out a low whistle of delight.

"Hey, now this is terrific, Guv." The young man raced around the room, checking the bathroom and walk-in closet. "We've only got ourselves a private little steam room in there, not to mention a friggin' Jacuzzi."

"Yes, very upmarket," said Quist, eyeing the decor. "I have to say, this unknown village hotel is reminiscent of the London Savoy."

"Whooo!" Watson flopped on one of the twin beds and jumped up and down to test it. "Wheee!"

"Are you actually feeling *alright*?" The detective gave him a puzzled look, aware that this was totally out of character. "First all the helpless laughter and now you're leaping about like an excited child."

"Yeah," he chuckled. "I just feel a little…"

"Giddy?"

"Something like that. It's a weird feeling." Watson bounced again on the bed, giggling. "Great mattress. I like them nice and thick like this. Those thin Japanese-style mattresses are no good for me. I think I might be Futon Intolerant."

"You really should be performing stand-up comedy." Shaking his head, Quist pulled on his overcoat and headed for the door. "Come along. We'll take a look around this place, starting here in the hotel. We need to mingle with the villagers, but I don't intend to ask any awkward questions. Instead we'll use our eyes and ears and go along with whatever scenario arises."

The pair descended the stairs to the bar area where another Christmas tree, smaller than the one in the hall, stood by the open fireplace. Gold festive trimmings hung from the overhead beams.

"Hello there," said a man's cheery voice. "Drink what thou wilt shall be the whole of the law."

Quist turned to the bar counter where a customer sat perched on one of the high stools. The detective stiffened. Silver-haired and well-dressed, the man looked to be in his late fifties. He *also* looked exactly like the late Aleister Crowley.

"I'm offering you a drink." The man held out his hand. "Mister Quist? Mister Watson? I'm very pleased to meet you at last. I'm Aleister."

* * * *

Chapter 16

The complex of cellars beneath Ravenspoint Castle extended through several chambers, all constructed from sandstone blocks and supported by vaulted ceilings. Ten sullen youths stood in the largest of these rooms, petty criminals on the Newcastle Young Offender Programme, along with their supervisor Alma Priestley. The guided tour of the building was almost over and, so far, the young men had shown little in the way of interest. As far as one or two were concerned, looking around this place was only marginally preferable to having bleach rubbed into their eyes.

Thirty-two years old and suffering from, what her managers referred to as, *chronic contempt*, Alma Priestley hated her job and the teenage felons she had to work with. Her department motto was: *Let's Give Something Back*, but she felt the residents of Newcastle would probably appreciate a say in the matter. Rather than cleaning graffiti, picking up litter and clipping hedges, the community might prefer these youths to *give back* the laptops, gaming consoles, phones and other items they'd stolen.

Alma nurtured many pet hates, but the current one to top her list was this new, progressive *Schooling Initiative*. Her work role had recently been broadened by management to incorporate these ludicrous educational trips, usually to stately homes and places like the Beamish open-air museum. As a supervisor, Alma had to drive the minibus and oversee the outings, all at the taxpayer's expense. The enlightened aim was to provide young felons with a fresh and healthy outlook on life, which would hopefully give them purpose and prevent reoffending. *That* was the idea.

Alma had her own idea of what to do with them – they could be put to work as scarecrows. Traditional scarecrows were worse than useless; the birds know the dummies aren't real. Instead of having offenders tidying gardens, where they can case the homes for future crimes, they could be ankle-tagged and sent into crop fields as living bird scarers. She'd entered this into the department suggestion scheme, but so far, there'd been no feedback. This was typical. She'd still heard nothing from her previous suggestion of offering vodka and rolling tobacco to offenders in exchange for sterilisation.

Alma looked around the castle cellar. A private dwelling, Ravenspoint had never been open to the general public as such, but local groups, such as schools and historical societies, could make website bookings and partake in these guided tours. Her boss had contacted the place to arrange this visit three months ago, but he'd given up hope of a reply when yesterday's unexpected email arrived.

Fortunately, this *educational* outing hadn't been as exasperating and dull as Alma had expected; their guide Richard Brunton had seen to that. She liked men who could make her laugh, and here was a huge alpha male with a dark sense of humour, not to mention deep blue eyes and a head of lustrous black hair. Dressed in a white Fair Isle sweater, his muscular frame towered over the group.

"So we're nearly at the end of our tour," said Brunton. "We started up there on the battlements and now, guess what? We're in the lowest part of the castle."

Tugging up his sweatshirt hood, Leyton Carter turned away from the guide to run his bored gaze over the underground room. Obscured by a tarpaulin sheet, something large and square – almost as big as a garden shed – stood against the wall.

"What a way to spend a fuckin' Friday afternoon," he grunted, walking over to lift the sheet. "Hey, what's this under here?"

"Don't touch that," snapped the guide. "There's nothing there that would interest you."

"And put your hood down," said Alma. "You little scu…"

"It's cold down here," moaned Leyton.

Alma bit her tongue; she'd almost said *scummer*. Apparently her delicate charges didn't like being referred to as *scummers* and, by way of a polite reminder, the department had issued her with two written warnings.

Another member of Alma's group, Josh Keegan, eyed the opposite wall where rows of bottles lay cradled in wooden racking, "I see the Laird likes his wine," he said, sizing them up to estimate if any could be secreted under his denim jacket. "Are there any free samples?"

Brunton gave a sarcastic smile that seemed to suggest there *weren't*. "The Mulgraves stored their wine down here in enormous wooden vats when the castle was first built. Rumour has it that they..."

"I like wine," interrupted Alma. She'd always been attracted to large guys like this: brawny young farmer types, rugby players and especially boxers. "Can you recommend anywhere around here that serves a decent glass? Maybe a place where *you* like to go drinking yourself?"

"We'll speak about that afterwards." The huge man winked at her and turned back to the youths. "As I mentioned earlier, the Mulgraves had this castle built in the early 1600s and Nathaniel Mulgrave was the first to live here."

Carlton Walker's ears pricked up. He enjoyed reading books, but he'd never dream of sharing such volatile information with the Community Payback group – it was best not to appear too clever or different amongst these people. Carlton had recently stolen a book named *Our Unexplained World*, one of those sensationalist 'coffee table' volumes about the supernatural, and Nathaniel Mulgrave's name was mentioned in the occult chapters. He'd been hoping to ask about this character during today's visit and this seemed like an ideal opportunity.

"Nathaniel..." he repeated. "That guy was really into the dark arts, wasn't he?"

"A black magician?" Brunton laughed, before opening a door

to reveal a flight of wide stone steps that terminated in a sandy soil floor some fifteen feet below. "Yes, I've heard all those spooky stories. His daughter was a black witch too, if you believe in that sort of thing."

"Hey, are you allowed to say *black* magician these day?" asked one of the thicker youths.

Brunton ignored him. "Okay," he said, gesturing down the steps. Dim bulbs drooped from the arched ceiling and he swung back the heavy door to provide additional illumination. "This is the final part of the tour, so down we go."

"You say witches lived here?" Carlton shivered slightly and edged closer to Alma, not realising he'd have found more human warmth spooning a mortuary corpse. "Er, you know what? I'd better not go down there. I'm kind of claustrophobic."

"Right," sighed his supervisor. Strangely enough, the claustrophobia had never stopped him squeezing through those tight bathroom windows when the homeowners were out. "Stay up here with me then. Everyone else form a line and follow your guide."

"Don't be silly," said Brunton. "You don't want to miss seeing the dungeon; it's the best part."

"A *dungeon*?" Leyton gasped excitedly. "Did lots of people die horribly down there on racks and shit?"

"Probably." Brunton winked at the supervisor. "They certainly don't build dungeons for folk to have fun and games in."

Alma winked back. She was no stranger to flirtatious attention and, over the years, she'd been gleefully triumphant in several harassment dismissals. *Yes, she'd definitely be giving this man her number before heading back to Newcastle.*

"This is the oldest part of our castle," said the guide. "The lower cellar hasn't changed over the past four-hundred years. We call it the dungeon, but in reality no one was ever held prisoner here. Shackles and chains were installed when it was built, just in case, and you can still see them down there."

"Well, just imagine that." Alma smiled sexily. "Manacled against a wall and completely helpless. Ooh, that sounds awful."

"It's wide enough to go down three-abreast," said Brunton, stepping aside. "But when you set off, take it steady, okay? The steps aren't slippery, but they're very worn."

"Er…" Alma pictured the morons under her charge pushing each other and stumbling. More to the point, she pictured piles of compensation claims sitting on her desk. "I assumed you'd be leading the way?"

"No, *I'm* not going," he chuckled. "It's much too scary for *me* down there."

A smell billowed up the tunnel as the youths descended, jostling and joking with one another. It was a musty stench of mould, damp, and something else – something reminiscent of a refrigerator when the fleshy contents are in the first sweet stages of putrefaction. Filled with a sudden anxiety, the supervisor opened her mouth to call the group back, but reason overcame the idiotic notion. *Of course it would smell. It was an underground room, and what possible harm could come from an unpleasant odour?* The last thing she wanted was to appear foolish in front of this gorgeous man.

Brushing back her hair, she smirked coquettishly. "So it's too scary, is it? I wouldn't have thought a big strong boy like you would be scared of the dark."

"Oh the dark doesn't bother me," he said, gesturing down the steps. "Just the things that the dark sometimes hides from us."

"Well I happen to like spooky things," said Alma. "Actually I love *anything* that makes my heart beat faster, if you know what I mean?"

Ignoring the insinuation, Brunton turned and stiffened to see that someone had silently walked up behind him. *His* heart certainly began to beat faster. He thought he'd have become used to Maria

Crane since their first meeting in Mexico last week, but this seemingly innocuous woman with the black eye-patch still made him nervous. Very few people had ever made Brunton nervous.

"They've arrived," said Crane. "You'll be pleased to know that Quist has just checked into the hotel with his young associate."

"Good." Brunton checked his watch. "We're almost finished here."

Alma peered icily at the newcomer, looking her up and down with barely concealed resentment. She'd always had a liking for designer clothes and this middle-aged woman clearly shared her expensive tastes. The black Italian suit and the boots must have cost more than a public servant like herself made in three whole months. With an indignant sniff, she turned back to the open door. Away from their supervisor, the group below had begun to grow noisy, but Leyton's voice could be heard above the jabbering.

"Hey, what tripped me up?" he shouted. "A root wrapped around my ankle."

Here we go, thought Alma. *Here come those fucking compensation claims.*

"I want to watch," said Crane, approaching the doorway.

"Huh?" Brunton frowned. "But you saw it last night."

"I saw one of your volunteers. No, I want to watch the real thing."

Carlton gave his supervisor a vacant look, baffled as to what they could be talking about.

"What the *fuck*?" yelled Josh from the lower chamber. "What *are* those root things?"

"I'm afraid there's nothing to see." Brunton clicked off the light switch. "We always do this in darkness."

"Spoilsport," said Crane, laughing quietly. "I've already told you I dislike you and you're doing nothing to change that."

Her words were drowned by the noise. At first Alma thought

the piercing shrillness was a siren – perhaps the light had fused the electrics causing the fire alarm to trip in – but the momentary idea was crushed by a sickening realisation. The youths down below were screaming. The entire group were screaming as one.

"Why did you turn off the light?" Alma started towards the dungeon door, but the huge man threw it shut. "What on earth…"

"Don't worry, sweetheart." He winked. "Believe me, it doesn't last long."

"They're terrified." Alma gaped at her tour guide and then turned to the woman with the eye patch. "You need to…"

"They're not terrified." Brunton struck a match, lighting a cigarette as the screaming abruptly stopped. "They're gone." He let out a cruel laugh. "I couldn't smoke during the tour. They were young offenders and we're supposed to set an example. What kind of role model would smoke in front of them?"

"I'm curious," said Crane, nodding to Alma and Carlton. "Why are these two still here?"

"We need their bodies intact." Brunton shrugged. "For the bus crash to appear genuine, the authorities need to find a couple of corpses in the wreckage."

"Crash? Corpses?" Alma's mouth fell open. The connections between her ears and her brain had quite obviously malfunctioned in some way. "Er, I'm sorry, but *what* did you just say?"

* * * *

Chapter 17

Quist gazed at the silver-haired man sitting at the hotel bar, his eyes widening in amazement. "I've been perusing internet photographs," he said, composing himself and cautiously shaking the outstretched hand. "Ballroom photographs of a gentleman named Adrian Crowther. I thought perhaps this Crowther was a descendant with a remarkable resemblance to you, but no. Here, in the flesh and close-up, I can see it really *is* you." He turned to Watson. "Incredible as it may be, this *is* Aleister Crowley."

"Ah, the one and only." Grinning widely, Crowley threw his arms apart like a stage performer. "Yes, I've been using the name Crowther for many years. As I'm sure *you* will understand, Bernard, it saves me the trouble of having to answer a host of problematic questions concerning longevity."

Watson ran a suspicious eye over him. Handsome and well-groomed, the magician appeared to be in his late fifties and in great health. He wore an expensive jacket, open-necked shirt and trousers, and, although it was late December, his skin glowed with a light brown tan. His perfect white smile appeared to be natural, as opposed to those fake sets of teeth favoured by celebrities, the sort that leave the mouth looking as though it's filled with a section of the Dover coastline.

"Speaking of photos..." added Watson. "I saw you with the camera in York."

"That's right, on Baker Avenue." Crowley jumped down from his bar stool and shook the youth's hand too. "Welcome to our lovely little village. I wonder if I could perhaps tempt the pair of you to a drink?"

"We were just about to take a walk and explore the area," said Quist. "But yes, you could certainly offer us a drink." He gave a tight smile as anger unexpectedly welled up within. "A drink and perhaps an explanation as to what the hell is going on?"

So much for going along with whatever scenario arises and not asking awkward questions, thought Watson.

"Yes, you certainly *do* deserve an explanation," said Crowley, smiling sheepishly. "Both of you, along with a huge apology, but let's be civil and begin with that drink. What will you have?"

The detective took a deep breath to calm himself and gestured to a bar hand pump. "I'll have a half pint of this Northumbrian ale."

"A half of lager, mate," said Watson. "And maybe a bag of beef crisps."

"Crisps?" Crowley muttered something and made a subtle hand movement. "No, you aren't hungry, young man."

"No." The youth shrugged. "That's right. I'm not."

"I'll kindly ask you to refrain from doing that," snapped his boss. "My assistant isn't some performing seal."

"Eh?" Watson looked puzzled.

"He's manipulating you," said Quist. "Entertaining himself by using magick. Your mind is obviously still susceptible to it from yesterday's ritual."

"I'm sorry, Bernard, but sometimes I just can't help myself." Crowley chuckled and waved to the barmaid. "Willow, my dear girl, halves of bitter and lager for my friends, please, and another small malt for myself."

"I see." Watson eyed the man warily as Crowley took the drinks and passed them to the two men. "So it's like a Jedi mind trick, is it? Well now that I know you're messing with me, that shit isn't going to work anymore."

"Um, Watson…" Quist gestured to his assistant's feet. "I wonder if you could do something about *that*?"

"Oh, for Christ's sake!" Looking down, the young man found he'd unknowingly unfastened his jeans and dropped them around his ankles. "Hey, just stop with your abracadabra stuff, okay?"

The magician laughed loudly. "Again I'm so sorry for that, but you're so deliciously easy to influence." He watched the youth quickly yank them back up. "I assure you, that's an end to my jesting. I know some would view such behaviour as a little juvenile, but I used to have a huge amount of fun indulging myself with this kind of nonsense in the old days."

"Really?" The detective sipped his drink. "The *old days* as you term them were quite some time ago."

"Indeed they were." Crowley smiled ruefully. "As you've deduced, our young friend here is still mentally open to suggestion from yesterday's hypnotic rite. The magick I used was simple enough. I had a photo of him and a few personal items which..."

"Yeah, we found them in your hotel bin," said Watson.

"Ah, you went there?" Crowley nodded. "I'm afraid I was tasked with the job of getting you to come to Ravenspoint. They knew Bernard would follow you and then..."

"They?" quizzed the detective.

"The Mulgraves. Reginald, the Laird of the castle, and his delectable daughter Rachel."

Watson frowned. "Don't you have to be in Scotland to be a Laird?" He turned to his boss. "There, I obviously did learn *something* in school."

"You're quite right," confirmed Crowley. "The Mulgrave family *were* originally Scottish and they brought the title with them when they moved to Northumberland four centuries ago. The people here have always been happy to be unofficially governed by a Laird, considering the protection his castle afforded them back in the more dangerous times."

"Would Rachel Mulgrave be the lady we met yesterday?" asked Quist. "The one who checked into Middlethorpe Hall with you and went by the name Rachel Penrose?"

"Of course." The magician's eyes twinkled impishly. "You'll

120

meet her again shortly, along with her father."

"Will we be meeting her hubby?" asked Watson, cynically.

"The husband will be conspicuous by his absence." Crowley winked at Quist. "As I'm sure the pair of you will have guessed by now, there *is* no hubby."

The detective shook his head. "I must say, you all went to a great deal of trouble to get me here."

"We did," agreed Crowley. "And now that you *are* here, the Laird of Ravenspoint has a proposition for you. Quite a lucrative proposition actually."

Watson laughed dryly. "And he couldn't have just phoned and invited him?"

"Time is very much a factor in this," said Crowley. "To be truthful, time is fast running out and you might have been busy, or refused their request for some reason. They really couldn't take that chance."

Quist's features darkened. "So instead…"

"So instead, the Mulgraves employed every means at their disposal to ensure you came." The magician gave them a guilty smile. "I won't attempt to sugar-coat any of this. Our young friend here was considered to be the easiest option; they decided to bring Watson to Ravenspoint and use him as a sort of bait to get you here. Failing that, they'd abduct you, which turned out to be a rather foolish idea. The Laird's daughter then approached your agency with a fake problem, although her visit was mostly to obtain a few personal items which I could use to…"

"You intended to *kidnap* Watson," snapped Quist. "Then you used your magick to mess with his mind. Believe me, I could get quite angry about this if I allowed myself. I'll only say this *once* – my friend here is very much off-limits."

"You wouldn't like him when he's angry," pointed out the youth. "Hey, Guv, cheers for saying *friend* instead of assistant."

"There was an accident at the station," said Quist. "Because of your *enchantment*, he almost broke his arm."

"Is that so?" Crowley noticed the compression bandage and gestured to the girl behind the counter. "I believe we can do something about that right now. Willow, my dear, a bottle of our water, if you'd be so kind."

"What's this?" quizzed Watson, taking the offered bottle from the barmaid and reading the label. "*Ravenspoint Spa?*"

"Try it," urged Crowley. "I guarantee this will take away all your aches and pains."

"Water?" The young man took a couple of gulps. "Yeah, it's just water, like it says on the label. Is this a joke?"

"Let me see that." Quist took the bottle to examine it and sniff the contents. "Yes, it *is* water, but there's something rather odd about it. Don't drink any more."

"Trust me, Bernard," smiled Crowley. "It won't cause him any harm. The complete opposite, in fact."

"*Trust?*" snorted Quist. "I really don't think so."

"Who are you?" asked Watson, peering blankly at his boss. "Will you bring an end to my pain?"

"Enough of this." The detective glared at Crowley. "For the final time, will you *please* refrain from doing that?"

"Hey, that wasn't me," laughed the magician. "I think your friend may be fooling around himself."

"Eh?" The youth gave a confused frown. "What do you mean?"

"Whatever," growled Quist. "So why don't we get back to the obvious question. Why do the Mulgraves want me here? What could be so *unbelievably* important that they'd go to all this trouble?"

"To most, the reason would *indeed* be unbelievable," said Crowley. "The Laird wishes to explain everything in person, but it very much centres around what you are."

Quist stiffened slightly. "A consultant detective?"

"There's no need to worry, Bernard." His eyes twinkling, Crowley leant closer and lowered his voice. "Your secret is perfectly safe and all will be made clear very soon."

"I can't imagine what you think you might know about me," said the detective, glancing around the bar for eavesdroppers. "But there's a definite elephant in this room and that's *you*, Mister Crowley."

"Well, I've been called many things," chuckled the magician, knocking back his scotch. "The Great Beast, the wickedest man in the world, but never, to the best of my knowledge, an elephant."

"He's asking how come you're still alive?" said Watson.

"I'm fully aware of that." Crowley took a folded overcoat from a nearby chair and pulled it on over his jacket. "But first let's take a walk. You said you were going to explore the village, so if you'd care to finish those drinks, I'd be delighted to be your guide.".

* * * *

Chapter 18

Quist strolled through the narrow streets of Ravenspoint with the collar turned up on his leather trenchcoat. "This village is an amazing little place," he said, looking around at the grey stone houses and interconnecting snickets and yards. The low-lying mist, that seemed to be ever-present here, drifted eerily across the cobblestones, almost luminous in the weak afternoon light. "So quaint and atmospheric."

"It is indeed," agreed Crowley, enthusiastically. "Yes, we're small and compact within our wall, but really rather beautiful. We have a population here of just 97."

"That's a precise figure," pointed out the detective.

"And easy enough to remember. We've had no births or deaths for quite some time. No one moves into our village and no one ever leaves. As a matter of fact, you've already met the last person to be born here."

"You mean Rachel?" Quist frowned. "It's hard to believe you've had no other births for twenty-something years."

"Er, *yes*." The magician gave an enigmatic smile. "Isn't it?"

Watson wasn't so sure he'd agree with the 'beautiful' description. *There were no clubs, Indian restaurants, or bars, so he was pretty certain the nightlife here would leave much to be desired.*

"Ravenspoint might be, er, *beautiful*," he said. "But you obviously like to keep it all to yourselves. You've got nowhere for the visitors to park."

"And nowhere for them to stay," added Quist. "No guest houses or similar establishments, as far as I can see."

"Very true," confessed Crowley, with a conspiratorial wink. "And, whenever outsiders enquire, our hotel never has vacancies; you probably saw their sign. The website yields similar negative results – restaurant tables are never available and the tours of the castle are always fully booked."

"Well, I'm sure you know what you're doing," said Watson, baffled. Zipping up his canvas jacket against the cold, he blew warmth into his hands. "There's no phone signal here either, apart from in the hotel."

"That in *itself* keeps the masses away." Crowley laughed heartily. "People need their phone signal in the way that some need insulin."

"This little gem should be a tourist Mecca," said Quist. "One of the Northumberland highlights, like Holy Island and Bamburgh Castle, and yet you openly discourage visitors."

The magician nodded. "As Watson says, we like to keep ourselves to ourselves, but we do have our reasons."

"I don't suppose you'd care to enlighten us?"

"Sorry." Crowley shook his head. "Not just yet."

The detective gestured to a nearby wall. "Would it be anything to do with this building damage and repair work that I keep seeing around the village?"

"You noticed that?" For a brief moment, the magician's confident smile slipped slightly. "Well, as I've already mentioned, the Laird wants to explain everything in person. Believe me, Bernard, he has a very good reason for this."

"So where the hell *is* he?" snapped Quist. "He went to all that trouble to get me to Ravenspoint, employing magick and attempting kidnap. You claimed he needed me here and that *time* was a huge factor, so why then are we strolling around the streets chatting?"

"You *are* needed," confirmed Crowley. "But not until tomorrow evening. The Laird needs you on the 21st of December."

"The longest night of the year?" The detective raised a curious eyebrow. "So I presume the Winter Solstice has some occult significance?"

"Indeed it does."

Watson noticed Quist's tight smile and knew he was biting his tongue. *Ali Bongo here was telling them nothing and appeared to be just stringing them along.*

They arrived at the small square outside the castle wall where the minibus was still parked. "I suppose you'd call this our marketplace," said Crowley, nodding to the wisps of mist drifting over the cobbles. "If Ravenspoint had ever hosted a market."

"This weird fog is always floating about at ground level," said Watson, looking around his feet as he walked. "It's like the ghost of a friggin' carpet."

"A ghost carpet?" The magician laughed loudly. "Oh, I do like *you*, young man."

"His humour is something of an acquired taste," drawled Quist.

"Hey, wait a minute…" Watson stopped halfway across the square and flexed his bandaged hand. "Whoa, I don't believe this…"

"Ah!" Crowley grinned. "Feeling better, are we?"

"I've only just realised…" The youth tugged at his elasticated bandage and yanked it off. "The pain's gone. The throbbing and that dull ache are both… well, it's like they were never there."

"Your wrist is feeling better," said Crowley. "But how about *you*?"

"What do you mean?" asked Watson.

"I mean are *you* feeling better? Are you, by any chance, feeling more healthy and far more *alive* since you've been here in Ravenspoint? Are you experiencing that joyous glow? That wonderful feeling of euphoria and exhilaration?"

"Er, yeah…" Watson turned to his boss. "He's right, Guv. It's kind of weird, but I really *do* feel like that."

"Intriguing," said Quist, smiling tautly. "Presumably this is something *else* which only your Laird can explain?"

Without waiting for an answer, the detective continued across the marketplace to the barbican tower that acted as the entrance to the castle courtyard. Crowley's BMW was parked inside, next to a red Porsche and three black Range Rovers. Noting the cement-pointed cracks in the tower stonework, he stood in the archway gazing at the building beyond. Movement caught his eye and he glimpsed a dark figure in one of the upper windows. They quickly stepped back as he raised his gaze.

"Yes, it's a fine-looking manor house." Quist turned to the magician. "Jacobean, I'd say?"

"That's right," he nodded, taking a pipe and matches from his coat pocket. "Completed in the early sixteen-hundreds during the reign of James the First."

"Is that a well?" Watson gestured to the Gothic structure in the centre of the misty castle yard. Raised on three steps, it stood beneath a decorative stone dome supported on four carved pillars.

"It is," confirmed Crowley, lighting his pipe in the shelter of the archway and puffing smoke. "They had a series of small earthquakes here back in 1906 and the original well collapsed. This one was built in the 1930s."

"And I see you have a portcullis." Quist eyed the gap in the stonework above them with its row of protruding metal spikes. "Does it still operate?"

"Oh, yes," said Crowley. "It's always lowered at sunset to shut off the courtyard. We close and bar the gates too, so no one can see inside. We like our privacy."

"*We?*" echoed Watson. "I see your car's parked in there. Do you live in the castle with this Mulgrave guy and his daughter?"

"As befits my exalted status of resident magician." Laughing, Crowley gave him a mock bow. "Yes, I have a private apartment in the east wing. Two others have similar flats in there and here's one of them right now."

Wrapped in a black Parka coat, Richard Brunton left the

castle and strode across the courtyard through the layer of ground mist. He smirked to see Quist in the archway.

"Hello again." The detective eyed him cynically. "So how did you enjoy your recent Yorkshire trip?"

"It had its moments," growled Brunton. He opened a metal box on the wall and pressed a button inside. "I really wouldn't stand there if I were you."

An electronic hum was masked by the louder clatter from above as the heavy portcullis began to slowly descend on two chains. Quist, Watson and Crowley stepped back, watching as the barred gate lowered in front of them. Brunton ducked underneath and joined the trio.

"How disappointing," said Quist. "It's clearly easier to use, but your dramatic medieval portcullis is now no different to a domestic garage door." He peered at Brunton's face. "It's strange, but I could have sworn I broke your nose yesterday morning."

"You did," said the big man, turning to head across the square.

"Interesting. A fast healer, aren't you?"

"Yeah." He looked back over his shoulder. "Much like yourself, I hear,"

"I wouldn't want to meet *that* big bastard in a dark alley," murmured Watson. "So he's the other guy from the Range Rover?"

"Yes, that was him." Quist lit a cigarette. "Oliver Tarrant's partner."

"Richard Brunton," confirmed Crowley, puffing a cloud of sweet, aromatic pipe smoke. "He's the Head of Security at the castle and Reginald's right-hand man. As I mentioned, he has a private apartment in there."

"And as *I* mentioned," said Quist, "his broken nose has completely healed since yesterday."

"Incredible," gasped the magician, feigning a comical show of amazement. "Just like Watson's wrist."

"Speaking of healing fast..." said the youth. "I don't reckon his mate Ollie will be healing at *all*. The last time we saw him, in York hospital, he looked as if someone had emptied a bucket of prawn korma on the bed."

"I can well imagine." Crowley winced, clenching his pipe in a pained grimace. "The deterioration process isn't exactly pretty, is it?"

"It wasn't exactly *natural* either." Quist drew slowly on his cigarette. "I don't suppose you'd care to enlighten us on that subject?"

"I'd love to, Bernard, but as you know, my lips are temporarily sealed..."

"Yes, yes," sighed the detective, once again experiencing the weird buzzing in his head. "You've already told us. Your Laird wants to explain everything himself."

"I'm wondering..." said Watson, fingering the wooden portcullis bars. "With the control box being inside the archway there, how do you get in here?"

"A good question." Crowley produced a remote from his pocket and pressed the button. The electronic hum sounded again and the gate began to slowly rise. "Everyone who lives in the castle has one of these handy little gizmos. Hello..." He pointed with his pipe to the village perimeter wall that ran, ten feet high, along the edge of the square. "Do I spy strangers? Who can this be?"

Steps ran up the stonework to a circular lookout point on top, where two young men in combat jackets were erecting telescopes by the waist-high railings. Watson followed them up the flight and peered over, breathing in the salty breeze. He saw how the castle's seaward elevation extended straight down into the ocean, a sheer stone face from the rooftops to the water, with window balconies jutting out over the waves.

Appearing behind him, Crowley smiled at the men. "Good afternoon," he said. "I see you're birdwatchers?"

"Hey, do you mind?" The larger, bearded character turned from adjusting his tripod. "The word is *birder*, not *birdwatcher*."

"Ooh, that must be an *enthralling* hobby," mumbled Watson, smirking.

"Yeah, *birder*." His tubby companion held up binoculars. "Modern birders are cool and in a different league to the birdwatchers of old." He grinned at Watson. "And it's a passion, mate, not a hobby."

"Why Ravenspoint?" asked Quist, smoking his cigarette and gazing over the railings. "I know the Farne Islands out there are famed for their wildlife, but is this a good birding spot too?"

"No idea," admitted the bearded man. "We're on our way home to Luton from Scotland and this is an ideal halfway break."

"Mmmh." Quist stared across the sparkling water towards the Farnes. "It *would* be ideal if there were any birds."

"Well of course there are birds," he laughed. "This is a coastal headland, which is why we stopped here. Birds have to fly past it if they're moving north or south."

"He's right, Tommo." His companion scanned both ways through his binoculars. "This is weird. There aren't any gulls, or other common seabirds. No turnstones on the rocks down there. *Nothing.*"

"There seems to be plenty of distant bird movement," said Quist, drawing on his cigarette. "Those scoters and other ducks are flying up the coast, but keeping their distance from this particular headland. Even the porpoises out there appear to be staying away."

"Maybe something's scaring them?" suggested Watson. "A phone mast giving off microwaves, or some such shit?"

"Incredible." Tommo squinted through his telescope. "How did you see those porpoise fins with the naked eye?"

The detective smiled. "I eat plenty of carrots."

"It might help if they had something to land in," said Watson. "I haven't seen a single tree or bush in the village. No grass either, come to think of it."

Puffing on his pipe, Crowley nodded to a middle-aged man in a woollen overcoat who was climbing the steps. "Oh, hello there," he said, turning to Quist. "This is Gavin Howell. Like Brunton, he works in the castle."

Watson looked the man over. Howell was hard-faced, with wild eyes, a full black beard and a neck stuffed with muscle. He reminded the youth of those American militia nutters who dislike dark-skinned people, but love stockpiling guns in compounds and having shoot-outs with the FBI.

Howell approached the birders. "Are you staying in the village?" he asked, aggressively. "Who are you?"

"Well, I'm Tommo and he's Pricey," said the bearded birder, frowning. "Not that it's any of *your* fuckin' business."

"It's *my* business if that's your car on the street back there." Howell's eyes flared angrily. "The white Nissan? You've left it in a no parking spot."

"Is there any *other* kind of spot around here?" asked Watson.

"Exactly," said Pricey. "There's literally *nowhere* to park, so what are we supposed to do?"

"That isn't my problem," said Howell. "You need to move it right now before…"

"Why not turn a blind eye?" Crowley slapped a friendly hand on Pricey's back. "I'm sure, in the present climate, so to speak, they'll be fine. Perhaps they were considering spending the night here?"

"Actually we *were* thinking of staying," said Tommo. "But the hotel has no…"

"No, no." The magician shook his head. "The hotel might have told you they have no vacancies, but that isn't true. I know the owner and I can promise you there are good rooms available tonight at half-price."

"Seriously?" The birders exchanged bewildered glances.

"Half-price? Why would they do that?"

"Why?" grinned Crowley, puffing pipe smoke. "Surely you've heard that old adage about mouths and gift horses?"

Quist and Watson descended the steps as the group chatted.

"Howell is quite the charmer, isn't he?" murmured the detective. "If he resides in the castle with that Brunton character, I'm sure the pair will get along famously. By the way, what do you think about the birdlife?"

"Yeah." His assistant peered up at the rooftops. "Like you said, birds are rarer than rocking horse shit around here."

"Not *rare*," corrected Quist. "They're non-existent. There was nothing on the sea and nothing here in the village either; no sparrows, starlings, or pigeons. Have you noticed any dogs or cats since you arrived?"

"With *you* about?" Watson grinned. "That's no big surprise, Guv." His expression glazed over. "You're different, aren't you? Will you help with my pain?"

"Oh, for crying out loud." Rolling his eyes and throwing down his cigarette, the detective gripped him by the shoulders. "Snap out of it."

"Huh? What's wrong, Guv?"

"What's *wrong* is that damned hypnotic ritual that Crowley used on you. You're still experiencing trance-like moments."

"Trances? Seriously?" Watson gave a nervous laugh. "So what am I doing? Not walking like a chicken, or impersonating Elvis, I hope?"

Crowley had descended the steps. "I overheard you," he said, smiling ruefully. "If there's some residual problem resulting from the rite, it will be quite harmless and only be temporary, I can assure you."

"Really?" Quist wheeled on him. "It had better be harmless, I can assure *you* of that."

132

"Once again, I apologise." Crowley sighed. "Perhaps it would be best if I performed another magickal working to set this young man right and..."

"I don't think so," snapped Quist. He looked around the square. "And further to our conversation up there, where *are* all the birds? Apparently there are no dogs or other animals either. Wait a moment; allow me to try something..." Walking to the base of the perimeter wall, he turned over a large stone to expose soil. "Just as I suspected – absolutely nothing. There are no insects either."

"No," said Crowley. "There's a very good reason for that." He pointed with his pipe to the seaward face of the castle. "Ah, there's Rachel, our Laird's daughter. Watch this."

Looking up in the direction indicated, Watson's eyes widened and his jaw fell open. Nine stone balconies adorned the side of the building and the girl he'd met the previous day had appeared on one of the lower ones, closing the French doors behind her. Her long red hair was tied back, but the most noticeable thing was her lack of clothing.

"Hey, nice view." The young man grinned. "But she's going to catch pneumonia out there dressed like that. What's she doing? Yoga?" He shook his head as she nimbly jumped up onto the parapet. "No way. Tell me she's not actually going to..."

Springing off, Rachel plunged in a perfect dive to vanish out of his line of sight behind the village wall. The two birders above him both whistled and clapped.

"Shit," gasped Watson, hearing the splash. "Is she crazy? How deep is the water below that balcony?"

"Oh, she's fine," said Crowley. "Rachel dives from there and swims most days, even in the winter like this. I wouldn't fancy it myself, of course. As you can doubtless imagine, the December sea is colder than a whore's kiss."

"Um, I have to ask," said Watson, slightly bewildered by the idea of anyone swimming naked at Christmas. "How does she get back up to the balcony?"

"Through the sally port," laughed Crowley. "It's a door at the base of the castle that leads out onto a small area of rocks. Rachel and I sunbathe naked down there in the summer months."

The youth pictured this, recalling the brief glimpse of her body that he'd just had, whilst trying his best to block out any mental images of this old man.

Puffing away on his pipe, the magician checked his watch. "Now, gentlemen, I would imagine you're both hungry?"

"We haven't eaten since lunchtime," admitted Quist.

"The Ravenspoint air is famous for sharpening the appetite," said Crowley. "Let's return to the hotel for dinner. My treat."

"Hungry?" echoed Watson. "Are you kidding? Right now I could eat a horse... and then the jockey."

* * * *

Chapter 19

The dining room in the Fountain Hotel was spacious, yet cosy, with its subdued lighting, red linen cloths and flickering candles on every table. Quist and Watson sat with Crowley by a stone fireplace where the latter perused an extensive wine list. The detective's leather trenchcoat hung next to Watson's canvas jacket on an upright stand by the door and, like his assistant, Quist wore a casual shirt with open collar. Several couples were eating dinner around them and Quist could see through the open doorway into the bar area where Tommo and Pricey, the two birders sat by the Christmas tree. The pair had obviously booked a room here and were now drinking beer at a table covered in ornithology notebooks.

Watson was far more interested in the woman who sat at a nearby table – amazingly, it was the Hollywood star Marcia Newley, *here* in the wilds of Northumberland. Her younger dinner companion was an actor too, one of the newer action stars who often shared the screen with helicopter gunships and slow-motion explosions. Looking at her, Watson would have guessed Marcia's age to be mid-fifties, but he'd seen her on television in late-night horror films – some of which were filmed in black-and-white – so God alone knew how old she *really* was. Those Beverley Hills surgeons often transformed their clients into hideously surprised plastic dolls, but they'd done surprisingly well with Marcia.

"I've got to admit, I feel amazing," laughed Watson. Finding Lestrade's gift in his jacket pocket – the small model starship – he tossed it up high and caught it. "Hey, look, Captain, the ship's in orbit around Planet Ravenspoint. You said the air here affected the appetite and it's certainly affecting *mine*. It's affecting *everything*."

"Or perhaps it was that water you drank earlier." Quist turned suspiciously to the magician. "One has to wonder what it might have contained."

"I'll be honest with you," said Crowley. "It's a unique combination of both. The feelings of euphoria stem from the spa water *and* our remarkable air."

The detective nodded curtly. "But, of course, you aren't about to expound upon that?"

"Not yet." Crowley beckoned one of the waiters and ordered a bottle of Burgundy.

"Don't you feel it, Guv?" Watson threw the toy higher and caught it again. "This brilliant buzz of excitement?"

"Unfortunately I don't," confessed his boss, opening one of the three leather-bound menus.

The youth noticed Quist's tetchy expression. *Whatever this feeling was, it clearly had no effect on the Guv, probably due to him being a little bit different and furrier than most folk.*

Quist *was* feeling something – that same peculiar buzzing in his head – but he decided to say nothing. He read through the menu, raising his eyebrows at some of the gourmet offerings: Anjou pigeon squab with winter truffle, teal with elderberries, wild venison loin with figs and red endive, smoked eel with quail eggs. Apparently this wasn't the place to come if you were an aficionado of the *Greggs* sausage roll.

"What's lobster cassoulet?" quizzed Watson, reading. "I'm betting it doesn't come with chips?"

"The chef has three Michelin stars," said Crowley. "I'm sure he'll be more than capable of whipping up a portion for you." He handed Quist a card from his own menu. "The kitchen prepared this especially for you, Bernard. A separate list of quite exemplary fare, but no animal products were used in the preparation."

"How thoughtful." The detective raised a questioning eyebrow. "I wonder how the chef knew I was vegan, but I suppose that's another of those questions that can only be answered by Reginald Mulgrave?"

Watson tossed up his model starship again and, irritated by the buzzing in his head, his boss snatched it from the air.

"Why don't I take charge of that for a while?" he snapped. "Before it ends up in someone's soup."

His jacket hung on the rear of the chair and he slipped it into a pocket as a pretty waitress arrived with a pad and pen. The detective ordered vegetable coconut curry, Crowley chose a rare Wagyu steak, and Watson went for the ginger chicken tagine… with chips.

"Your Laird wishes to explain everything." Quist waited until the girl left the table. "But does *everything* extend to how *you* are here, alive and well? The world believes you died in 1947."

"Now *that* I can tell you about." said Crowley, watching the waitress's taut bottom. "Well, most of it, at any rate. I first became aware of Reginald Mulgrave way back in 1906 when he approached me in London. His village required my help with a problem, a problem, in fact, that was pretty much identical to their current one. I was paid handsomely to make a brief visit here and perform a magickal ritual, it went well and that was that. I didn't see the Mulgraves again for four decades."

"Until 1947?" asked Quist. "The year of your supposed death on December the 1st?"

The magician looked up appreciatively as a waiter appeared with a bottle, uncorked it with a *plop* and allowed him to taste the wine. He nodded his approval and waited as it was steadily poured.

"Not for me, thanks." Watson waved a hand over his glass. "A pint of lager here, please, mate."

"This is a truly superb Burgundy." Crowley sipped the wine and watched as Quist tried it. "Cote De Beaune, 2016. You'll notice the raspberry and blackcurrant, but there's also a subtle hint of truffle on the finish."

"Indeed," agreed the detective, closing his eyes to swallow.

Smiling warmly, Crowley continued with his story. "Now I

was in something of a predicament after the war," he said. "To put it bluntly, it was growing difficult for me to find somewhere to live. It shouldn't have come as a surprise, I suppose, as my life had always been rather disreputable. The occult, the ritual magick, my constant experimentation with sex and drugs…"

"Conjuring demons and shagging women on altars." Watson nodded. "The Guv told me about you. Most normal folk would have kept it quiet, but you liked to shout about it all."

"Quite so," agreed the magician, laughing quietly. "I confess, I *did* revel in broadcasting my darker exploits. Fortunately, just before my seventieth birthday in 1945, I found an excellent retirement home prepared to take in a scandalous character such as myself."

"Netherwood," said Quist, drinking his wine. "In Hastings."

"Yes, the house stood on a high ridge in a quiet suburb above the town. It was a large Victorian place owned by a rather Bohemian couple, Vernon and Kathleen. When I moved in, I insisted upon room number thirteen, not only because it amused me, but it was at the front and I had good views of the castle, the ocean and Beachy Head."

The detective nodded. "The cliffs, which I understand, you climbed in your younger mountaineering days?"

"I did indeed. Netherwood was like a little socialist commune filled with poets, painters, musicians and other eccentric types. I enjoyed the relaxed atmosphere and marvellous cuisine and, best of all, I had a monthly supply of heroin sent to me from a London chemist. Yes, Hastings was delightful. I joined the chess club, I watched the ballroom dancing on the pier and, to be truthful, I genuinely assumed I'd end my days there."

Watson's drink arrived and he sipped the lager. "Exquisite," he murmured, sniffing. "Yeah, this has a good nose, not unlike yourself, Guv, and I'm getting a hint of hops and summer malt, with a subtle aftertaste of pretentious bollocks."

"Oh, yes, I *do* like you," laughed Crowley, squeezing the

youth's shoulder. "Not only are you a rather appealing young man, but you really amuse me."

"Ah, that's right," said Quist. "I recall reading about your rather broad bisexual tastes."

"I like girls," pointed out Watson, very quickly.

"As do I," said the magician, raising his glass. "But I like both snails *and* oysters, so to speak. It's a tired old adage, I know, but don't knock it if you haven't tried it."

"I haven't tried dowsing myself in petrol and lighting a fuckin' match," drawled Watson. "But to be honest, mate, I'd probably knock *that*."

Quist waited until Crowley had finished laughing. "So you were in Hastings for two years?"

"I was," he nodded, wiping his eyes. "My health started to deteriorate with bronchitis towards the end of 1947 and pneumonia had begun to set in. I'd developed a real love for dancing and I visited the pier ballroom for what I thought might be the last time in late November. I couldn't believe it when I was approached that night by Reginald Mulgrave. He'd tracked me down and booked himself into a hotel there. Forty years had passed since I last saw the Laird and yet he looked exactly the same; he hadn't aged one bit."

"He needed you to perform a ritual again?" asked Quist. "Like in 1906?"

"Yes, but I told him I'd be of little use," said Crowley. "I explained how my bronchitis was too serious. It was almost December and I knew I wouldn't see Christmas. Reginald, however, disagreed with my gloomy prognosis. He invited me to come here to live in their community where a very different future would await. Any future, of course, would have been preferable to coughing my way into a cremation oven."

"Speaking of which…" Quist sipped his wine. "Your funeral took place in Brighton on December the 5th."

"Yes, at Woodvale Cemetery." Crowley grinned impishly. "I watched from outside and it was a lovely send off. My friend Louis read the *Hymn to Pan* which I thought was a rather nice touch."

Watson raised his eyebrows. "So who exactly *was* cremated?"

"A volunteer," said Crowley. "A Ravenspoint resident with more than a passing resemblance to myself. They shaved his head in the right places and used make-up before smuggling him into Netherwood and injecting him with an overdose of my heroin. No one looks *too* closely at an elderly corpse when they know the person is sick and they're fully expecting them to die."

"A volunteer, you say?" Watson snorted. "Who the hell would volunteer for *that*?"

"Oh, you'd be surprised," said Crowley. "You'll soon be discovering how volunteering is a way of life here in Ravenspoint."

"I can't wait," admitted Quist. "So you faked your death and here you are, all these years later, alive and well."

"Extremely well." The magician's eyes twinkled. "I look less than sixty years old and I feel even younger. I'm not yet at liberty to tell you the full story, but I *can* tell you that Reginald gave me a bottle of their water to drink that night on the Hastings pier."

"The same water I drank?" asked Watson. "The stuff that you say cured my wrist?"

He nodded. "Apart from its curative properties, that water is far better than heroin. I wasn't shown it on my 1906 visit, but I quaffed an entire bottle on the pier and went on to watch the dancing with my feet tapping away like crazy. I remember it was a rumba competition. Because I've always associated it with the start of my new life, the rumba became my favourite dance."

"Magick, writing, poetry and mountaineering," said Quist. "You're famed for many things, but I was never aware that you had a love of ballroom dancing."

"Oh, not only ballroom." Crowley swayed his hips on the

chair. "I loved the discos of the 1970s. But this isn't something *any* disreputable black magician would go out of their way to advertise. Just imagine the CV – he performed the dangerous Abramelin ritual, he summoned the demon Choronzon, and he won the Bournemouth Rialto trophy for his rather exquisite Quickstep."

"We saw some of the dance websites," said Watson. "You look to have won loads of competitions under your new name, Adrian Crowther."

"I have," confirmed Crowley. "Usually accompanied by the Laird's exquisite daughter."

"You visited York together." The youth recalled how his boss had sniffed their hotel bed, not a snippet of information he'd care to share with many people. "Is she your, um, girlfriend?"

"Rachel Mulgrave has never been anyone's *girlfriend.*" The magician chuckled. "She's very much a sexual free spirit, as you may very soon discover for yourself, young man."

"Really?" Watson thought about this for a moment and cleared his dry throat. "Oh, I don't know. I'm quite particular about who I sleep with."

"As am I." Crowley gave him an amorous wink. "Here in Ravenspoint we have a rather liberal attitude to sex in general. One of my light-hearted stipulations, as their resident magician, was that Rachel would partner me to the larger dancing events. We're appearing tomorrow night in Newcastle at the *Dance Away* finals. It's televised live and I can guarantee you, we'll be taking the trophy."

"*Dance Away?*" echoed Watson. "That's a top Saturday night show, isn't it? My mum watches all that crap."

"Appearing on television?" Quist shook his head. "So you've been living here as Adrian Crowther since 1947 and no one has ever recognised you?"

"When people know you're dead and they know they won't see you again, they *don't* see you." Crowley leant forward. "I once had a house on Loch Ness named Boleskine which eventually came into the possession of the Led Zeppelin guitarist Jimmy Page. He was a fan of mine and I was glad the old house had a worthy new owner. I loved his music and managed to gate-crash one of his parties there in the 1970s." He let out a disgruntled laugh. "As I say, Page was supposedly an aficionado and, although I chatted with him, the bastard didn't recognise me. Can you believe that?"

Quist smiled thinly and gave a fake tut. "What an insult."

"There you are," boomed a deep voice. "Mister Quist and Mister Watson."

Watson turned in his seat to see a huge, bulky man over six feet in height. A mass of untidy auburn hair brushed the collar of his tweed jacket and a bushy red beard covered the front of his Arran sweater. This robust character exuded power and, unable to help himself, Watson pictured him swinging a Viking axe.

"I'm Reginald," he announced loudly. "Reginald Mulgrave. It's so good to meet you both. I'm the Laird of the village, as I'm sure Aleister will have told you."

"He hasn't told us *much*," said Watson.

"I thought it was time to come along and introduce myself." Grabbing their hands, Mulgrave vigorously pumped them up and down. "I really must apologise for our inexcusable behaviour – it truly *was* unforgivable – but we really need you here, Mister Quist."

"That much I've been told," said the detective, inspecting his crushed fingers. "But, as my colleague here says, very little else."

Mulgrave nodded. "We need your assistance with something of the utmost importance. We couldn't just *ask* you to come to Ravenspoint, because we honestly couldn't afford to take any chances. Instead, I'm ashamed to say we tried force and we attempted to bring Watson here knowing that you'd follow. Again, I apologise profusely for everything and beg your forgiveness, but you're the only one who can help us."

"Why *me*?" asked Quist.

"Not here." Grinning broadly, the Laird looked around the dining room. "I think it will be prudent to discuss such, um, *delicate* matters tomorrow in the privacy of my castle."

Watson glanced at his boss. Although this was supposedly conspiratorial, Mulgrave didn't lower his voice. The youth found it difficult to imagine this loud character ever whispering. *So, like Ali Bongo the magician, this guy also knew about the werewolf stuff.*

"Tomorrow morning?" suggested Mulgrave. "Could I invite you both for coffee in the castle after breakfast? You really don't want to miss the breakfast here in the Fountain. It's superb."

"Alright." Quist nodded slowly. "But can you give me some indication of what this is about?"

"It's difficult to explain our problem in words," confessed the Laird. "Soon you'll see just *how* difficult. No, rather than attempt an explanation, it will be far better to simply show you the problem. Once you discover what's at stake here, you'll understand why we went to such elaborate lengths."

Arriving with a trolley, two waiters set down plates in front of the diners and simultaneously lifted three chrome cloches to reveal the exquisite food. Watson rolled his eyes to see that his ten chips had been stacked upright, like the *Jenga* game, and decorated with edible petals. Crowley's rare steak appeared to have been *cooked* by someone holding it near a light bulb. Blood pooled around the meat and the youth watched his boss staring longingly at the flesh. He was clearly tempted, but centuries of practise kept his dark urges in check.

"I'll leave you to enjoy your meals," said Mulgrave. "So can I expect you tomorrow morning at the castle? Shall we say around ten?"

"Ten o'clock it is," said Quist, still gazing at the steak.

"Hey, Guv..." Watson gestured through the restaurant doorway into the bar area where the television on the far wall was showing the local news. "Isn't that the bus we saw today?"

The detective tore his eyes from Crowley's plate to see a female reporter standing on a windswept coastal cliff. It was a live report, the sound was muted, but text scrolled along the bottom of the screen.

"Yes, you're right," he said, reading. "The minibus was involved in an accident on the Craggan Headland after leaving here. They don't appear to know what happened yet, but no other vehicles were involved. It left the road somehow and crashed into the sea. They're currently searching for survivors."

"Good Lord!" The Laird shook his head, horrified. "I need to contact the relevant authorities right now and make a statement about this. I don't believe it. Those poor people were in the castle this afternoon on one of our guided tours." He turned to leave. "This is truly terrible."

"Indeed," agreed Quist, narrowing his eyes. "Indeed it is."

* * * *

Chapter 20

The gates to Ravenspoint Castle were locked and the barbican portcullis had been lowered to close off the private courtyard. It was midnight and bright moonlight twinkled on the frozen white cobblestones and the row of frosty parked cars. The pale lunar rays combined with the golden glow of the castle windows to illuminate the central well, where Crowley stood gazing sadly at a shrivelled old lady.

Wearing only a thin blue nightdress, Victoria Packham sat on the waist-high parapet wall of the well, trembling uncontrollably in the freezing temperature. Her wizened ribcage rose and fell beneath the thin cotton as she painfully drew in rasping gasps of air. Over the years, Crowley had slept with countless women, and quite a few men, and Victoria had been one of his sexual partners. He smiled at the woman, recalling their recent night of raunchy fun. Although it had been less than six months ago, she hadn't looked anything at all like *this*.

"It's time to begin," said the magician, quietly.

Dressed in a purple ceremonial robe and holding a stiletto dagger, Crowley appeared bizarrely out of place next to the silent spectators in their modern overcoats, woollen hats and scarves. Most of the villagers were present in the icy courtyard, a tight huddle of almost one-hundred people. Reginald Mulgrave and his daughter Rachel stood at the front of the crowd, watching keenly with Brunton and Howell.

A tremor shook the cobblestones underfoot and Crowley glanced at the row of parked cars. Since the *problem* began again, two weeks ago, the security systems had been turned off on all the Ravenspoint vehicles – it was the only way to prevent the villagers from being continuously deafened by alarms. He noticed the Laird's worried expression and began to loudly chant unintelligible words, esoteric phrases from a powerful forgotten language. The ritual was only short and, turning to the smoking incense burner on the wall of the well, he rotated his knife in the aromatic fumes.

"Are you ready, Victoria?" he asked, in a reassuring voice.

The old lady nodded slightly.

Tugging back the sleeve of his robe, the magician made a small incision in his forearm; a sticking plaster covered a similar cut. A silver chalice stood beside the incense thurible and he swiftly dribbled his blood into it before turning again to the shivering woman. She whimpered as he dipped a finger into the hot liquid and dabbed her wizened brow and cheeks, marking out magickal symbols, before presenting the chalice to her. She took it with shaking hands, sipping at the contents and swallowing with difficulty.

Don't drop it, he thought, uneasily. *Don't you dare drop it and ruin this.*

Crowley felt another underground shudder as the woman sucked in a deep breath to compose herself. She nodded again that she was ready and, taking the cup from her, he watched as she gritted her teeth. *A remarkably good set for her apparent age*, he found himself surreally thinking.

Screwing her eyes shut and moaning with fear, Victoria leant backwards and toppled down the well. Seemingly indifferent to this shocking finale to the ceremony, the crowd watched without emotion, listening for the hollow splash. A few moments of thrashing and terrified screaming followed, before silence once again descended upon the courtyard. The magician intoned the final words of his ritual and paused for several seconds with head bowed before descending the three steps.

"Is that it?" asked Rachel, wrapping her fur coat tightly around herself. "Are we done here?"

Crowley tutted. "Well so much for reverence, my dear girl, but yes, that's it. The rite is complete."

"Goodbye, Victoria," said Mulgrave, walking over to the Gothic structure and peering into the mouth of the well. "Another courageous volunteer who will be remembered for their selfless..."

The ground shook violently and two dislodged tiles fell from the roof of the castle to shatter on the cobblestones, narrowly missing one of the parked Range Rovers. The gathering of villagers looked around and began to grow agitated.

"What the hell," growled Brunton. "I don't believe this."

"Her termination doesn't seem to have helped us," sighed the Laird, turning dejectedly to his magician. "What's more, the tremors feel as if they're growing worse."

"That shudder came straight after the ritual." Brunton glared at Crowley. "Victoria was rejected, wasn't she? She was obviously too old for this, just like the last volunteer."

"Richard's right," said Rachel, angrily. "We should have done like he said and snatched a whore from Edinburgh or somewhere."

"This was nothing more than a termination rite," snapped Crowley. "At this late stage, I never really expected Victoria to make a difference. But if you really want to argue about age, the Newcastle group weren't too old. If those nine youths didn't halt the deterioration, then why would a prostitute?"

The Laird nodded. "We're fast approaching the time and date. Things are accelerating and whatever we do now to prevent the destabilisation, the chances are it won't work. Still, we can but try."

"You don't need to try," said a woman's voice. "Now that you have Bernard Quist."

Mulgrave and Crowley turned warily to see Maria Crane walking across the courtyard to them. She wore a sable fur coat and smoked a cigarette.

"I was watching you from back there." Crane mounted the steps to peer down the well and irreverently tap her ash. "You're clearly wasting your time with these pointless sacrifices, so why do you bother?"

"We still have two more," said the Laird. "We have to take every opportunity we can to buy ourselves time and keep these quakes at bay until the ritual."

"Whatever," snorted Crane. "You'll only have to wait a little longer and your problems will be over. Didn't I tell you Quist would come here of his own free will? Curiosity is something of an Achilles' heel with this private investigator. I told you to simply *invite* him before you tried anything stupid, but you didn't listen. There was no need for those frantic abduction attempts."

"It's easy for you to say that." Mulgrave shook his head, careful that he didn't say anything that might anger the woman. "This situation doesn't affect you and you know we couldn't take the chance. You must appreciate we have so little time left before the 21st."

"That's tomorrow," pointed out Brunton. "You've felt how bad things are getting. This time it's far worse than ever before and we may not *have* another day. I say we should do it tonight."

Rachel nodded. "I agree."

"But we *can't*," sighed Crowley. "You know that it has to take place on the solstice. You know we have to wait."

Brunton and Rachel both turned to glare at Maria Crane.

"Yes," she said, seemingly reading their thoughts. "You could always try subduing me again, couldn't you? Who knows? Perhaps *this* time when you try to Taser and imprison me, things might go better for you."

Rachel seethed, remembering how six good men had been lost the last time they'd attempted it. "No," she said, gritting her teeth. "Perhaps not."

"Trust me," said Crowley. "For the Mulgrave Ritual to work, we *have* to perform it on the 21st. It has to be the *correct* date at the *correct* time."

Another sickening shudder ran through the castle courtyard and another falling tile smashed on the cobbles.

Brunton laughed, but there was no humour in the harsh sound. "Well…" he said, coldly. "It looks like we'll have to get the builders out again with their cement and pointing trowels."

* * * *

Chapter 21

Breakfast in the Fountain Hotel was served in the main restaurant where the red dinner tablecloths had been changed for crisp white linen. The faint aroma of fried bacon filled the air, light classical music played over concealed speakers and, in place of the evening candles, small vases of flowers stood on every table. Watson wondered where they might have come from. Apart from the greens in the Guv's dinner last night, this was the only vegetation he'd seen in Ravenspoint. He fingered one of the blooms and realised they were upmarket fakes.

Watson and Quist had been served with fresh orange juice and coffee and were now waiting for their food to arrive. Visibly wincing when his boss ordered muesli with almond milk, the youth had chosen the Full English with extra sausage, fried bread, and a side bowl of ketchup. His appetite was better than ever this Saturday morning and the inexplicable feelings of glee and exhilaration hadn't diminished. From the moment he opened his eyes, the sensation had returned to supercharge his young system.

Pricey and Tommo, the birders from Luton sat at the next table, both reading through bird guides and scribbling in notebooks. Watson nodded cheerfully to them and then looked around the half-empty room. The politician Nigel Drummond sat eating with the young girl from the previous evening, and Marcia Newley, the American actress, sat with her much younger friend. From the knowing looks and body language, both couples had clearly enjoyed a *restless* night together.

Reading through the BBC news on his phone, Quist turned to his assistant. "I meant to ask earlier, but you were showering" he said. "I don't suppose you felt anything unusual in the night? I was roused briefly just after twelve by the building shaking slightly."

"Really?" Watson shrugged. "That's weird. No, I was dead to

the world."

"Yes, I guessed as much. What with your horrendous snoring and those tremors, I thought perhaps Russian tanks were invading." The detective massaged his temple. "It's highly peculiar, but I awoke with a throbbing headache. By the way, I presume you weren't speaking to me in the night?"

"No." Watson sipped his orange juice. "To be honest, Guv, I don't usually chat with blokes when they're sleeping."

"I don't understand it," said Quist, frowning. "I know I wasn't awake, yet someone was speaking to me. They were speaking as clearly as if they were in the bedroom, but I've no idea what they were saying."

The youth gave him a puzzled look. "Um, I feel a bit daft pointing this out," he said. "What with *you* being the clever one at this breakfast table, but if you were fast asleep, then surely it was a dream?"

"No, I can assure you it wasn't," said Quist. "Then, as I say, I awoke with a headache. This is truly bizarre."

"Yeah, we didn't drink *that* much in the bar last night."

"No, you don't understand." He lowered his voice to a whisper. "It's due to my, er, unique *condition*, but I *never* dream and I *never* get headaches."

Tommo leant across from the neighbouring table. "Morning," he grinned. "How are we doing today?"

"Well, apparently, *he's* had a headache." Watson nodded to his boss. "But I'm doing great." He raised his coffee cup in a toast. "No, I'm feeling *really* great. It must be this amazing sea air that they brag about."

"I know what you mean." Tommo stretched up his arms. "We knocked back quite a few drinks last night in the bar, but there's no hangover today. We both woke up alive and buzzing."

"It feels like we've both had shots of adrenaline," added his friend, Pricey. "I don't get it, but hey, I'm certainly not knocking it."

"So how's the birding going?" quizzed Watson, pointing to the identification guides on the table. "Seen anything good?"

"Absolutely." Tommo winked. "We saw a stark-naked redhead dive off a balcony and swim around in the sea. It doesn't get much better than that."

"You're not kidding," agreed Pricey. "But as for birds, no, certainly not around Ravenspoint. Christ knows why, but birds seem to avoid this place like the plague. At first light we were up on the village wall again to do a bit of sea-watching."

"Right." Watson smirked. "That would be watching the sea?"

"Got it in one," confirmed Tommo. "You don't miss a trick, do you? Everything that flies up or down the coast likes to hug the land, so you find yourself a headland that sticks out, like this one, and you get to see them up close."

"Well, that's the idea," said Pricey, bemused. "Except, as I say, they don't come anywhere near *this* Craggan headland. On the plus side, we got a great show from the redhead and this superb hotel was unbelievably cheap. We couldn't believe it."

"We've been touring Scotland," said Tommo. "Photographing eagles and harriers. It's been a good trip, but it's safe to say our next trip will beat it. We fly out to the Philippines on Wednesday for two months."

"That's further than Benidorm." Watson whistled. "All that way to watch birds? For *two* whole months? Wow, your jobs must pay well."

"We do contracting work on the highways,' explained Pricey. "It's flexible and the money is brilliant. Once we've built up enough cash, we pack the rucksacks and head off for a few months out east."

"Sounds like a good life, eh, Guv?" Watson turned back to Quist. "Well, apart from the crap birdwatching part, of course."

"Mmmh? Er, yes." Quist had only been half-listening to the

conversation, his attention being focussed on his phone where he'd brought up the local news. "I'm reading about yesterday's awful accident. It was a group of young men from Newcastle and the crash happened just along the coast after they'd left Ravenspoint. They were young offenders on one of those community payback schemes."

"What were they doing here?" asked Watson. "They usually have those guys cleaning graffiti in towns, or picking litter."

"They were on a guided tour of the castle, apparently. It's some new educational initiative where teenage offenders are taken on such visits to give them a better outlook on life. So far they've only found two bodies, one of the youths and the supervisor. Incredibly, nine of them are still missing."

"Bloody hell." Watson frowned. "Hey, do they get sharks up here?"

The detective narrowed his eyes. "I told you about a similar accident that happened somewhere near here last week. That young couple that ran off the clifftop road in their car and crashed into the sea, just like this."

"Yeah, you said neither were found." Watson grimaced. "It's horrible, but accidents *do* happen."

"Yes, they do." Quist tapped at his phone. "Ah, here's the news report I'm speaking of. A witness, following in another vehicle, claimed they were driving erratically, so it was assumed the driver was intoxicated."

"Well, there you go."

Quist nodded slowly. "The witness was from Ravenspoint."

"Um, right. So what are you thinking, Guv?"

"I don't know, but *this* latest accident with the minibus raises a few questions. Why on earth did they decide to take the coast road along the Craggan headland? The main road that we used yesterday is the obvious route back to Newcastle."

* * * *

Chapter 22

"Not one blade of grass anywhere," said Quist. He smoked a cigarette as he walked along the main street to the castle, his long leather trenchcoat flapping about him. "This isn't right."

"Yeah," agreed Watson. "The headland was covered in grass as we drove to Ravenspoint, but it vanished as soon as we went through that arched entrance. There are no weeds anywhere either."

"I've always disliked the term *weeds*," said Quist. "They're British wild flowers and most are quite beautiful, but you're correct. There are no plants anywhere to be…"

"Wow!" Watson shot his boss a concerned look. "Hey, did you feel that, Guv?"

"It would have been difficult to miss, wouldn't it?" The detective looked around. "That was a similar shudder to the one I felt around midnight, only I'd say this was more powerful."

"Do they mine for stuff around here? It felt like an underground explosion or something."

"No, that was a definite seismic tremor, although Northumberland isn't exactly famed for its earthquakes. How very peculiar." Quist pointed up a shadowy snicket on their right. "Speaking of strange phenomenon, I notice that low-lying mist hasn't dissipated. I assumed it was some atmospheric anomaly – perhaps the damp sea air reacting on the ice-cold stonework – but it shouldn't be lingering here constantly."

Arriving at the market square, they walked through the barbican archway into the castle grounds. A police car was leaving and they stepped aside to allow the two officers to drive past.

"I wonder what the cops were doing here?" said Watson, walking across the courtyard. "Maybe they were warning Redbeard and Ali Bongo about using magick to kidnap good-looking black guys."

Close up, they could both see how various parts of the castle walls sported cracks and areas of repaired damage, just like the rest of the village. A sandstone porch housed two large oak doors and Quist killed his cigarette underfoot before thumbing the bell.

His assistant grinned at the large bronze door knockers – ferocious dragon heads clasping heavy rings in their jaws. The installation of an electric bell had downgraded these to ornamentation, which was a pity. He felt it would have been fun to slam them hard and hear the echoing booms. Once again, the peculiar feelings of exhilaration tempted him to laugh out loud and try it.

"Redbeard's knockers," he chuckled, the weird elation bubbling up as he thought of the juvenile term for breasts. His employer's critical glance only added to the hilarity. "Ginger Reg's big knockers."

Brunton opened the door, his muscular size and aggressive air instantly killing the childish excitement.

"Good morning," said Quist. He decided against mentioning the failed abduction attempt unless this character brought it up. "I believe the Laird is expecting us for coffee."

"It's probably percolating as we speak." Brunton looked the two men up and down, smirking as he swung the heavy door wide. "So you're Watson, eh? I saw you in the square yesterday."

"Yeah, mum told me how you called on us in York." The youth smiled cynically. "Sorry I was out."

Brunton replied with a short laugh.

The three men walked through an entrance lobby and along a short passage into a banqueting hall, with huge leaded windows and a wide staircase sweeping up to a balcony above. Despite its lofty size, the oak-panelled room was comfortably warm; due, no doubt, to the gigantic fireplace where Gavin Howell toiled at the blazing grate with a scuttle and poker. Expensive Persian rugs covered the stone floor and a black metal chandelier hung centrally from a chain, lighting the vast collection of paintings, shields and swords.

"You haven't gone overboard with the Christmas trimmings, have you?" drawled Watson, noticing the lack of festive decorations. "Is the Laird allergic to tinsel, or something?"

"Try the hotel if you want all that garbage," said Brunton, sarcastically. "They put on a show for the guests there, but no one here in Ravenspoint bothers with Christmas."

"We saw the police car leaving," said Quist, unbuttoning his trenchcoat. "I presume they were making enquiries about yesterday's tragedy up on the headland?"

"The minibus crash?" Brunton nodded. "Yes, it was a bunch of Newcastle teenagers that were here for a tour of the castle. I was their guide, so I had to give the cops a statement and I'll be appearing at the inquest."

"I wonder what could have caused the accident?" The detective gazed at the big man, reading his sardonic expression. "Or why they chose to take that particular backroad along the cliff. I'm fairly certain it couldn't have been the most direct route home."

"You're right, and I was able to help the officers with those very questions." Brunton attempted a sorrowful smile and failed badly. "I explained how the group supervisor was clearly depressed and acting oddly. I don't like to speak ill of the departed, but she was probably on medication for the condition and shouldn't have been driving. She was the one who decided upon that road, so we have to ask ourselves whether it was deliberate or not. Who knows?"

Quist bit his tongue, watching as Brunton went over to speak quietly to Howell.

Watson peered at the two men, wondering why the staff here were so large and brawny. *Brunton was supposedly 'security', but what exactly was his job? He had the square jaw and chiselled good looks seen on the covers of those shit romantic novels, but he appeared more suited to causing brain damage in boxing gyms than helping out in a castle.*

"Mulgrave Castle," murmured Quist, walking slowly into the centre of the hall and gazing around. "Yes, I must admit, it's quite outstanding."

The detective moved closer to the fire and gazed at the oil portrait above the mantelpiece. The violent-looking subject, a man with long red-hair and beard, clutched a sword against a background of stormy sea. The stylised subject and setting belonged on a *Rob Roy* movie poster.

"That ferocious gentleman is Tobias Mulgrave." Brunton walked up behind him and lit a cigarette. "Would you like one?" He held out the pack. "A smoke, I mean. Not a painting."

Quist took one as a tremor shook the room causing swords and other wall decorations to rattle. "We keep feeling those vibrations," he said, allowing Brunton to light the cigarette. "What are they?"

"Oh, that's just our underground railway." The big man smiled glibly. "It's similar to the London Tube." He noticed Watson's surprised look. "Well, of course it isn't, you idiot. The Laird will…"

"He'll explain everything," broke in Quist. "Yes, I've grown quite familiar with that phrase now."

"I'm sure you have," laughed Brunton. "Hey, by the way, no hard feelings for the other morning, I hope?"

"Not at all." The detective smiled tightly. "*My* nose wasn't broken and *my* partner didn't suffer a terrible death."

"And how about *you?*" Brunton turned to Watson. "I hear you bust your wrist in the station. How is it now?"

"It's fine," admitted the youth. "Like it was never injured."

"Good to know." He laughed again. "So I guess you can get back to your favourite pastime?"

"Tobias Mulgrave," said Quist, ignoring the crude insult and gesturing to the painting. "So this is an ancestor of the Laird?"

"His father," confirmed Brunton.

"Really? It looks like a rather old portrait." Smoking his cigarette, the detective studied the subject's clothing and the general artwork style, before reading the signature aloud. "Allan Ramsay."

"The famous Scottish artist." Brunton nodded. "He was the guy who painted George the Third's coronation."

Quist frowned slightly. George had been crowned in 1760, so the man definitely had something wrong here, but he saw little point in mentioning it.

"Ginger Reg' likes his art, doesn't he?" whispered Watson, strolling from painting to painting. "I'm guessing they'll all be worth a few quid?"

"*That* one certainly will be." Quist walked over and looked closely. "It's a view by Degas."

"Degas view. eh?" The youth supressed a giggle, as the odd elation bubbled once again. "That's weird, Guv. I've only just seen this, but I have the strangest feeling that I've seen it before."

"Hello again."

The two men turned at the sound of the girl's voice to see Rachel Mulgrave at the head of the staircase, one hand on her hip and the other resting casually on the banister. Red hair flowed over the shoulders of a black mini dress, cut low to expose her cleavage. Watson unintentionally licked at his lips as she descended the stairs like a professional model, her stilettos locating each step without looking down. A tingle of sexual excitement joined his exhilaration and he stifled another giggle This entrance was straight out of some Hollywood melodrama.

"You owe me a hair brush," he said, winking.

"Yes, sorry about that." Rachel walked up close, a subtle waft of her high-priced perfume transmitting a direct message from his nostrils to his loins. "I'll get you another. I'm told by Aleister that you saw me dive from the balcony yesterday?"

"Yeah. I've got to say, it was pretty impressive."

"From *there*?" she scoffed. "Not at all. I've taken part in the famous cliff diving in both Acapulco and Hawaii. Those 30 metre heights are a little *more* impressive. You could have watched again today, but I'm afraid I'll be far too busy to swim."

"That's a shame," said Watson. "I could have guarded your towel."

"He also told me about your wrist." Smiling sweetly, Rachel reached for his hand and lifted it. "You poor boy. Perhaps I should kiss it better?"

"Um, yeah." The young man gulped as she gently brushed it with her soft lips. "That sounds like a good idea."

"But, I'm forgetting..." She let go, laughing quietly. "There's no need, is there? After drinking our water and just being here in Ravenspoint, the damage will have simply vanished."

"True," agreed Watson. "But I can't see how a kiss would do any harm."

"I'm sorry to interrupt," sighed Quist, tossing his half-smoked cigarette into the open fire. "But when you've finished teasing my assistant, we're here to see the Laird."

"Of course." Rachel laughed again and headed for one of the doors leading off the hall. "If you'd like to follow me, Reginald is in his study."

"*Reginald*?" echoed Watson. "Don't you call him *Dad*?

She turned and smiled sexily. "I imagine you'd love it if I called *you* Daddy?"

Watson uncomfortably cleared his throat.

"Calm yourself down." Quist lowered his voice to murmur in the youth's ear. "Or I'll insist that you start calling me *Mister Wolf*."

* * * *

Chapter 23

The Laird's study was situated on the ground floor of the castle, but due to its position above the sheer cliff, the windows looked over the bay from a fair height. Watson noticed the stone balcony outside the French doors and realised this could be the spot from where Rachel performed her naked dive the previous afternoon. A large antique desk was the room centrepiece, mahogany bookcases covered one of the walls, and three leather couches were set out around a red marble fireplace.

Wearing his tweed jacket, Reginald Mulgrave stood by the glass doors, stroking thoughtfully at his thick beard and gazing at the sea. Crowley sat on the sofa closest to the fire and raised his coffee mug to Quist and Watson as they entered.

"A very good morning to you," boomed the Laird, setting down his own mug and walking over to shake the detective's hand. "Thank you both for coming. Considering recent events, it's very gracious of you to accept my invitation."

"Not at all." Quist's hair rose on the back of his neck. Something here immediately filled him with unease and he realised it was a faint scent on the air. A fading scent of strong tobacco. "It's our pleasure," he said, casting off the feeling of disquiet. "It's probably due to the mysterious build up, but I must admit, I'm extremely curious to hear what you have to say."

"I take it you slept well," said Crowley, sipping his drink. "Thanks to our unique air, everyone here has the most restful of slumbers."

"That's quite true." Mulgrave waved a hand towards the couches. "Please sit. Tell me, how do you take your coffee?"

"No, that's alright." Quist glanced at Watson who also shook his head. "We're both fine for now."

"Unlike the people of this village." Rachel flopped on the sofa

160

beside the magician and crossed her shapely legs. "We have a problem and you're the only one who can help us."

"*Problem* is somewhat understating our crisis," said the Laird, walking to a cigar humidor on the bureau. "We can explain everything to you, but first you need to see something. Believe me, it will make the explanation so much easier."

"And *I'm* the only one who can help?" repeated Quist, slipping off his overcoat and sitting with Watson opposite Crowley and Rachel. "I honestly can't imagine what this could be about."

The entire room began to shake, the tremors lasting around four seconds, much longer than the previous occasions. Quist shot Mulgrave a questioning look.

"Yes, Bernard," he nodded. "That really couldn't have been timed any better. Yes, *that* is part of our problem." He took a cigar from the desk humidor and clipped the cap. "Before we begin, could I tempt you with a Cohiba? They're rather good."

"I prefer cigars in the evening," said Quist, taking out his cigarettes. "I'll stay with these, if that's acceptable?"

"Perhaps Mister Watson would care to try one?" Mulgrave held out the cedar box. "These were a recent gift from Hollywood, where Cohiba has always been the movie star's favoured brand. Cigar smoking is quite fashionable in Los Angeles amongst cool young men such as yourself."

"Well thanks for the description, mate." The youth laughed. "But no thanks to the cigar. The smell makes me want to puke and that hardly fits in with my *coolness*. Talking of Hollywood, I see you've got Marcia Newley in your village hotel."

"We have," confirmed Crowley. "She's the one who kindly brought Reginald the cigars. You'd be surprised at some of the famous guests we get staying in the Fountain."

Quist watched as the magician lit two cigarettes and passed one to Rachel. He'd picked up a tobacco scent when he entered the study, but it wasn't anything being smoked here. No, he realised it was the faint, but distinctive smell of French Gauloises cigarettes. *But why should that make him feel uneasy?* He looked up at the splendid oil portrait above the fireplace, a Jacobean gentleman with the obligatory short beard, black tunic and white lace collar.

"Nathaniel," said the Laird, lighting his cigar. "The gentleman you're looking at there is Nathaniel Mulgrave, the 16th century occultist. He's the one who had this castle built."

"An occultist?" Watson raised an inquisitive eyebrow. "Um, you mean like Aleister here?"

Mulgrave nodded. "Some would say my ancestor was far more proficient in the dark arts."

"Oh, Reginald." Crowley clasped at his chest in a sham display of hurt. "Your words wound me, like arrows to the heart."

Laughing quietly, the Laird sat next to him. "Nathaniel," he said, "was born into the wealthy Mulgrave family of Scotland in 1560. Around the age of sixteen, he met and romanced a gypsy girl, a *wise woman*, by all accounts, and she initiated him into witchcraft and the occult basics. Unlike many, he had the money to take his interest much further. He invested in rare books from across Europe and soon began to study the more complex forms of ritual magick."

"Nathaniel became an accomplished practitioner," said Rachel. "But by this time, James the First was on the throne. The King had a fanatical hatred of the dark arts and it was a sensitive time to practise the occult. If you were discovered, torture and a grisly death were guaranteed."

"So here's a thought…" Watson gave a dry laugh. "Why would anyone be daft enough to risk it?"

"The rewards," said Crowley. "And for Nathaniel, those rewards far outweighed the risk."

"His early magick was performed to accumulate wealth and wisdom," said Mulgrave. "But eventually, Nathaniel became obsessed with healing and prolonging life. His father and wife both died of consumption at an early age and Caroline, his only child, was gravely ill with the same condition. He decided to do something about this."

"Tell me..." Crowley sipped his coffee and gazed at Quist. "Are you aware of the Abra-Mutar ceremony?"

The detective shook his head.

"It's one of the, um, *nastier* and more dangerous of the ancient blood rituals. A way of conjuring up a dark elemental entity in an attempt to cure illness."

"Are you saying he had success with it?" asked Quist.

"Huge success," confirmed the magician. "He managed to completely heal his daughter, but there were certain side-effects which were..."

"How old would you say I am?" interrupted the Laird.

"Ah." Watson narrowed his eyes suspiciously. "Because you're *asking* that, I'm guessing you're older than you look?"

"One-hundred and eighty-eight," said Mulgrave, stroking his red beard. "Actually, I'll be one-hundred and eighty-nine this coming February."

"Whatever you say." The youth gestured to his cigar. "The doctors are obviously wrong about smoking being bad for us."

"No, smoking is most definitely harmful." He puffed a thick cloud. "The point is, it doesn't harm *me*."

"It's true," said Crowley. "Like most cigar smokers, Reginald doesn't inhale, but it wouldn't really matter if he did."

Rachel held up her cigarette. "These are filled with toxic tar and countless poisons, but here it doesn't matter. Here in Ravenspoint they're totally harmless."

Watson glanced warily at his boss. *Was it his imagination, or had they all suddenly started talking bollocks?*

Mulgrave smiled at the youth. "Tell me, young man, do you have any tattoos?"

"Er, kind of." He shrugged. "A pretty crap one, to be honest."

Aged fourteen, Watson had been dating Mia Grimes and had decided to commemorate their lifetime of love together by using a needle and ink to self-tattoo a letter *M* on his left forearm. Two weeks later, Mia and her new boyfriend were long gone, but fortunately the romantic gesture looked kind of like a *W* for Watson when his arm hung by his side.

"May I see?" asked the Laird.

"Um, well, if you must." Watson tugged up the sleeve of his canvas jacket and froze. "What the fu…" he mouthed. "No, I don't understand…"

"Something wrong?" asked Mulgrave, grinning broadly.

"You could say that." Rubbing his arm, the youth shook his head. "It's gone. How's this possible?"

"Something is clearly going on here," said Quist. "You've told us your supposed age, and Brunton said the portrait in the hall was your father. He told us it was by the artist who painted George the Third. So that would make your father Tobias some incredible age too." He turned to Crowley. "I take it this longevity is connected to the Abra-Mutar ceremony that you mentioned?"

"It is," confirmed the magician.

"Interesting." Nodding slowly, the detective drew on his cigarette. "So what is it that you intend to show us?"

"The Fountain," said Rachel.

"I'm sure you don't mean your hotel, so what might *that* be?"

Ignoring the question and standing, the Laird puffed again on his cigar before leaving it in an ashtray to expire. "I've told you *my* age," he said, gesturing for them to follow him. "I'm now about to introduce you to someone considerably older."

* * * *

164

Chapter 24

Quist and Watson descended the wide sandstone steps into the castle cellars with Brunton and Rachel leading the way. Mulgrave followed with Crowley, the latter quietly humming the Bolero dance music to himself.

"So painful," whimpered Watson, quietly. "So much pain in my dark prison."

His boss shot him a puzzled look and saw the glazed expression. Taking his arm, he shook him slightly.

"Eh?" The youth snapped back to normal. "What's up, Guv?"

"Nothing," murmured Quist. Glancing around, he saw that no one else had noticed the exchange. "Forget about it for now."

Subterranean cold flowed out as Brunton held open the door at the bottom of the staircase, allowing them into the complex of chambers beyond. Quist had pulled on his lengthy overcoat before leaving the Laird's study and he turned up the leather collar before stroking at his temple. For some reason, the irritating buzz in his head had begun to return with a vengeance.

An electric cable crossed the vaulted ceiling to supply three dim bulbs and, pausing beneath one of the lights, Watson checked his arm again for the letter M. He turned his wrist in case it had somehow sneakily moved, but no, it was still missing. Shaking his head, he frowned curiously at Mulgrave. *So what the hell could have happened to his tattoo, and what did old Ginger Reg' intend to show them down here? Rachel had mentioned a fountain.*

The youth followed Quist into a second larger chamber where something big and square-shaped was hidden beneath tarpaulins in the far corner. Howell, the brawny castle worker, stood waiting by a door with five smartly-dressed people, three men and two women.

"I'd like you to meet the Peterson family," said Mulgrave. "They've been residents here in Ravenspoint for quite some time."

Quist's eyes were drawn to the eldest woman, a wizened, bald lady who sat hunched and trembling on a stool, a raincoat covering her crooked frame. "What is this?" he asked. "When you said you wanted us to meet someone older…"

"One moment, please." Striding to the woman, Mulgrave saw the nosebleed and milky cataracts. "Thank you all for your patience, especially *you*, Joan. Is the pain bad?"

She nodded, the slight movement visibly adding to her torment.

Quist and Watson watched with growing alarm.

"My dear lady, we've left it too long, haven't we?" Mulgrave turned sadly to the Petersons. "With your permission we'll proceed immediately. I assume you're prepared?"

"We're ready," confirmed the eldest man. "We've already said goodbye."

Although unable to see any resemblance in the crumpled skull that was Joan Peterson's face, Watson guessed the man was her son, and his heart quickened at the mention of *goodbye*. He glanced about the chamber, wondering how they'd carried her down here and, more to the point, *why? What the hell could be going on?* Turning to his boss, he gulped to see his tense expression. For some time now, Watson's all-purpose strategy had been: *Try to stay calm and stand behind the Guv.* It was probably time to worry when the big bad wolf was *also* feeling apprehensive.

The youth cleared his throat. "Er, I'm no doctor," he said. "But should this old girl really be down here? I mean, what with the cold and…"

"Don't worry," said Rachel. She walked over to stand beside him and slide an arm around his waist. "Trust me. Joan won't be here a moment longer than necessary."

Joan's son smiled sympathetically. "We appreciate your concern, young man, but our mother is here willingly. Honestly, it really *is* fine."

Mulgrave squat by Joan's stool. "Are you ready?" he said, softly. "Richard will assist you and we'll be as swift as possible."

She gave a feeble nod, as the Laird slipped off her coat to reveal a living skeleton. A pale cotton nightdress covered a collection of bones held together by desiccated dead skin. Stifling a gasp, Watson was reminded of the Egyptian mummies he'd seen on television. He'd never set eyes on anyone so emaciated, and winced at the tumours covering the withered flesh.

"This is ludicrous," snapped Quist. "The cellars are freezing." He'd felt such cold many times before and he knew it wasn't natural. "You can't have this lady down here in a nightdress."

"I agree." Mulgrave helped the woman up onto fragile, stick-like legs. "Joan is two-hundred and seventy." He opened the door behind her stool. "Below this room is the lower cellar, or the dungeon, as we call it."

"Are you lot serious?" Watson peered down the sloping tunnel beyond, his heart racing as he felt the unnatural ice-cold air. *It reminded him of when the boss shapeshifted.* "A fucking *dungeon*? Tell me you're not thinking of taking her down there?"

"Stay calm," said Rachel, taking his hand and squeezing

Quist turned to the Petersons. "Look, I've no idea what your intentions are, but your mother needs medical care and..."

"No, I'm afraid she needs *this*, and *you* need to see it." The son gave a placid smile, mirrored by the other family members. "It really *is* alright, Mister Quist."

Watson had seen similar serene smiles on the owners of the Jehovah's Fitness gym in York. Seemingly *normal* people often smiled like this before revealing themselves to be members of religious cults, or *nutters* as he referred to them. The youth just *knew* that something very wrong was about to happen.

"Aleister?" said the Laird. "If you'd be so kind?"

167

Crowley stepped forward to swiftly recite a short ritual, the same words he'd spoken the previous evening at the courtyard well. Taking out a dagger, he made a small cut on his arm and dabbed bloody symbols on Joan's forehead and cheeks. Brunton waited until he'd finished before scooping up the ancient woman in his arms and carrying her down the steps into the dungeon, taking care how he gripped. At this age the bones would be as brittle as old biscuits.

The bizarre fizzing sensation grew in Quist's head, but he fought it down and turned to Crowley. "So what's going on?" he demanded. "What was that ritual?"

"Just wait and see," said the magician.

"Joan," called out Mulgrave. "I need to leave the lights on for our two guests, but you can keep your eyes closed." He gestured for everyone to accompany him down the wide stone staircase. "This way, please."

"We've chosen to remain up here," said the head of the Peterson family. "I'm sure you'll understand?"

"I don't like this," muttered Watson, following and wrinkling his nose at the musty odour. "Not one friggin' bit."

The dungeon was circular, over thirty feet in diameter, with a stone domed ceiling and five tunnels leading off it into darkness. The arched passageways sloped slightly and appeared to be flooded after a few feet. Two steps from the bottom, Brunton placed the woman down in the amber glow of the staircase light bulbs and hurried back to join the group.

Mulgrave gestured to the sandy ground beyond Joan. "This is as far down as we dare stand," he said. "It's unsafe to proceed further into the dungeon."

"Unsafe?" Quist watched the old lady negotiate the last step with effort and totter across the floor. He pulled a sour face as the stench grew stronger. "What do you mean?"

"Don't move, either of you," said Rachel, taking Watson's

hand again. "This will be quite shocking, I'm afraid, but you mustn't attempt to get any closer."

The chamber shuddered and bubbling puddles formed on the earthen floor around Joan, as if water pipes had ruptured below the sandy surface. The vibration was only slight, but more than enough to unbalance the unsteady geriatric. She stumbled onto hands and knees, and Watson winced to hear the sickening snap of a bone in one of her arms.

"*Fuck!*" he snarled. "No, this is crazy. You've got to stop this right now."

Rachel's grip on his hand tightened and Brunton grabbed his arm. They'd obviously been instructed to prevent any interference, but Mulgrave had wasted his breath. Watson froze as five sinuous tentacles snaked up from the deepening puddles. Slender, fleshy, and sickly-pale in the dim light, they reminded the petrified youth of bizarre mutant vines as they entwined the old woman's limbs.

"Oh, my God!" mouthed Watson. "What *are* they?"

Quist watched with eyes wide. One tentacle curled gracefully and hypnotically to the kneeling woman's posterior, seemingly sniffing like a dog, before worming between the withered buttocks taking the nightdress with it. The ground shuddered violently, the puddles widened into one large pool, and Joan screwed her eyes tightly shut. Her breath came in agonised pants, as more of the repulsive tendrils appeared from the liquid to quickly wrap her shivering body.

Watson shook his head, his jaw dropping at the sudden realisation – she *knew*. Whatever these ghastly things were and whatever was about to happen, Joan Peterson had known all about this. Everyone here, including her family, had known this was going to happen.

"What the hell is it?" Quist glanced angrily at Mulgrave. "You brought us here to watch a woman die, didn't you, you bastard?

What *is* this thing?"

Joan squawked as the grisly tendril nuzzling at her posterior rammed deep. The nightdress tore, a scarlet carnation blooming on the cotton. More tentacles rose from the now bubbling pool to burrow through her parchment skin like gigantic maggots. Whipping and twisting, rippling and pulsing, they greedily sucked out organs, siphoning off whatever nourishment they could locate in the ancient body.

Mesmerised and numb, Watson stared at the twitching woman as the thrashing tendrils frenziedly tore apart her flimsy frame. The limbs, intestines, and scraps of flesh fell into the frothing pool to be quickly dissolved and digested. The liquid was clearly some sort of acid. *He'd seen some weird and unpleasant shit during his time working for the Guv, but to be fair, this would probably take some beating.*

The acid was absorbed back into the dungeon floor, which began to undulate and rise up. No longer was it sandy ground, but sulphurous wrinkled skin. Spasming capillaries and darker tube-like veins covered the grotesque surface, all surging now with the liquefied geriatric. Leprous and ulcerated, the leathery hide quivered and pulsed with life, the forest of pallid tendrils snaking out through pore-like holes and searching blindly for further food. In the centre of it all was an eye – a large, dull yellow eye."

"Gentlemen," said Mulgrave, turning to Quist and Watson. "This is the Fountain."

The detective winced as a painful jolt shook his system, an electrical jolt similar to the one he'd experienced on entering the village.

Watson turned away from the monster, wrenching his hand from Rachel's grip, to press his shaking back against the wall, cold sweat pouring down his face.

The yellow eye closed, the tentacles retracted and the final acid puddles were absorbed back into the creature as the skin flattened into an even surface. Thick puffs of sand-like powder erupted like fungus spores to settle back over the vileness in a dry layer. Less than thirty seconds after it had begun it was over; the cellar floor lay flat and still once again, covered in dusty sand as if no one had ever been there.

"Goodbye, Joan," said the Laird. "Thank you for your courageous sacrifice."

Rachel smiled at Watson, a manic glint in her eye. "Yes, that was the Fountain," she said. "Terrifying, yet quite stimulating, isn't it?"

These days, no matter what supernatural horror he experienced, the youth was always quick to recover. "Terrifying?" He shrugged. "Ah, I've seen worse, luv."

* * * *

Chapter 25

Watson and Quist walked along the castle corridor, following Mulgrave, Rachel and Crowley.

"So what the hell *was* it?" demanded the youth, his body shaking as adrenalin pumped. "You let it eat her alive."

"Don't worry," said Rachel, slipping an arm around him. "*Daddy* is about to explain everything."

"Yeah, well, top marks for the cabaret, luv." He shrugged her off and let out a dry laugh. "It's not the first time I've been invited to see *something special*, but it usually turns out to be a pirate download of a new *Star Trek* movie. I don't know what I expected here, but it definitely wasn't *that*."

"My friend asked a question," snapped Quist. "What *is* that thing down there? Why did you take us to watch a woman die?"

"As you know, we call it the Fountain." Mulgrave led them back into his study. "I apologise for subjecting you to that, but it happened with the full approval of Joan and her family; I'm sure you could see that?"

"It's never pleasant," added Crowley, settling himself back on the fireside couch.

"*What?*" gasped Watson, incredulous. "You're saying that shit down there was fairly normal."

"It isn't *normal*," said Rachel. "But it isn't rare either. Yes, someone died, but someone who should have died two centuries ago."

Mulgrave nodded. "Death was close and her pain was unbearable. Joan chose to end her suffering in that consensual manner and I wanted you to see it to understand why we need you. Had I simply told you what you're about to hear, you'd have thought me insane." Taking his cigar from the ashtray, he relit it and gestured to the couches. "Please sit down."

"I know it was supernatural." Quist lit a cigarette and sat with

Watson opposite the Laird. "But what *was* it exactly?"

"As we mentioned earlier," said Crowley, "Nathaniel Mulgrave performed the Abra-Mutar ritual to heal his sick daughter Caroline. On the Winter Solstice, a pentagram was carved into the floor of that lower cellar and a dark elemental was called up."

"Today is the solstice," said Quist. "I presume that isn't a coincidence?"

"No it isn't," admitted the magician. "Now I don't know what mistakes he made, but something went wrong and the entity materialised in solid form. The aim had been to cure Caroline's consumption and Nathaniel kept it imprisoned in the pentagram until she recovered. Over the next week she *did* heal, but a nasty boil on Nathaniel's neck also vanished and he noticed how he'd begun to look younger and feel fitter. The same went for his servants and everyone else in close proximity to the elemental."

Rachel nodded. "The creature produces a gas which slows the aging process and cures the ailments of anyone spending time near it, Everyone who breathes the vapours is affected by them. Have you noticed the mist that always lingers here in Ravenspoint?"

Quist drew on his cigarette and nodded slowly.

"It emits the healing mist, but it also secretes a liquid. You must have seen those bubbling puddles down there? It's a strong acid to dissolve its, um, *food*, but after a short time it transforms into harmless water which can be bottled."

"That's your spa water?" gasped Watson. "*That's* what I drank? Monster piss?"

"And *that's* what cured your wrist," said Rachel. "Breathing our misty air for a couple of days would have been enough, but your healing was accelerated. Nathaniel realised he'd created, for lack of better words, a fountain of youth – hence our name for it – and he decided to keep it here permanently."

"Impossible." Quist shook his head. "From what I know

about such matters, elementals can't exist in our world for very long. They're usually placed inside human hosts to prolong their..."

"So every occultist believes," said Rachel. "But here it is."

"You'll be aware of the stress hormones that promote healing?" said Mulgrave. "We secrete them in response to illness and trauma. The mist released by the entity contains hormones far more advanced, and the more it feeds, the more mist it produces."

"Elementals feed upon psychic energy," said the detective. "I couldn't help noticing how *yours* feeds upon flesh."

"It mutated with age," explained Crowley. "After the first decade it had become a basic, mindless organism and Nathaniel could no longer communicate with it. That's when the change in its, um, *diet* occurred."

Watson shook his head in awe. "It stops people aging? Your pet monster can heal *anything*?"

"Anything," confirmed Rachel. "The Fountain even cures baldness. This is also why your tattoo vanished; it *cures* tattoos just as it would any other skin damage."

"But the healing and longevity are actually side-effects," said Crowley. "As the entity developed its taste for meat, it began to produce more mist to attract prey. People *are* attracted as the air gives the most wonderful feelings of elation."

Watson glanced at Quist. So *that* was it. *Even now, after the horror he'd just witnessed, he still felt exhilarated.*

"I see," said Quist, presuming this explained the buzzing in his head. "So you're telling me that creature down there is the original elemental from four-hundred years ago?"

Mulgrave drew on his cigar and nodded. "Nathaniel's daughter Caroline owed her health to ritual magick and she studied hard to become an occultist herself. Eventually she married into a noble English household, but her consumption returned when she moved away from Ravenspoint, forcing her to make regular return trips to recuperate."

"You make this place sound like a spa resort," said Watson, still feeling queasy from the knowledge of what he'd swallowed.

"That pretty much sums it up," said Rachel. "Eventually she returned permanently for her health. Caroline was the mother of my grandfather Tobias."

"This area was plagued by raiders for centuries," said the Laird. "People built fortified mansions to keep the Scots out, but Ravenspoint had far more to guard and the village constructed the defensive wall and a circle of trust. Everyone inside the wall benefitted from the Fountain and protected it."

"They also realised they could profit from it," said Rachel. "They knew they couldn't conceal such a secret without outside assistance, so a few well-selected authority figures were approached, powerful people who could keep Ravenspoint isolated and protected. We didn't even appear on the maps for two centuries. They quietly helped us in exchange for health and longevity, and it's an arrangement that continues to the present day."

"The politician at the hotel?" said Quist. "Nigel Drummond?"

"A perfect example," said Mulgrave. "As is the actress Marcia Newley."

The detective frowned. "How do actors benefit you?"

"Money, of course. We approach the *right* people and you can imagine what they pay for our cures. They come here to convalesce and our *mineral water* is available on the Dark Web and mailed to exclusive customers around the world. The hotel accommodates our visitors in luxury and the cuisine is superb. The palate is sharper here and anything less than the best would taste remarkably dull."

Rachel nodded. "We cure our clients and prolong their lives, but never by *too* much. In this anonymous community no one notices our longevity, but celebrities would provoke suspicion. Movie stars can only attribute *so* much to their surgeons. They're all unaware of the elemental, of course, and they have no idea *how* we're able to do what we do. They're just grateful for our help. Only a privileged few, such as yourselves, get to see the Fountain."

"Drummond is a real asset," said Mulgrave. "He thwarts all the planning submissions that propose developments or roads near Ravenspoint. He has a tumour, you see, and should have died a decade ago. We say the Fountain *cures*, but to be strictly correct the ailments become dormant and harmless. If Nigel stopped his occasional visits, or stopped drinking the bottled water we provide, his tumour would return."

"Are you like that?" asked Watson. "If you left here…"

"I'd die," confirmed the Laird. "The entire village would, either from old age or dormant illness."

"Not me," said Rachel, winking. "I'm only fifty-five."

"Bloody hell!" Watson peered at her, his eyes wide. *She was gorgeous, but far older than his Granny.*

"The Fountain provides extended life," continued Mulgrave. "It gives perfect health, but it requires food in return. Animals sense the supernatural aura of the elemental and avoid it. Plant life won't grow here either. A few hardy lichens cling to our stonework, but most vegetation can't tolerate the mist. In any case, the entity will no longer consume animal flesh. Only human."

"Like Joan Peterson?" Watson grimaced. "Why the hell didn't you wait until the old girl was dead?"

"It *will* digest the dead," said Crowley. "But it no longer emits the healing mists unless we provide *living* tissue."

"That's right," confirmed the Laird. "Everyone here lives to an advanced age, but we *don't* live forever. Towards the end, our bodies begin to break down and Joan was virtually dead when you saw her, just a mass of decomposing tissue. She had a few hours left at the most. The ending accelerates quickly and it's extremely unpleasant. I'm told you witnessed the awful culmination of this deterioration process with the unfortunate Oliver Tarrant."

"Yeah, *that* was fun," mumbled Watson.

Mulgrave puffed his cigar and smiled. "We've all agreed to voluntary termination before we reach that stage, to ease our agony and to provide the Fountain with its needs. My father died at the age of two-hundred and fifty. He began the termination tradition by walking into the dungeon. Some choose to throw themselves down the courtyard well."

"Incredible," murmured Quist. "How did they feed the creature prior to these voluntary sacrifices?"

"Ah, they were less civilised times," said Rachel, with a smirk. "I'm afraid they used tinkers, gypsies and other passing travellers. Fortunately, the Fountain never required *too* many meals."

"We're all able to leave the village, of course," said Mulgrave. "But never for very long and we *always* take a supply of water. Any more than two weeks or so and we'd start to become like Joan Peterson."

Quist grimaced. "As you mentioned, we watched your friend Tarrant expire. It wasn't pretty."

The Laird nodded sadly. "Oliver's injuries vastly accelerated the decomposition and prevented him from returning in time. He'd spent too long attempting to, um, persuade you to come here."

"Speaking of which," said Quist, "isn't it time we touched upon why I *am* here?"

"We have a dilemma," said Crowley. "A problem that has occurred intermittently since the very beginning. Caroline Mulgrave's journals record how, after about a hundred years, the elemental started to behave abnormally, shuddering and vibrating at intervals just before the Winter Solstice. She consulted her late father's magickal papers and found it had happened before, a year after he'd conjured it up. Nathaniel had realised the elemental was destabilising and…"

"Er…" Watson frowned. "It was…?"

"It was beginning to slowly vanish. For some reason, the entity was returning to its own plane of existence, so her father had devised and performed a blood ceremony to prevent this."

"Luckily he'd written it down," said the Laird. "It became known as the *Mulgrave Ritual*. Caroline used Nathaniel's ceremony on the solstice and it was successful." He puffed slowly on his cigar. "Everyone believed the problem was over, and indeed it *was* until 1906. Our series of minor earthquakes in December that year weren't natural; the Fountain had begun to deteriorate once again. As with the previous two occasions, this was just prior to the Winter Solstice and this time the tremors were quite violent. Many buildings in the locality were damaged."

"They attempted the ritual," said Crowley, smiling smugly. "It didn't work, but that wasn't surprising. Centuries had passed since the last destabilisation and no one expected they'd need to use magick again. Nathaniel had been an occultist, so had his daughter, but Caroline's son Tobias didn't see any point, and Reginald here has no occult knowledge whatsoever. Ravenspoint knew it needed to bring in a *real* magician."

"Yes, we invited Aleister here," said the Laird, "but we didn't tell him the full story. He was simply paid to perform the ritual. The thing is, we didn't want this to happen again, so, as well as stabilising the entity, we asked him to strengthen it too."

"For that," said the magician, "I had to use extra rites from my book, the *Black Equinox*. The Mulgrave Ritual is a blood ritual. Nathaniel used his own blood, his daughter used hers, but in 1906 I used a more *specialised* blood to stabilise and fortify the creature."

"And Aleister *did* strengthen the Fountain," said Mulgrave. "But he changed it too and it began growing at an incredible rate. The creature is best described as a leathery starfish – it took the shape of the pentagram that held it – but after 1906, it began expanding. The centre of its body fills the dungeon and we quickly constructed the tunnels down there to accommodate the five developing arms. They now extend beneath the entire village, like broad, flat paddles, stopping only at the deep foundations of the perimeter wall."

"It waits down in the dungeon like a spider in a web," said Rachel. "There's no mouth and, as you saw, the prey is absorbed through its skin using those feeder tentacles and the gastric acid it secretes. As we built the tunnels in front of those expanding arms, we left an opening beneath the castle well that allows us to feed it from there. Joan sacrificed herself in the dungeon so you could properly see the Fountain, but the voluntary terminations usually take place at the well with the whole village spectating."

"Lovely," muttered Watson. "Most villages hold a school play, or a craft fair. In the cellar, you couldn't see its skin to begin with. It looked like a sandy floor."

"It conceals itself," said Rachel, nodding. "It doesn't need to, of course, because *we* feed it, but it has no way of understanding that. It produces the gritty camouflage dust to imitate normal ground and hopes something, or *someone* will walk on it."

"You mentioned *specialised* blood?" said Quist.

"*Supernatural* blood." Crowley smiled. "The Mulgrave Ritual only requires enough to half-fill a chalice, but for special blood you require a special *type* of person. Back in 1906, I was aware of such a gentleman living with gypsies in the Welsh mountains."

"Aleister rectified our problem," said Mulgrave. "But only forty-one years later, the destabilisation happened again. Once more, we asked him for assistance, but this time we explained everything and invited him to remain in Ravenspoint; to live here as our resident magician in case it should ever reoccur."

"That was November 1947," said the magician. "I wasn't exactly in the best of health, so, as you can imagine, I leapt at the offer."

"We knew supernatural blood would be required again," said

Mulgrave. "Aleister had lost contact with his 1906 acquaintance, but we'd anticipated this and located another individual. We brought him here, paid him well, and his blood was used in the rite."

"I see." Quist sat quietly for several seconds, smoking his cigarette. "We've felt the earth tremors, so clearly the elemental is destabilising once again?"

"I'm afraid so," said the Laird.

"And today is the Winter Solstice, so you're about to perform the Mulgrave Ritual?"

Crowley nodded. "I'll be conducting the ceremony at six o'clock. Whenever the ritual is required, it's always performed at the same time as Nathaniel's original rite."

"Tonight?" Watson turned to Rachel. "I thought you two were performing in some television dance special?"

"We are indeed," confirmed the magician. "But that's later. The ceremony doesn't take long."

"But perhaps now you can understand our urgency?" said Rachel. "Why we went to such dramatic lengths to get you here? The ritual *has* to happen at six tonight, we need supernatural blood for this, and individuals such as yourself are rather difficult to come by."

"That's why Joan gave herself," said Mulgrave. "It was to delay the destabilisation and prevent the tremors becoming worse. To buy some time until Aleister can perform his ritual tonight."

"We can't force you to help, of course," said Rachel. "But I'm sure you can imagine how wealthy we are? Naturally we'd pay anything you asked. After all, it's only a splash of blood and you'd be saving all our lives."

Quist stroked thoughtfully at his large nose for several seconds. "This destabilisation?" he said. "It's been happening more often this century. Don't you think there might be a reason for that? Perhaps it's time for the elemental to go?"

"If it goes, then the people of Ravenspoint will die," said

Mulgrave. "Yes, the majority of them, including myself, should have died many years ago, but the fact is we didn't. We could philosophise at length over such matters, but first I feel we should rectify this pressing matter. Will you help us with this, Bernard?"

"There's a rather *pressing* question here." Quist drew on his cigarette. "One I need answering before we go any further. How, pray tell, did you become aware of me?"

"Ah, that was a friend of yours," said Rachel. "Rex Grant."

"*Rex?*" The detective froze. "Rex actually told you about me? No, I can't believe he'd be so indiscreet and stupid."

Watson raised his eyebrows. "Really?" he muttered.

"I met Rex at a London party last year," said Rachel. "He seemed like a nice guy. We ended up in bed and he told me his secret and how you were responsible for his, um, *condition*. Er, to be honest, he was a little bit drunk."

"So if you know Rex, why didn't you ask *him* to help?" quizzed Watson.

"Obviously, he was our first choice," admitted Rachel. "I phoned him, but he's currently on a yacht out in the Indian Ocean and, as you've heard, we need someone right *now*. I gave him a condensed version of our rather unique problem and he mentioned how *you* might help us. He said you were a kind and caring soul who…"

"Rex actually *told* you about my lycanthropy?" broke in Quist, shaking his head. "I still can't believe it." He pondered for a moment. "But, just assuming I agreed to do this, how would it work exactly?"

"I'll perform the ritual in the dungeon," explained Crowley. "We'll be on the lower steps where we watched Joan earlier. At the finale, I'll cut your arm and collect a little blood in my chalice which I'll then cast over the surface of the elemental. It's as simple as that."

"I see," murmured the detective. "You'll doubtless be aware, from your previous rites, that my *special* blood becomes powder when it leaves my body."

"Of course." Crowley nodded. "And the powdered blood works perfectly."

"This is huge." Quist sighed. "I've yet to get my head around the ethics of this."

"Ethics?" laughed Rachel. "This isn't a person we're holding prisoner here, or some dog that we're cruelly mistreating. It isn't even a battery chicken. It's a mindless creature that…"

"That we all know *shouldn't* be here," interrupted Quist.

"But it *is* here and it cures people," said Mulgrave. "Yes, we obscenely profit from it, but many people are alive and well because of it."

Quist nodded. "People that are living far, far longer than they should…"

"Seriously?" The magician laughed. "Surely you're the last one to talk about that, Bernard?"

Smiling thinly, Quist pondered again for several seconds, before stubbing out his cigarette with a sigh and climbing to his feet. "Watson and I are going back to the hotel," he said. "I need to consider this fully, but I must admit, I don't see any problem with what you're asking in principal. Once I've thought about it, there *will* be a price, however. A very high price that will be divided between several charities."

"I know a good charity," said Watson. "It's called *I'll Buy My Favourite Assistant A Car.*"

* * * *

Chapter 26

People often refer to the Winter Solstice as *the shortest day*, which seems to weirdly suggest that it has less hours than the conventional twenty-four. What they *actually* mean is, the Winter Solstice, December the 21st, is the day of the year with the fewest hours of light. It was a little after three-thirty on the Northumberland coast and the sun had already vanished beneath the Cheviot Hills. Afternoon had melted into deep twilight and the brighter planets and stars had appeared between the snow clouds.

The guest bedrooms at the rear of the Fountain Hotel had excellent views over the hotchpotch of village rooftops to the ocean. Quist stood at the window, drinking a coffee and staring out at the expanse of dark water. Watson lay on one of the beds behind him, keeping a low profile and allowing his boss to silently deliberate. The only noise was the rhythmic tinkle of a signet ring as Quist unconsciously tapped his finger on the mug, that and the sound of munching. The youth had raided the room minibar and sipped at a tin of Coke whilst chomping on two KitKats.

"So what do you reckon, Guv?" he asked eventually. "You've been thinking about it for ages. Are you going to do it, or what?"

The detective sighed. "Taking everything into consideration, I don't see how I have much choice. If I don't help these people with this ritual, then many of them will die. Obviously, I don't want that to happen when I can easily prevent it, but I still feel this whole supernatural scenario is ethically wrong. By their own admission, most of these villagers should have died years ago."

Watson grinned. "Like Ali Bongo the magician pointed out, Guv, you're hardly in a position to criticise *that*."

"There's also the obvious moral question of keeping that creature imprisoned down there. Trapped for centuries and..." Quist frowned thoughtfully, his signet ring tapping once again on the coffee mug. "But like they said, it's just a mindless entity... or maybe..."

"At least they *feed* it." Watson let out a mirthless laugh. "I keep remembering how that old woman was torn to bits. I have to remind myself that she actually volunteered for that horror film shit." He shook his head. "I don't really understand why this Fountain thing is top secret. Surely everyone should know about something as fantastic as this?"

"Open it up to the entire world, you mean?" Quist gave him a lopsided smile. "Bottle the waters and cure all the ailments? Can you imagine a world with no illness and everyone living over two-hundred years? How long would it be before this vastly overpopulated planet was unable to cope?"

"Yeah, I know what you mean," conceded Watson, crunching a crisp. "But I'm not talking about *everyone*. What about sick scientists and brilliant people who deserve to be cured?"

"People who *deserve* it? Now that's the issue right there, wouldn't you say? How can you possibly play God and decide who lives and who dies?"

"This bunch have *definitely* decided," scoffed Watson. "If someone can help the village, or if they're incredibly rich, then they get to live. Everyone else can simply piss off."

"Yes, Ravenspoint wouldn't win too many prizes for moral principles." Quist laughed dryly. "You're correct, of course. It isn't right that a handful of billionaires and wealthy politicians should benefit from the Fountain, whilst poor people are left to die, but I suppose the elemental *does* technically belong to the Mulgraves. We don't really have any say in how they use it for profit. All I can do is charge them a huge fee for my blood and then put that money to good use later."

"Like a nice car for your favourite assistant," Watson reminded him, through a mouthful of chocolate. "BMW and Audi are both *very* nice cars."

184

"I have Rachel's number," said Quist, glancing at his watch. "We have over two hours before this six o'clock ritual. I'd better ring and tell her my decision to help them before we head over there."

"How do you fancy going along to watch Ali Bongo dancing with her afterwards?" asked Watson. "I wouldn't mind seeing Ginger twirling about in a tight skirt."

"Let's try to keep our minds on more pertinent matters." The detective narrowed his eyes. "There's something I haven't mentioned. I picked up a faint scent in Mulgrave's study earlier which I found to be quite unnerving and I don't know why."

"What did you smell? Eau De Cellar Monster?"

"Gauloises," murmured Quist.

The young man frowned. "What the hell is *that*?"

"What the hell are *they*?" he corrected. "They're French cigarettes. The unfiltered Turkish tobacco produces a strong and rather individual smell, unmistakable to someone with my heightened olfactory senses."

"So someone in the castle smokes French fags?" Watson shrugged. "So what?"

"As I say, I don't know why it should unsettle me. What with seeing the elemental and everything else, I haven't had the chance to think about it." Quist finished his coffee and set down the mug. "By the way, you're still entering those odd trance-like states from time to time. You had another brief episode in the castle cellar, but I was the only one who noticed."

"You mentioned this yesterday." His assistant jumped off the bed. "You mean trances like a sleepwalker, or…"

"It's almost like a form of possession," said Quist. "At first I assumed it was Crowley still fooling around, but the things you say at such times lead me to suspect something else entirely."

"*Possession*?" The youth's eyes widened fearfully. "Does my head spin around? The things I say? Like *what*?"

"Nothing that makes any real sense," The detective peered down into the dark street. "Hello, there go another seven. Where could they all be heading?"

"Huh?" Watson joined him at the window. "What are you watching?"

"The villagers." Quist pointed to another passing group. "As I've been standing here, I've noticed scores of them walking by below. They're all heading east."

"Towards the castle?" Watson gazed down at them. "Maybe they're gathering to watch Ali Bongo's big magick ceremony? It isn't even four o'clock yet, but they might be rushing to get a ringside seat. This lot aren't exactly *normal*, are they? To them, the Mulgrave Ritual might be like the final of the World Cup."

"The venue leaves much to be desired." Quist laughed quietly. "They won't fit many spectators on those cellar steps."

"True." He turned back to his boss, hands on hips. "So come on – what exactly have I been saying in these *possessed* trances? Do I have a demonic voice, or some shit?"

"No, apart from you pleading with me to end your pain, you sound perfectly normal." The detective kicked off both shoes and unfastened his trousers. "I'm developing a theory, but right now I shouldn't worry about it."

"Actually, *right now* I'm more worried about you pulling down your pants in front of me." Cringing, the youth quickly averted his eyes. "Oh, yes, there it is, winking at me."

"I was going to ring Rachel, but it can wait for a short while longer." Quist clicked off the bedroom light and tugged his shirt over his head. "I've heard what the Mulgraves have to say and now I'd like to see a few things for myself."

"Such as?"

"For one thing, I want to find out what's happening with the villagers out there, so I'm going to take a quick look around. It won't take me long and it's dark enough now, especially with those heavy snow clouds passing across the moon."

"And you don't fancy taking a look around on *two* legs?" asked Watson, realising what he was doing. "You know the moon's full."

He shook his head. "And *you* know that I'm in full control of the urges."

His assistant nodded warily. The bestial and evil side of the lycanthropy exerted a constant seductive pull, which was always at its strongest during the full phase of the lunar cycle. Quist's regime of yoga meditation and his strict vegan diet had always kept things in check. *Mind you*, thought Watson, *there was always a first time for everything. A first time for forgetting oneself and carelessly tearing out a young black guy's throat.*

"I'm faster and stronger in my lupine form." The naked man slipped off his signet ring and watch. "I don't want to be seen, so I'm going across the rooftops where I'll get a much better view of everything."

"The rooftops," muttered Watson, nodding. He watched his boss bend over, grunting and gasping. "Yeah, the natural habitat of the wolf. A bit like dolphins in trees."

Illuminated by the street lamps outside, bones visibly altered beneath Quist's skin and his face sprouted into a monstrous animal muzzle. The youth shuddered to feel the temperature fall as the detective's body grew in bulk, muscles expanding and thick fur covering his swiftly changing form. An enormous werewolf finally rose on two legs and turned to him, its amber eyes smouldering eerily in the dark room.

"Few people look up at rooftops as they walk," growled the wolf, opening the window wide. "Besides, darkness has fallen and I'm black. No one will spot me up there."

"Hey…" Watson laughed uneasily. "If you really want to talk

about being *black*."

Baring his fangs in a wide smile, Quist held up his front paws, the bones crackling as taloned fingers sprouted. He glanced over the windowsill and, satisfied that the street was empty, climbed onto the ledge and grabbed the guttering above to quickly pull himself up.

"So, a night on the tiles, eh?" whispered Watson, watching him vanish onto the roof. "Have fun, Guv."

Silently making his way to the apex, the wolf peeped over, checking for observers in the rear car park, before crossing the hotel roof to the gable end. The street below was narrow, enabling him to crouch low and spring onto the adjacent building, a terrace of eight houses. He bounded along the ridge on all-fours, negotiating dormer windows and chimney stacks, to arrive at an alley that separated the end house from the clifftop rampart wall. The moon began to emerge from its silvery shroud of cloud and the wolf moved back into the shadow of a chimney, squatting like a shaggy gargoyle to look over the village.

Hiding appeared to be pointless. Quist's eyesight was greatly enhanced in lupine form and, from this lofty vantage point, he could see that the streets were empty; there was no sign of light or movement in any windows, almost as if the community had been hastily evacuated. Shrugging, he jumped the gap and landed on the ten-foot high perimeter wall, pausing to peer over the seaward side. Waves crashed on the rocks below, the salty breeze tousled his fur and he breathed it in deeply, all the time fighting the powerful urge to throw back his head and howl at the sky.

Glancing accusingly at the full moon, the wolf continued along the top of the ramparts to the small marketplace where this village wall abutted the castle wall. He sniffed at the air and came to a sudden halt, sinking low for concealment and lifting his muzzle to smell again. He'd just picked up the strong scent of humans and smouldering incense.

There were people ahead, lots of them.

Sinking lower still, Quist shuffled forward on his furry belly to peer furtively into the castle courtyard.

So this was why Ravenspoint appeared empty. Al those people he'd seen passing the hotel had obviously been heading here.

The barbican gates were closed, the portcullis had been lowered, and most of the villagers were congregated in the private square, their silence and stillness creating an eerie spectacle. He spotted Rachel in the centre of the throng with Crowley, the latter wearing a long purple robe. The pair stood by the central well where an incense thurible smoked on the parapet wall. The dense crowd made it difficult to see what was happening, but the magician held a ceremonial dagger and chalice and seemed to be performing some occult rite.

Quist frowned in puzzlement. *This couldn't be the Mulgrave Ritual, as that had to be performed at six o'clock, over two hours away, and they'd made it perfectly clear that he was required there to provide the blood.*

As usual, a row of cars were parked against the castle wall and the tailgate was raised on one of the three black Range Rovers. Something was happening behind the vehicle, but he couldn't see what. The assembly suddenly parted, creating a channel through the crush, and allowing Brunton and Howell to drag forward two struggling figures. Both were handcuffed and the wolf stiffened as their faces came into view. Gaffer tape covered their mouths, but he could see it was the birdwatchers, Tommo and Pricey.

"What the…" he growled. "What the hell is *this*?"

Quist jumped to his feet, but before he could act, three villagers stepped forward to grab their legs and assist Brunton and Howell in throwing them into the well.

"No," hissed the wolf.

It was too late to save them. Pricey plunged headfirst into the darkness, but Tommo managed to grip the parapet with his cuffed hands. It bought him two extra seconds of life, before Rachel swung her leg in a wide arc and kicked away his fingers. She laughed gleefully as he followed his chubby friend down the shaft.

The wolf closed its amber eyes, anger rising as he thought about the horrific supernatural creature that waited at the bottom. This had all happened far too fast and there was nothing that he could have done to prevent it. Trembling with rage, he pictured how the two men must have been Tasered in the hotel and brought here in the boot of the Range Rover. He thought about the group of missing youths from the minibus and how Brunton had glibly blamed the crash on their *depressed* supervisor. He remembered the young couple from the previous week who had vanished here following a similar car *accident*. Having seen this, he now knew what had happened to them all.

The wolf bared its fangs, snarling and salivating as the wave of fury intensified and began to take over. Quist wanted to give in to it, to spring down into the courtyard and to tear into this crowd. More than anything, he wanted to claw and rip these murdering bastards to pieces. He wanted to devour their...

Screwing his eyes shut and gritting his huge teeth, the trembling wolf took several deep breaths and managed to supress the ferocious urges. The full moon was exerting its pull and drawing out his dark bestial side. For an awful moment, it had almost succeeded.

"Right," he growled, turning to leave. "This ends tonight."

* * * *

Chapter 27

Watson almost choked on his minibar peanuts to see the glowing yellow eyes at the open window. The shock only lasted a second. He knew it was his boss, but still found it momentarily horrifying to watch a huge furry monster clamber into his hotel bedroom.

"Everything okay, Guv?" he asked, coughing on the snack. Werewolves tended to have permanently furious expressions, but Quist's lupine features appeared darker and angrier than normal. "Um, I can't help but notice you look a little…"

"No," snarled the wolf. "As a matter of fact, everything is very far from being *okay*."

"What's that supposed to mean?" Watson closed the window behind him. "Ah, it's time for a change, is it?"

The room temperature dropped and the youth backed away, waiting whilst the beast shapeshifted. Fur and fangs fell onto the carpet and crumbled instantly to dust, expelled by the sprouting growth of human teeth and hair. The wolf twisted and writhed, its bone structure crackling and transforming, as it swiftly shrank back into the smaller form of a naked, middle-aged man.

"I've said it before…" laughing quietly, Watson shook his head in wonder. "That's a hell of a party trick."

"I should put the jokes on hold for the time being," snapped Quist, pulling up his trousers. "Believe me, I'm in no mood for humour right now. Mulgrave and his friends are killing people."

His assistant looked puzzled. "Well, we saw the old girl die, but she was a…"

"I'm talking about those birdwatchers."

"*What?*" The young man's jaw fell. "Tommo and Pricey? You're telling me they're dead? No way. Did you actually see…"

"Yes, I saw it happen. The pair were thrown down the castle

well to feed that *thing* and I was unable to prevent it." Quist angrily snatched his shirt from the chair. "Most of the villagers had gathered in the courtyard to enjoy the *entertainment*."

"*Shit*," whispered Watson, gesturing to the window. "All those people that passed by here? They were on their way to watch Tommo and Pricey die? So what the hell are we going to do about this?"

"*We* are doing nothing." Quist buttoned his shirt and tugged on his jacket. "As soon as I know you're safe, I'll be dealing with this alone."

"Hey, I'm a big boy." Watson smiled nervously. "I don't know what it is you're planning, but I can help with…"

"Not a chance in hell," said the detective, firmly. "This entire community is involved in cold-blooded murder and it's far too dangerous for you to be here. I'm responsible for your safety and I'm getting you out of this place right now They're unaware that I witnessed the killings in the courtyard so no one will be expecting us to leave."

"No, don't go," moaned Watson, his voice quavering. "You can help me. Please. I'm in so much pain in my prison and you *must* help me."

"What the…" Quist paused in lacing his shoes, and looked up to see his assistant's blank expression. "Who are you?" he asked, quietly. "Tell me what I can do. Tell me *how* I can help you."

"*Help me*?" The youth shook himself. "What do you mean?"

"Never mind," sighed Quist. "It just happened again. You briefly entered another of those trances and spoke to me in a creepy voice."

"I don't get it." Watson frowned. "Why don't I know it's happening? Why don't I remember this shit afterwards?"

"I'm not entirely sure," admitted Quist. "But when Crowley performed that hypnotic rite in York, he obviously opened your mind in some way. You became receptive to these messages..." He narrowed his eyes. "These pleas from *something*."

"So am I picking up ghosts?" The youth let out a frightened laugh. "Am I tuning in to *Radio Dead Folk*?"

"No, it has to be the elemental. This began the moment you arrived here and whenever you enter the trances, you mention *pain* and a *prison*. That entity in the cellar must be attempting to communicate through you." Quist glanced out of the window, then grabbed his trenchcoat and car keys. "But whatever it is, we don't have the time to find out. Come on, we're going right now."

"You're running out on the Mulgraves *and* taking your blood with you." Watson took his bag from the wardrobe and grinned. "This will really piss them off."

"Leave the rucksack," instructed Quist. "I'll get you another back in York. If anyone should see us carrying our bags, they'll know we're leaving."

"Good thinking." Watson pulled on his windcheater jacket and stowed his indispensable phone charger in a pocket. "Like you, I didn't bring much. Just this charger, a toothbrush, and a tube of Pringles, which I've already eaten."

Quietly leaving the room, they made their way down the hotel stairs, past the empty bar, and out into the rear square. It was bitterly cold and a shimmering frost covered the parked vehicles and the cobblestones. Quist unlocked his car, tossed his overcoat onto the rear seat, then flipped open the glove compartment to take out a torch and a small ice scraper.

"Be a good chap and clear the screen, would you?" He passed his assistant the tool and began to circle the car, crouching and shining the light beneath the wheel arches. "We found that transponder on Wednesday evening, but Lestrade told us they'd purchased several devices from the electronics store."

"That's right," said Watson, cleaning the glass. "He checked the shop records for you. So you're thinking…"

"Yes, I am. Ah, here we go." Reaching under the chassis, the detective pulled out a small black box identical to the one he'd discovered in Hull. "This would alert them immediately if our car moved."

"Like if we decided to leave." Watson glanced about warily as his boss slid the tracker out of sight beneath a Bentley. "Yeah, that needs to keep on transmitting and stay right here."

They jumped in the car and Quist pulled out of the hotel grounds. "I very much doubt anyone will see us," he said, motoring slowly through the dark village with the lights switched off. "From the size of the crowd, it looked to me as if everyone was in the castle courtyard."

Negotiating the winding tangle of deserted streets, they reached the barbican tower in the perimeter wall, the only way in and out of Ravenspoint. The detective drove under the archway and onto the open expanse of headland beyond.

"Hey, look at these roadside verges, Guv." Watson grinned as his boss clicked on the headlights. "I never thought I'd be so pleased to see green grass and bushes."

"Absolutely," agreed Quist. He pulled over on the narrow lane and took out his phone. "This will only take a moment. I need to check the satellite map."

"Okay, my phone's low on juice so I'm going to plug it in." The youth connected his charger lead to one of the vehicle's power outlets and looked out over the Craggan peninsula, squinting into the darkness. "So now we're away from those murdering twats, what's the plan?"

"The train is the plan," murmured the detective, scrutinising the area on his phone screen. "This lane leads to the main road where we turn left. There's a railway station in a village named Chathill near Bamburgh. It's only small, but looking at this, it's on the main line between Edinburgh and York." He pocketed the phone and pulled away from the verge. "I'm going to put you on a train home."

Watson nodded. "And then you're coming straight back here?"

"Yes, I intend to..." Quist glanced in the mirror. "Damn it! A car is right behind us with its lights off."

"*Guv*," squawked the youth. "Watch out."

The warning was almost too late. Ahead of them, a van had pulled out from behind a thick clump of gorse bushes to park sideways across the lane. Quist stamped hard on the brakes and skidded to a halt on the icy tarmac just feet away from it.

"*Shit!*" hissed Watson, as cars appeared on either side. "What the hell is going on?"

The detective realised he'd been wrong. *Three* vehicles had been following them in the darkness, not *one*, the three black Range Rovers from the castle courtyard. Two swerved left and right to pull up tightly and flank his car, preventing the doors from opening, as the third stopped close behind to box him in. Smiling gleefully, Rachel sat in the passenger seat of the vehicle on the right. She shoved a handgun through her open window and tapped the muzzle on Quist's door.

He lowered his window. "Good evening," he said caustically. "Are you lost and seeking directions?"

"Naughty boy," giggled Rachel. "Driving off without telling us. We didn't think you'd try leaving like this, but we've had that van waiting here all day just in case."

Watson's eyes were fixed on car to his left, or rather the man who leant out of it. Brunton was holding a compact Uzi machine gun and, although it was dark, he could see where it was pointing. He tried to swallow, but his mouth and throat were drier than talc.

Rachel smiled sweetly at Quist. "As you can probably see," she said, "Richard isn't aiming his gun at *you*. It's trained on your friend. If you try anything at all, he won't hesitate to..."

"Enough of all this," snapped a woman's voice.

The driver of Rachel's car pushed the girl roughly aside and fired an automatic pistol through the window. Watson yelped with shock at the sound of the gunshot and the bright muzzle flare, then saw that his boss had been hit in the chest.

"Guv?" He grabbed Quist's limp arm as he slumped forward over the wheel. "Guv, are you..."

"You shot him," gasped Rachel.

"How observant," said Maria Crane. "What's more the bullet was silver."

"*What?*" The girl shook her head, confused. "But you knew we needed him alive for the..."

"Don't be stupid," hissed Crane. "I know where the vital organs are and exactly where to aim. The bullet will kill him if it's left inside, but the silver poisoning will keep him safely unconscious until you get him back to the castle and I dig it out. Much more effective than silver handcuffs, wouldn't you say?"

Brunton reversed his Range Rover several feet, enabling him to open Quist's car and drag out Watson. "Stand there and don't try running," he snarled, slamming the terrified youth hard against the bonnet. "Speaking of running, we knew you'd gone. You're both carrying miniature transponders on you. They were left in your pockets last night when your coats were hanging in the hotel dining room."

Watson remained silent, watching Brunton haul Quist from the car, drag him to the Range Rover and dump his lifeless body in the boot. Rachel appeared at the youth's side and slipped her arm around him.

"Ooh, are you cold?" she giggled, sexily. "You seem to be shaking."

"Silver?" he stammered. "Did I just hear some woman say

196

she'd shot the Guv with silver?"

"That's right," confirmed Rachel, turning. "I understand you know the lady."

Watson turned too, his eyes widening as he saw who was standing behind him. He'd been unable to see her properly in the dark car and things had been a little too intense for him to recognise her voice. This was someone he hadn't seen for a while, but the passing of time hadn't clouded his memory. It was very hard to forget Irana Adler.

* * * *

Chapter 28

Quist emerged from the depths of unconsciousness, his eyes fluttering open to a blurry kaleidoscope of sparkling confetti. He recalled someone firing a gun, the intense chest pain as he was hit several times, and then icy blackness. He briefly wondered if he was in the car, but no, he was lying on a cold, hard surface, and from the corrugated feel beneath his shoulder blades, it wasn't the ground. The swirling fuzziness in his head began to swiftly dissipate, and he realised he was sprawling on the barred floor of a large cage.

"Aargh!" He winced as his hand touched the metal and his fingers painfully sizzled. "What the *hell*..."

Incredibly, it was a cage completely constructed from *silver*. His jacket had been removed and stuffed beneath his head to prevent his skin making contact with the bars.

"How thoughtful," he muttered, massaging his eyes.

The air reeked of musty damp and, as the detective's vision cleared, he saw he was in the castle cellar. He climbed unsteadily to his feet, taking care not to touch anything with bare flesh. The bars in the base of this seven-foot cage were spaced closer together than the rest, making it possible to stand on them. His shirt was undone and he spotted a nearby dish on the floor containing a used 9mm bullet. It too was silver, and from the powdered blood on the platter, it must have been dug from his chest.

"Guv?" Watson's anxious voice came from behind him. "Are you okay?"

He turned to see his assistant sitting on a plastic chair with Brunton standing beside him. "I'm in better shape than my shirt," he said, fingering the hole in the cotton and fastening up the buttons. "It isn't the first time I've been shot with a silver bullet, but I see someone has been considerate enough to remove it from the wound before the metal poisoned me and proved fatal. How about you? Are you hurt?"

"Oh, he's doing great," said Brunton. "For now."

"Er, Guv…" Watson cleared his throat nervously and pointed to Quist's left. "They've laid on a bit of a surprise for us."

Three more chairs had been set out facing the cage. Mulgrave and his daughter occupied two, but Quist was more interested in the woman who sat cross-legged on the third. Wearing an indigo suit and matching silk eye-patch, she smoked a cigarette and fixed him with a cold stare. Genuinely astounded, he gazed back in silence for several seconds. He'd known this bizarre situation was highly dangerous – that's why he'd attempted to get Watson out of harm's way – but things were far, far worse than he could ever have imagined.

"Well, hello again, Colonel." He managed a taut smile. "I can't help but notice you're still alive."

"It would seem so," she said.

"It's been a while, hasn't it?" His composure returning, Quist reached into his pocket and found his cigarettes and lighter were still there; they must have decided there was little point in confiscating them. "I have to say, you look much better than the last time I saw you, and it's nice to see you've made some new friends too. So I presume you're the one who ruined my shirt?"

"That's right." She drew slowly on her cigarette. "That's the second time I've shot you with a silver bullet. It doesn't matter where you're hit with conventional rounds; I know that from experience. But my aim is always precise and I made sure to avoid anything too vital."

"You're a Colonel?" asked Mulgrave, peering at the woman.

"Colonel Irana Adler," said Quist, lighting a cigarette of his own. "The sociopathic daughter of a loathsome Nazi war criminal, a mercenary soldier, a multiple murderer and, perhaps best of all, a werewolf. But apart from that, she's a truly charming lady, as I'm sure you already know. When last we met, we didn't exactly part on the best of terms."

"So you're not called Maria Crane?" asked Rachel.

"I'd say we've just established that, darling," snapped Adler, sarcastically. "I change my name so often these days, I never bother to use my German army rank."

"I ought to have known," said the detective, inspecting his sturdy cage and the lock on the hinged door. Small rotational wheels were fitted beneath each corner, to move it around the cellar floor, and a long length of chain was attached to the base. "I noticed someone watching from a castle window yesterday. They stepped back when I looked up, which suggested it was probably someone known to me. Then I picked up your scent this morning. I must be slipping, because I really should have put those two together."

Adler raised a curious eyebrow. "You're able to smell other wolves?"

"No, luv," said Watson. "Those shitty cigs of yours."

Quist nodded. "The last time I saw you, your house stank of Gauloises. They're an uncommon brand and it isn't often that I smell them, but I did today and it left me disconcerted. Everything has happened so fast and I didn't have the time to work out why." He looked around the enclosure. "The very idea that anyone should possess a silver cage intrigues me. I saw this contraption earlier, but I'd no idea what it was hidden away beneath the tarpaulins. It looks quite old."

"It was manufactured in 1908," confirmed Rachel.

"Bloody hell," muttered Watson. "How many candelabras did you have melt down for that? I'm guessing it was Adler here who gave you the Guv's name, not Rex Grant, like you said?"

"Yes, she told us all about you both," confirmed the Laird.

"But she didn't tell us how rude you were," laughed Rachel. "You left us. You decided to drive away without so much as a goodbye. That was rather impolite, wasn't it?"

"They knew we'd gone, Guv," said Watson. "They planted

trackers in our coats."

"I see," said Quist, smoking his cigarette and staring at Adler.

"Was it something we said?" continued Rachel, mockingly.

"Something you *did*." The youth glared at her. "He says you killed those guys who were staying at the hotel."

"Ah, you saw that?" Mulgrave smiled ruefully. "We have a different version of events prepared. Those men left here and traffic cameras will record them speeding in Norfolk tomorrow. If they aren't seen after that, who knows where they are? If you check their backgrounds, as I did, you'll find they were well known for their unconventional behaviour; they often vanished to chase rare birds."

"You'll have someone drive their car to Norfolk?" gasped Watson. "To cover your tracks.?"

Mulgrave nodded. "We've grown rather adept at *covering tracks*. Ever since the Fountain began to grow, it's destabilised more often than we had you believe. Not to the dangerous levels we're experiencing now, but several times a year we feel tremors. Whenever it happens, something more substantial than a voluntary sacrifice is required – a young prostitute from Newcastle, or something similar."

"It's far better if the sustenance is young," chuckled Brunton, squeezing Watson's shoulder. "You're quite young, aren't you?"

"They were young too," said Quist. "The couple in the car accident last week and those youths in the minibus yesterday."

"I'm afraid your suspicions are correct," admitted Mulgrave. "The authorities keep asking for safety barriers on the headland, but I've spoken to the right people and nothing will ever be installed. We need that dangerous stretch of road for our occasional *accidents*."

"*Jesus*," muttered Watson. "You lot are unbelievable."

"The Fountain has to be fed," sighed the Laird. "We tried to keep it stable until the ritual could be performed by giving it those two men and the youths. Unfortunately, neither offering worked, but we weren't to know that. None of us enjoy the killing. We have to accept it as a distasteful, but necessary evil to protect the village."

Watson glanced at the smirks on Rachel and Brunton. He wasn't so sure about the lack of *enjoyment*.

"After the first killing it becomes easy," said Mulgrave. "Since you can't change the act that you've committed, your subconscious changes your attitude to the act and you become desensitised."

"The psychiatric term is *cognitive dissonance*," said Quist. "It was common amongst Nazi guards in their camps. I'm sure *she* could tell you all about that." He gestured to Adler. "But you can't balance one life against another. You can't play God by choosing in that way."

"Of course we can," snorted Mulgrave. "One homeless junkie from Edinburgh dies and our entire village lives. Joan Peterson's voluntary termination had arrived and you watched as she gave herself. Unfortunately, there aren't enough old people nearing the end to sustain the Fountain."

Quist laughed incredulously. "So don't feed it."

"Don't be stupid," sneered Rachel. "Whenever we've denied it nourishment in the past, or attempted to substitute corpses or animals for live humans, it stops producing the mists and we begin to age."

"We deteriorate rapidly," added Mulgrave. "This symbiotic relationship can't be broken or the village dies."

"But this elemental shouldn't be here," said Quist. "You know that. Many of you are around two-hundred or more. If you die of old age or some dormant illness, then that's the way it has to be."

"You can't just keep murdering people," said Watson.

"People die all the time," said Brunton, grinning. "Every second someone dies." He snapped his fingers in Watson's ear. "There, another one just died, and another. Do you have any idea how many young dickheads like you die in car smashes?"

"Seriously?" Quist peered at him. "Are you trying to condone this with statistics?"

"Some die in their sleep," said Mulgrave. "Over one-hundred and fifty thousand die every day because their hearts simply stop beating. And a few, an unbelievably miniscule few of all those thousands who die every hour of every day, are fed to the Fountain."

"Well..." said Quist, sarcastically. "When you put it like that, it sounds perfectly acceptable and..."

"Enough," laughed Irana Adler. She stood up and approached the cage, drawing on her cigarette. "None of this matters. They already have your blood. They filled a chalice while you were unconscious and their magician is in the dungeon right now performing the Mulgrave Ritual."

"I see." Quist glanced at the door that led down to the entity.

"The thing is..." Adler blew smoke through the bars. "They haven't been entirely honest with you. You wondered why they have this silver cage? There's a second part to this ceremony that they neglected to mention." She smiled at Mulgrave. "Isn't it time he knew?"

The Laird cleared his throat. "You recall how I told you about that first werewolf back in 1906?"

Puffing on his cigarette, Quist nodded slowly.

"Aleister needed shapeshifter blood to strengthen the elemental and he'd heard rumours of just such a creature in Wales, a young gypsy in a travelling fair. This youth had been killing people, but his parents had covered up his crimes. We tracked him down and paid him a small fortune to come here to take part in the ceremony. The ritual worked, but things didn't go as smoothly as we'd hoped."

"It was a full moon like tonight," said Brunton. "This guy was half-mad to begin with, but he started to grow crazy and vicious after the ceremony and we had to kill him. I took his head off with one of those decorative swords up there in the banqueting hall." Unable to help himself, he glanced at Adler.

"Yes, you'd like to do that to me, wouldn't you?" Staring coldly, she nodded slowly. "I've told you before, I really don't like *you* at all."

"No, I'm sure Richard bears no animosity towards you," said Mulgrave, continuing with the story. "A werewolf corpse was too good to burn in the castle furnace, so we fed it to the Fountain and it absolutely loved the meal. Normally the entity doesn't respond to dead meat, but with this it produced *huge* amounts of mist for months afterwards. We decided that, if the ritual was ever needed again, we'd feed it a *living* werewolf and we had the cage constructed just in case. The elemental remained stable for decades, but in 1947 the problem returned and, once again, we searched for a lycanthrope."

"We had a friend in the London police," said Brunton. "He was also a wealthy Satanist and he knew of a werewolf living in the East End. Throughout the war, this character had been killing and eating people and using the bombings to conceal the evidence. We invited him to Ravenspoint and managed to trap him in the cage. We used his blood in the ritual and then gave his living body to the Fountain."

"Which brings us to the present," said Rachel, grinning broadly. "Same old problem, same old need for a werewolf. We made discreet enquiries through certain of our clients..."

"Clients?" Adler laughed. "They sell their bottled water on the dark web and many of the customers are unsavoury, to say the least. Dictators, underworld kingpins, corrupt African leaders, Russian Oligarchs and heads of drug cartels. That's how they found me – through a Mexican cartel boss who had hired me." She gave Mulgrave and Brunton an icy glance. "I work solo these days, eliminating problems for those kind of people. They brought me here under false pretences and tried to get me into that cage. It was a very bad idea."

"I can imagine," admitted Quist.

"Unlike you, I've no aversion to killing and several villagers were lost in the attempt." Adler smiled at Brunton. "They couldn't use silver bullets because they couldn't risk harming me when they needed my precious blood." She touched one of the bars with a fingertip and grimaced. "They didn't know how a silver bullet can be used to subdue a lycanthrope, provided you know where to aim and you dig it out quickly before it proves fatal."

"You only killed *several*?" said Quist. "You surprise me."

"Ah, we came to an understanding," laughed Adler, blowing cool air on her red finger. "They'd offered me money to come here for a fake assignment. I kept their cash and, once I'd discovered *why* they needed a werewolf, I naturally thought of *you* and your friend Grant. Grant is stupid and he'd have been easier for this, but he's away on a yacht somewhere near the Maldives. Plus, I knew if *he* vanished, you'd probably come looking for him like the last time. I decided it was best for them to use you and keep Grant in reserve. Who knows? This destabilisation problem might reoccur at some point in the future."

"It's nice to know you were thinking of us," said Quist, derisively.

Adler nodded. "I always intended to kill you and Grant, but I never got around to it. I was far too busy making money in various exotic parts of the world."

"So I'm on the elemental's dinner menu, am I?" Quist drew on his cigarette and gestured to the dungeon door. "How exactly does this work? Do you expect me to walk into the cellar at gunpoint like the old lady this afternoon?"

"Don't be silly," chuckled Mulgrave. "We can't take the chance of letting you out of there. No, you'll remain locked inside the cage which, as you can see, is mounted on small wheels. The last two lycanthropes were fed to the entity two hours after the ritual ended. The cage will be pushed down the dungeon steps and onto the elemental at exactly eight o'clock. Those bars will stop you escaping, but they won't stop the feeder tentacles from entering."

"And then the empty cage will be hauled back out using that attached chain." Rachel giggled. "Bon appetit, Monsieur Fountain."

"Good Lord!" Quist peered thoughtfully at the girl. "You really *are* a deranged little psychopath, aren't you?"

All heads turned, as Watson's plastic chair clattered across the floor, propelled by him slumping off it. Looking as if he'd been shot, the youth clutched at his chest and collapsed sideways to the floor.

* * * *

Chapter 29

The door to the dungeon swung open and Crowley emerged dressed in his purple robe. "What's going on here?" he demanded, seeing Watson sprawled on the floor. "What's happened to our young friend?"

"Yeah, what *is* this?" Brunton nudged the youth roughly with his boot. "Are you pretending to faint so that we…"

"It isn't pretence," snapped Quist. Dropping his cigarette, he reached instinctively for the cage door, then jerked back his hand as the skin sizzled. "Can't you see there's something wrong? Check him, one of you. Make sure he's alright."

"Things must have got too much for him," laughed Brunton. "Looks like he's passed out."

"Move back, Richard," said Crowley, rushing to the young man and kneeling to feel the carotid pulse in his neck.

"Make sure his airway is open," instructed the detective, watching with heart racing. "Is he breathing normally?"

"No, Richard's right," admitted the magician, gently lifting an eyelid. "It does indeed appear to have been a faint. He'll be fine."

"Oh, that's so good to know, Aleister," sneered Rachel. "But now that we've got your Florence Nightingale impression out of the way, don't you have something slightly *more* important to tell us? Like how the fuck did it go down there?"

"Absolutely." Climbing to his feet, Crowley turned to the girl and her father. "You'll be pleased to know that Bernard's blood worked perfectly, as I knew it would. I've just successfully completed the Mulgrave Ritual. The yellow eye shimmered, as it always does at the culmination, and the elemental has completely settled down. The destabilisation is finally over."

"Wonderful," said the Laird, clapping. "I can't wait to make the announcement."

Crowley walked to the cage. "It's one of Reginald's little traditions," he explained to Quist. "Every time the Mulgrave Ritual is completed, he hosts a lavish party in the castle for the entire village."

"To honour the Fountain," said the Laird. "And to celebrate many more untroubled decades, They're all upstairs right now, waiting to hear the news in the banqueting hall."

"A party?" Quist smiled sarcastically. "Well, how lovely, but I assume I'm not invited to these celebrations?"

"Er, right…" The magician grimaced. "I'm sure they've told you by now that there's a little more to the ritual than…"

"Yes." The detective nodded. "They've explained how you intend to murder me."

"This has nothing to do with me," said Crowley, quickly. "The ceremony is complete and my part is done. I've made it perfectly clear that I don't agree with what they intend to do, but I'm afraid to say it's out of my hands."

"Oh, Aleister," giggled Rachel. "Don't be so squeamish. I thought you were once known as the wickedest man in the world?"

"You know my views." The magician returned to Watson's limp form and gestured to Brunton. "Can you help me with this? We can't leave the young man unconscious in the cold down here. Could you give me a hand to carry him upstairs?"

"That's a good idea," admitted Mulgrave. "We're not callous monsters. Take the boy up to one of the bedrooms. Make sure he's alright and then lock him in securely."

"Thank you for that," said Quist, nodding begrudgingly to Crowley.

"Whatever," grunted Brunton. Sighing with exasperation, he grabbed the youth's arm, yanked him up and threw him over his shoulder like a side of beef. He pushed the magician to one side and set off for the adjoining room and its staircase. "Get out of the way. It's much easier if I do this myself."

Crowley gave Quist a final remorseful glance, before following Brunton through the door and brushing past Gavin Howell.

The castle worker carried an Uzi machine pistol and smiled at the Laird. "You asked me to come down around now," he said. "Did all go well with the ceremony?"

"Yes, Gavin, the ritual was a success." Mulgrave rose to his feet and pointed to the silver cage. "But I need you to remain here and watch him with the gun. He can't get out of there, but nevertheless, you should stand guard until the appointed time. Don't speak to him or go anywhere near the bars."

"Eight o'clock, I believe you said?" Quist gave him a sardonic smile. "I'll try to ensure my schedule is free."

"Yes, I'll see you then." Mulgrave handed Howell the cage key, then checked his watch and set off for the steps. "As you've heard, there's a celebratory party upstairs and I don't wish to be accused of being a poor host."

Adler gave her cigarette a final puff and flicked the stub at the detective. "See you soon," she said. "I'll be here too."

"I presume it was you I saw watching me from the castle window yesterday?" said Quist. "You scurried away when I looked up."

Adler nodded slowly. "It was so good to see you again. Unfortunately, it doesn't look as if our reunion is going to last long, not with what they have planned for you." She gestured to the dungeon door. "Trust me, I wouldn't miss their eight o'clock show for the world. It's going to be like feeding time at the zoo, but for a more *adult* audience."

* * * *

Brunton carried Watson's limp body into a small room on the castle's upper floor and unceremoniously dumped him on the single bed. "There," he growled, glaring at Crowley. "Unless you want me to tuck him in and read him a story, I'll be heading down to the party now. The key's in the door, so make sure you lock it before you leave."

"I will," confirmed Crowley, stroking the youth's head. "I'll also be locking the room in my own special way."

He waited until the huge man had left, before plucking two black curly hairs from Watson's scalp. Standing by the open door and muttering a few lines of incantation, he drew invisible symbols in the air with flamboyant hand gestures, before placing a hair on his palm and gently blowing it through the doorway. He moved to the window and repeated the short magickal working with the second hair.

"Are you talking to yourself?" muttered Watson, sitting up and rubbing his eyes. "Or were you saying all that bollocks to me?"

"Ah, you're awake." The magician perched himself on the edge of the bed. "How are you feeling?"

"Oh, never better," grunted the youth. "I was out of it, but I felt you pull my hair. What the hell was that for?"

Crowley ignored the question. "I must admit, I was quite worried when I saw you'd collapsed. I also found it a little odd, but I didn't say anything down there in the cellar. You don't seem like the fainting type to me."

"Worried?" Watson laughed. "Yeah, right."

He definitely *wasn't* the fainting type. *He knew the cellar episode hadn't been a faint. It was something far, far weirder, but he wasn't going to tell this guy. He really needed to speak to the Guv about it, but that was a little hard at the moment.*

"Look, I know how you must be feeling," said Crowley. Smiling tightly, the magician stroked his shoulder. "I'm truly sorry about all of this. If it's any consolation, I really like Bernard and I didn't want him harmed. I was all for paying whatever he asked, as was originally agreed, and allowing him to leave."

"It's not *much* consolation," snorted Watson, shrugging off his hand. "It looks like someone had other ideas."

210

"I'm afraid so," sighed Crowley. "The annoying thing is, he doesn't need to die. Feeding a lycanthrope to the Fountain was never a part of the Mulgrave Ritual, but ever since that messy episode with the Welshman in 1906, they've convinced themselves that it *is*. The last two werewolves were given to the elemental at eight o'clock, two hours after the completion of the rite, and it's now become a tradition. I think the Mulgraves are worried that the ceremony might not fully work anymore without this somewhat macabre addition."

Watson turned to the open door as Rachel appeared. She'd followed them upstairs and had clearly been listening.

"It's a chance we're not prepared to take," she said, leaning on the jamb and smirking. "We always intended to feed your boss to the Fountain, but your one-eyed Colonel friend insisted upon it too. She really wants him dead. I'm guessing you two must have upset her at some point."

"She isn't the nicest of women." Crowley pulled a sour face. "A truly sociopathic bitch."

"Who?" snorted Watson. "Adler, or this ginger twat?"

"Yeah, keep that up," laughed Rachel, blowing him an exaggerated kiss. "Just see where it leads."

."By the way," said the magician, "can you drive?"

"What?" Watson frowned at the unexpected question. "I don't have a license, but yeah, I can drive. Why?"

"Good," he nodded. "We didn't want to leave Bernard's car out there on the headland road, seemingly abandoned and attracting attention, so we brought it back here. It's in the castle courtyard and the keys are in the ignition." He waved a hand towards the door. "Off you go."

"I don't understand." Confused, the young man stared at the magician, before turning to the girl. "Is this some sort of joke?"

"Not at all." Crowley shook his head. "If you can get to the car, you can drive away from here right now."

"*If* I can get to it?" Watson laughed dryly. "Is she going to shoot me in the back or something? Why would you let me go when I could get the police to come and…"

"Oh, for fuck's sake." Rachel walked into the bedroom and folded her arms impatiently. "There, the route is clear and I assure you, no one is going to stop you."

"Yeah, right," muttered Watson, jumping off the bed. "Okay, I don't know what you're planning, but I'll play along."

Keeping a wary eye on the pair, he walked to the open door and then stopped abruptly. Something felt very wrong. Goosebumps covered his spine as he tried moving forward, but for some inexplicable reason he couldn't do it. He couldn't cross over the threshold.

"What the hell is this?" he muttered. "A friggin' *Star Trek* force field?"

He tried again, but something was preventing him. He began to tremble, his legs refusing to carry him any further forward, almost as if an invisible wall blocked his path.

"I can't go through the doorway," he growled. "But I'm guessing you already know that?"

"Sorry about that," nodded Crowley. "I performed a simple magickal rite to prevent you leaving, either by the door or the window. I needed to know it was effective."

"Speaking of leaving…" Rachel smiled cruelly at Watson. "You know we can't let you go. My father still hasn't decided what we're going to do with you, although I'll be honest, it probably involves the courtyard well."

"No," snapped Crowley. "That won't happen. I've told you how much I like him."

"But of course you do," she purred. "You like *all* attractive girls *and* boys."

"Snails and oysters, as you know, my dear." Crowley

squeezed the youth's arm. "Trust me when I tell you I'll do everything in my power to ensure no harm comes to you."

"You're so considerate," scoffed Watson.

"You've made quite an impression upon Aleister," said Rachel. "He's been telling me how he wants you to remain here voluntarily as part of our little community. He has an ulterior motive, of course, as I'm sure you've realised."

"Yes, I have," admitted the magician. "The only family you have is your mother and I believe, if I speak with Reginald, we could see about bringing her here too. It's the least we can do for you after Bernard's sacrifice. According to Richard, she's quite attractive and I'm sure the idea of perfectly preserving those looks for many decades would appeal to her."

"Aleister's sex parties would appeal to you both," purred Rachel. "They're quite something."

"You've actually been discussing *my mum* with Brunton?" gasped Watson, utterly appalled. The image of her garden gnomes in the castle courtyard flashed briefly into his head. Even worse was the image of himself and her at the *same* sex party. "I really don't believe it."

"Believe *this*," warned Crowley, sadly, "the alternative won't be pleasant. I need you to give the concept some serious thought whilst we're away. We'll talk about it properly when I return."

"Yes, we have a dance competition to win." Rachel checked her wristwatch. "It's six-thirty and we need to get to Newcastle for the finals of *Dance Away*."

"Sex parties and dancing?" Watson glared at them both. "They're going to feed the Guv to that monster and you're talking about orgies and now you're going fucking dancing."

"That's precisely why I *am* going," sighed the magician. "I don't want to be in Ravenspoint at eight o'clock. I want no part in Bernard's death and the dancing will provide a distraction. We're doing a rumba tonight. You might call it *the Rumba of the Beast.*"

"Normally I might," said Watson. "But I'm not in what you'd call a jokey mood."

"No, I suppose not." He smiled weakly and then hugged the youth tightly. "Goodbye for now and, once again, I'm so very sorry about your boss."

"Yeah, whatever." Watson struggled free of his embrace. "Just so you know, he's my boss, but he's also my friend."

* * * *

Chapter 30

Quist stood in the cellar cage with Howell sitting quietly on one of the chairs watching him. The Uzi machine pistol lay on the guard's lap like a rather intimidating cat.

"I have to say, this prison of mine isn't very large, is it?" drawled the detective, looking around his silver enclosure. "What do we think – about seven feet square, perhaps? I don't have enough room for pacing."

Scratching at his bushy black beard, Howell tutted irritably, but didn't answer. As instructed by the Laird, he hadn't spoken a word since beginning his sentry duty.

"Pacing," repeated Quist, eyeing the door lock and gauging the diameter of the bars. "I mean, it's the customary practise of the condemned man, isn't it? Pacing nervously up and down."

The guard folded his brawny arms and remained silent.

"Do you mind if I were to smoke instead? That *other* tradition in these circumstances – the famous last cigarette?" Taking out his pack and lighter, Quist shot him an enquiring look. "No, I don't suppose you're going to answer, so I'll just go ahead and light up. If you've been ordered not to speak to me, then I suppose it's unlikely that you'll complain about breathing in passive smoke, or…"

"Shut up," snarled Howell, finally breaking his silence and lifting the gun. "I'm sick of hearing your annoying drivel. These bullets aren't silver, and I know you'll heal straight away, but they'll hurt like fuck if I fire a couple of bursts into your kneecaps."

"Quite true," admitted the detective. "With that in mind, I think I'll do my legs a favour and remain quiet."

Slowly sliding out a cigarette, he ran his eyes over the cage again, estimating the spaces between the bars. If he tore up his shirt and wrapped the cloth around the silver, he probably had the strength to bend them, but they were set too close together. He wouldn't be able to open them wide enough to squeeze his body through. The large mortice lock was built into the cage door, with a slight gap between this and the cage itself where the key-operated deadbolt was visible. He could see it was too substantial to snap by kicking or shoulder-barging and, in any case, he couldn't do anything like this with an armed guard watching. Quist lit his cigarette and weighed the small red lighter in his palm, a strategy swiftly forming.

Howell had the cage key in his pocket and he needed to get this man out of the way. Could he kill those two birds with the same stone, so to speak?

This LPG lighter was the cheap plastic type and no use for what he had in mind, but slipping it back into his jacket, he felt something heavier at the bottom of the pocket and furtively lifted it out.

Of course. He'd taken this from Watson during dinner last night and then forgotten about it.

The detective turned his body slightly, partly to conceal the die-cast metal toy in his right hand, but mostly to adopt a bowler's stance. He took a couple of draws on his cigarette, then without any warning, utilised his supernatural strength, agility and coordination to throw the starship straight through the bars like a high-speed cricket ball. It happened far too fast for Howell to react and the USS Enterprise smacked him hard in the centre of his brow. His head snapped back, as if the man had been shot, and he collapsed sideways from the seat, his gun clattering on the stone floor.

"Damn," snarled Quist.

He'd hoped that the stunned man would topple forward, enabling him to reach through the bars and drag him close. There was no way now that he could get to his pocket and fish out the key.

"Wait a moment," he muttered, seeing how the rebounding toy had landed between Howell and the cage.

If this silver enclosure was constructed in 1908, as Rachel had claimed, then the lock wouldn't be too sophisticated. He'd seen the key when Mulgrave handed it to Howell and it had been large and crude.

Tossing away the cigarette and carefully sliding a hand through the bars, the detective turned his head and squeezed his shoulder against them to provide more reach. The jacket protected his arm, but he winced as his naked ear briefly touched the silver.

"Where are you?" he mumbled, groping around on the damp cellar floor.

Locating the model with his fingertips and managing to gently tease it closer to him, Quist grabbed it and pulled his arm back through the bars. He broke one of the long engine nacelles from the starship fuselage and crouched by the lock, only to find that his improvised key was too short.

He let out a bitter sigh. *For this L-shaped piece of metal to turn the internal levers, his hand would have to be touching the outer casing. His fingers were going to burn here, but it couldn't be helped.*

The detective took a deep breath and clamped his teeth tightly together. Sliding it deep into the keyhole and wiggling, he grimaced as his skin painfully sizzled, then smiled as, after only six seconds, the internal mechanism rotated with a satisfying click. The deadbolt had retracted from its housing, enabling him to push the cage door wide with his foot. His throbbing fingers had taken on the scarlet appearance of tandoori chicken and, blowing cool air over them, he waited for the hand to rapidly heal.

"Ah, I see you're already beginning to wake," he said, walking to the groaning Howell. "I'm afraid we can't have that." He grabbed a handful of shirt, lifted the man from the floor and punched him hard, feeling his jaw fracture beneath the thick beard. "Damn it! If it's any consolation, your chin just really hurt my burnt hand."

The detective headed through the door into the adjoining cellar chamber, checking his fingers again to ensure the damaged flesh had finally vanished. He paused at the stone steps, looking up the flight and frowning thoughtfully.

These people were dangerous and Irana Adler was somewhere up there. He had to find Watson, but there was little point in doing so in human form. There was no secret to protect here – everyone in the castle was fully aware of his lycanthropy – and he was far faster and stronger in lupine form.

Quickly stripping off, he placed his wristwatch and signet ring on the ground, and bent double to grunt and twist through the supernatural transformation. The huge wolf glanced again at the comatose guard in the next room, before popping the two personal items under its tongue for safekeeping and running up the flight of steps on all-fours.

Quist eased the cellar door open a couple of inches and peered out into the castle corridor. This was the wide passage he'd walked along earlier today on his way to and from the Laird's study. He listened cautiously, twitching his pointed ears, and sniffed the air for the scent of nearby humans. The study was away to his left, as was the banqueting hall where Mulgrave had said the party was taking place. He could hear the distant sounds of music and many voices. Sniffing again and, satisfied he was alone, the wolf crept out and turned right, bounding along the corridor.

The castle appeared to be empty, but if everyone had been invited to the Laird's celebration, then this was to be expected. The strong scents of Crowley, Brunton, Howell and the Mulgraves were everywhere, but arriving at a flight of stairs on his left, he detected the familiar smell of his assistant. *It was only faint, as Brunton had been carrying Watson, but this was definitely where they'd headed. He'd been told to take him to an upstairs room and lock him in.*

Despite its huge size, the werewolf raced silently up the steps, following the scent trail to the upper level of the castle, which also seemed to be devoid of life. Watson's smell was much stronger here and, trotting along a corridor, he quickly located the correct bedroom. The door was locked and Quist raised himself onto two legs, checking left and right for onlookers, before shouldering it open.

"*Fuck!*" The startled youth jumped back, peering up at the wolf. "Is that you, Guv?"

"*What?*" Quist closed the door behind him. "Who the hell did you *think* it might be?"

"Well, I dunno," snapped Watson. "Adler's here, isn't she?"

"You mean the one-eyed werewolf?" He gestured down to his furry genitals. "The one-eyed *female* werewolf?"

"Look, I'm scared shitless, aren't I? I'm hardly thinking straight right now." The young man narrowed his eyes. "Anyway, why are you walking around in your wolf form? It's the full moon and you always say if…"

"Yes," growled Quist. "You keep pointing this out and unfortunately I believe you could be right. Your warm flesh smells so delicious…"

"*No…*" moaned Watson, his legs buckling. "No, no, please don't…"

"Sorry." The wolf held up a paw. "Um, I'm sorry, but that was a somewhat misguided attempt at humour. You've been making so many jokes recently, I thought I'd try it myself to alleviate your obvious anxiety." He wagged his tail and gave a friendly grin, but the rows of gleaming fangs didn't help. "By the way, I wonder if you could keep these safe for me?"

Watson's eyes widened as he spat out the watch and signet ring into a furry palm and passed them to him.

"Yeah, I thought your voice sounded funny," croaked the youth, stowing them in a pocket. "Oh, how lovely. They're covered in werewolf spit." He managed a relieved smile. "Listen, it's really great to see you, Guv. I don't know how you managed to get out of that cage, but I honestly thought you were going to die down there and…"

"Now don't be getting all tearful on me." The wolf lowered its huge head. "If you'd like to stroke me or give me a loving pat, let's get it over with."

"No, I think we'll give that a miss," grinned Watson. "Okay, now I have something really important to tell you. Something kind of weird and unbelievable happened when I fainted..."

"Crowley appeared just after your collapse," broke in Quist. "By my calculations, you passed out as he completed the Mulgrave Ritual."

"Probably so," agreed Watson. "But as soon as I was unconscious, batshit crazy as I know it must sound, that Fountain thing actually *spoke* to me. I was out cold and it started talking to me in my head. I say *talking*, but there weren't any words. It just sort of made me understand what it wanted."

"Telepathic communication?" The wolf nodded slowly. "I see, and what *does* it want?"

"It needs *you* to help it. It says it wants you end its pain and to release it from its prison."

"Of course," sighed Quist. "The elemental has been trying to contact me directly, but it was unable to get through. All I experienced was a buzzing in my head. It made an unsuccessful attempt as I slept; I told you about the voice in my dreams, but I remembered nothing when I awoke. It's probably because I'm a lycanthrope, and that's why it used you instead. Ever since we arrived here, that creature has been attempting to speak to me through you."

"You're talking about those trances I keep going into?"

Quist nodded again. "Crowley's enchantment opened your mind in some bizarre way. It unlocked the latent psychic abilities that all humans possess and made you receptive to the Fountain's communication. I assume you haven't told anyone about this?"

"No, of course not." Watson frowned. "But why me and why now? Why hasn't it spoken to anyone before?"

"They actively discourage visitors here," said the wolf. "These people believe it to be a basic, mindless lifeform, but it appears to be far more, doesn't it? The entire village need it to remain here and perhaps the elemental could somehow sense that. Perhaps it knew that no one in Ravenspoint would ever assist it, so it remained silent and waited."

"Until someone like *us* showed up?" said Watson. "You mean the Fountain could tell that we were nice guys and that we'd probably help?

"That wasn't a normal faint you experienced," said Quist. "The Mulgrave Ritual was performed to stabilise and strengthen the elemental, but it strengthened it in *every* way, including its powers of communication. The creature was finally able to cause your blackout in order to contact you directly make itself understandable."

"Wow," whispered Watson. "Hey, does that mean I could be psychic now?"

"It's probably temporary," said Quist. "But if not, we'll change your name to *Watty Rose Lee* and rent you a booth on the Shambles Market." He gave the youth another toothy, and very unnerving, grin. "So the Fountain wants my help? What exactly did it say to you?"

"It's in loads of pain and distress, Guv." Watson grimaced. "It doesn't want to be here and it's been trying to leave for a really long time. It says it wants to be *banished*."

"Banished?" echoed the wolf. "Yes, *banishing* is the term magicians use when they return elementals to their own plane of existence. This explains why the creature has been destabilising more and more over the last century. It's attempting to depart our world. It's also been stretching itself beneath the village, seeking a physical way out as best it could."

"The thing is…" said Watson. "As far as I can make out, banishing the Fountain is a pretty easy job. It says it's bound to its

221

prison by magick and, daft as it sounds, it just needs to be ordered to leave. It's a supernatural creature and a magician conjured it into being here. Only a magician or a supernatural creature like itself can command it to go."

"Ah." Quist smiled knowingly. "A supernatural creature such as myself?"

"Yeah, but, um, there *is* a bit of a catch." His assistant gave a sheepish grin. "The supernatural creature, er, such as *yourself*, needs to be actually *touching* the Fountain when they order it to leave."

"I see." The wolf grimaced. "So I'd have to be down there on top of the thing like that old woman we saw. As you say, *a bit of a catch*."

"So what's the plan, Guv?"

"The *plan* hasn't changed." Quist quietly opened the bedroom door and checked outside. "I'm going to get you to safety and then deal with this. We need to move now, before anyone decides to check on my guard in the cellar. Everyone is gathered here for the celebrations, so you should have a clear escape route through the village. Once we get you out of the castle, you need to find a vehicle and get away from…"

"Apparently *your* car is in the courtyard." Watson peered warily at the open door. "But, um, I can't leave. I know it sounds daft and it's a bit embarrassing really, but I can't get out of the room."

"I'm sorry?" The wolf narrowed its eyes. "But what…"

"Ali Bongo did something with his abracadabra shit and made it so I can't walk through the doorway."

"Ah, I see." Quist scooped up the youth in his front legs, lifting him like a bride at the threshold. "Then please allow *me*. Just close your eyes for a moment."

Watson screwed them shut, partly because of the instruction, but also from the inevitable terror of being tightly embraced by a werewolf at the full moon. He felt an intense tingling sensation followed by a jolt as Quist set him back down.

"Well…" The youth looked around and saw he was outside in the passage. "That was easy enough. Cheers, Guv."

"That type of magick works on a mental level," explained the wolf, quietly. "Once again, Crowley influenced your mind. Your head wouldn't allow your body to leave, but as I just demonstrated, someone else could easily carry you out." He dropped onto all-fours and trotted along the corridor. "Come on, follow me and don't make a sound."

They arrived at the rear staircase and Quist led the way down the steps.

"Everyone should be in the banqueting hall," he murmured. "We'd need to go through there to reach the main entrance, which probably wouldn't be the cleverest idea. When we called earlier, however, I noticed another door in the corner of the courtyard. That will probably be a kitchen entrance where they take their deliveries."

"Great." Watson glanced nervously over his shoulder. "But what if there are servants in there?"

The wolf paused on the next landing and peeped around the corner. "I don't believe anyone actually *works* here as such," he whispered. "Yes, the village is maintained with electrics, plumbing and suchlike, and people staff the hotel, but I doubt anyone is paid. This isolated community is reminiscent of a cult, with the Laird in charge and everyone pulling together as they share the same dark secrets. Besides, like I say, anyone that usually tends to the kitchen will be at the party right now."

The pair reached the ground floor, where the indistinct sound of voices and music could be heard down the passage to their right. Quist turned left instead, and followed the faint smells of food and cooking to find the white-tiled kitchen rooms. Ensuring the place was empty, he closed the door behind them and hurried past cupboards, ranges and freezers to try the external door.

"It's unlocked," he whispered, opening it and rushing around checking drawers. "You were right. My car is parked out there, so you're good to go as soon as I find...Ah!" He smiled triumphantly and held up a remote control. "*This*, the control for the portcullis."

"Running out on you doesn't feel right, Guv." Watson shook his head. "I don't like the idea of leaving you to..."

"Don't worry about it." The wolf pointed the control through the open doorway and pressed, nodding as the portcullis began to lift in the barbican tower. "Mmh, a good range. Right, you need to..."

"Don't *worry*?" laughed the youth. "Guv, they've got guns with silver bullets and another werewolf here, a psycho, nutter bitch werewolf."

"You've neglected to mention the best part." Quist widened his smile, exposing huge razor fangs. "I have to get all close and personal with a giant flesh-eating monster."

"Listen, why don't you come with me and..."

"You know I have to do this," sighed the wolf. "But first I need to know that you're safe. You have to go now, drive with the lights off and go straight out of the village. Wait for me out on the headland where they captured us earlier."

"I don't know..." Watson hesitated. "If you're sure..."

"I *am*," insisted Quist. "Go *now*."

He watched as his assistant ran across the courtyard and jumped into the car. The wolf gave a relieved sigh to hear the engine start – the keys had obviously been left inside – then closed the kitchen door as it drove away beneath the portcullis.

"Right," he murmured. "It's time to meet the Fountain."

* * * *

Chapter 31

Quietly closing the passage door behind him, the wolf ran down the stone staircase and into the cellar complex where Gavin Howell still lay unconscious beside the silver cage.

"Sleeping on the job?" muttered Quist, opening the door to the dungeon and clicking on the light. "Sorry about the broken jaw, although I strongly suspect that will soon be the least of your problems."

He raised himself onto two legs and descended the steps, peering dubiously at the low fog that swirled over the floor of the circular chamber below. The layer hadn't been this dense on his previous visit here; presumably it was due to Crowley strengthening the entity. Through breaks in it, he could see how the *floor* still appeared to be earthen with a sandy texture, but he now knew this was the Fountain's way of camouflaging itself.

Quist paused on the bottom step. *Werewolves could only be killed by silver, fire and decapitation, but he was fairly sure that being ripped apart and dissolved in supernatural gastric juices could probably be added to that short list.*

"Alright," he growled, taking a deep breath and steeling himself. "Here we go."

The wolf stepped onto the misty surface of the elemental, feeling a pulsing sensation beneath his paws and immediately noticing movement to his left. Acid puddles had begun to bubble up and, snaking silently through the fog, a winding tentacle wrapped around his ankle like the pallid sucker root of some alien plant.

"Damn it," snarled Quist, dropping into a squat.

The milky-white tendril instantly tightened and began to nuzzle at his calf muscle. Heart hammering, he sprouted fingers on his front right paw and grabbed it. No fatter than a human thumb, it felt muscular and tough, the loathsome fleshiness twisting and bending in his grip.

"Listen to me," he said, grimacing. It wasn't often that his lupine side was repulsed by anything, but this eyeless thing resembled some gigantic maggot – an incredibly powerful maggot. "Listen. I'm the one you've been trying to contact. I can help you to…"

He froze, suddenly transfixed by the terrifying, yet strangely graceful movement all around him. The impression was of being on a fog-covered lake surrounded by a dozen swans, their bodies concealed by the mist and their pale necks curling up elegantly above it. The bizarre notion lasted little more than a second before the feeder tentacles darted like striking cobras to twist around the wolf.

"No, listen…" shouted Quist, snatching hold of one of the thicker tendrils. He grunted in pain as his hand sizzled; the release of feeding acid felt like the touch of silver. "You need to listen to me now."

Coils instantly formed around his limbs. Wrapping and tautening, seizing and constricting, they began their attempts to burrow into his body.

What the hell was happening here? This creature had pleaded for his assistance. It had attempted to speak with him directly and had then tried contacting him through Watson. It had wanted his help to escape, but all that appeared to have changed and now it seemed to want him as a spot of lupine lunch. Why wasn't it listening to… ah, of course – his blood.

Quist bit deeply into his front leg, the arterial spurts turning instantly to red powder as they splattered over the elemental's skin. The surface of the creature lurched beneath him and a low mound rose in the centre of the chamber, the sandy dust falling away to reveal the eye, the large, sulphurous yellow eye.

"Apparently I have your attention now," growled the wolf. "You know who I am and *what* I am." Raising his voice, he squeezed two of the tentacles tightly. "You will listen to me and you *will* do as I command."

The banqueting hall in Ravenspoint Castle hadn't seen an actual *banquet* for the best part of two centuries, but many gatherings and parties had been held there over the years. Suspended by its chain from the lofty ceiling, the massive iron chandelier illuminated the oak-panelled chamber, classical music played through concealed speakers and a table was crammed with countless bottles and platters of cold snacks. The entire community chatted in groups, over ninety people enjoying the drinks and celebrating many more decades of extended life.

The Laird had dressed for the event, sporting a smart Harris tweed jacket and tie, and a Mulgrave kilt in the blue and green family tartan. He stood talking to Irana Adler by the stone fireplace, where logs blazed and spat in the crib-like dog grate. Wearing her indigo silk suit, the Colonel smoked one of her French cigarettes and sipped a glass of wine. Sensing the familiar supernatural drop in temperature, she was the first to notice the werewolf.

"Ah." She raised her Malbec in a mock toast. "We appear to have a gatecrasher."

Mulgrave turned to see the creature in the hall doorway. "What the hell?" he hissed angrily. "How can this be?"

The villagers shuffled back, a mixture of shocked gasps and frightened muttering running through the assembly.

"The Colonel is right," confessed the wolf, strolling in on four legs. "I'm afraid I don't have an invite."

"I don't believe this." Brunton had been filling a whisky glass at the drinks table. Dropping the bottle and lifting his shirt, he quickly tugged a small pistol from the rear of his jeans. "How the fuck did you manage to get out?"

"That doesn't matter," said Quist. "I'm here with a warning for you all. I doubt any of you believe in the concept of a God, but if so, now would be an ideal time to ask for forgiveness."

"Oh, yeah?" The big man pointed the compact automatic. "Well, I should warn *you* – these bullets are silver."

"Don't shoot, you fool," barked Mulgrave. "You know we still need him."

"No, you'd better not shoot." The wolf began to slowly pad around the Persian rugs that covered the stone floor, the alarmed crowd parting as he slowly approached. He paused below one of the huge leaded windows. "If you do, you won't hear what I have to tell you."

"And what's that?" sneered Brunton.

"Your elemental has grown so large," said Quist, sitting on his haunches like a dog. "Those five expanding *arms*, for the lack of a better word, have widened, flattened out, and broken through the stonework of the tunnels you constructed to accommodate them. In many places the arms have become the actual foundations of the buildings above."

"We're fully aware of that," said Mulgrave, guardedly. "The expansion has caused all that deterioration and those cracks that needed to be repaired."

"That's right." The wolf nodded. "But there's something you *aren't* aware of. As the creature shrinks and vanishes, there will be nothing to hold up the castle and most of this village."

"Shrinks and vanishes?" Brunton shook his head. "What's that supposed to mean?"

A subterranean rumbling shook the banqueting hall. The chandelier began to swing, a spider's web of cracks appeared on the high ceiling and scabs of plaster fell, some exploding on the heads of the gathering. Completely unfazed, Adler looked up at the damage, smoking her cigarette.

"This is over," said Quist, watching as the villagers began to panic. "The elemental is returning to its own world. I've seen these entities vanish before and the process creates a supernatural energy vortex. Because this one is solid and so immense, I honestly can't predict what will happen when it goes."

"It can't *go*," shouted the Laird. "Crowley has just performed the Mulgrave Ritual to strengthen it. How can it possibly go?"

"I could explain it to you." The wolf shrugged. "But I really can't be bothered."

The underground rumbling grew and the shaking became more intense. Paintings, shields and decorative weapons fell from their mountings as the walls visibly shuddered. More ceiling plaster dropped and the distant thunder of tumbling masonry sounded outside the building.

"Well," said Quist. "It feels like the elemental is writhing around down there as it leaves. I don't imagine this will be too good for your castle."

The terrified throng pressed themselves against the walls as a jagged crack suddenly zigzagged across the stone floor between the rugs. Some started to flee the hall, heading for the passage to the main exit.

"This is interesting," said Adler, walking closer to Brunton as the majority of the screaming villagers struggled to push through the door. "Why would you be carrying a concealed weapon with silver bullets?"

"Isn't that obvious?" He kept the gun trained on the seated wolf. "It's for *him*."

"Really?" She raised a curious eyebrow and turned to look at Quist. "He was safely locked away in a cage and ready to be fed to that thing of yours. You had no need for that gun…" She paused, still watching the wolf. "Unless, of course, you intended to use it on me at some point when I had my guard down."

With her back towards him, Brunton silently brought the gun around, aiming instead between the woman's shoulder blades. Adler twisted with incredible speed and smacked the pistol out of his grip.

"Yes, like then," she said. "Except my guard *wasn't* down. I may have been facing away, but I was watching your reflection in the window over there." She snatched hold of his wrist and pulled him close to her. "But enough of all this. I need to slip into something more comfortable. Don't go away, will you?"

Mulgrave and the last remaining villagers watched in horror as the woman shapeshifted, maintaining her grip on the man's arm as she bent forward and burst out from her silk suit. The Laird would normally have been excited by the sight of an attractive female tearing off her clothes, but not tonight. The terrifying creature emerging from the tattered apparel would have done very little for *anyone's* sexual libido.

Rising to full height on its rear legs, the she wolf resembled Quist, but the black fur was sleeker and the single eye gleamed bright red, not amber. Mulgrave had been backing away towards the door and, taking one final terrified look at the two werewolves, he raced out. Quist watched from across the hall as Adler pulled Brunton closer.

"Mmmh, this is intimate, isn't it?" The she wolf licked the trembling man's face. "But I think I might have mentioned before how I don't like you."

Brunton glanced down, confused, as the creature gently fondled him between the legs. He looked into the red eye, wondering what on earth she could doing, then squealed as she wrenched her talons up through the clump of abdominal muscles, raking open his torso from testicles to sternum. Adler stepped away as he looked down again to see a mass of steaming offal tumble from the gaping wound onto the Persian rug.

Quist winced at the ghastly sight, watching as Brunton crumpled to his knees by the intestines. Adler saw the wolf's appalled expression.

"Oh, get over it," she snarled, licking the blood from her claw. "You didn't like him either, we both know that, so don't tell me you wouldn't have loved to kill him. What a shame that you have that stupid code that doesn't allow you to take life. You could have torn him apart long ago."

Brunton knelt, sweating and shivering, staring at his pile of innards in wide-eyed shock. Part of his spinning mind debated the best way to scoop them up and push them back inside. He wondered if he should clean off the ceiling plaster dust first, but he didn't wonder for long. Another huge rumble shook the room as Adler stepped behind him. He felt her vice-like jaws clamp onto the back of his neck, her fangs slowly biting through, until his screaming became a choked gargle and his severed head bounced across the hall towards Quist.

"Delicious," said the she wolf, snaking out her tongue to lick over her furry muzzle. "But I've saved the best until last and now it's finally your turn. I must admit, I'd have enjoyed watching you being eaten alive by that cellar monster of theirs, but I'm so glad now that you somehow escaped from that cage. Now I get the pleasure of killing you myself."

"I knew this day would eventually come," said Quist. "You clearly assume that fighting me will be a simple task. Remember, I'm much older than you, Colonel, and that gives me quite an advantage here."

"No, you're wrong," growled Adler. "Your human decency and lack of killer instinct are both big disadvantages in a fight to the death. *Fatal* disadvantages, in fact." She began walking slowly towards him on her hind legs. "Now me, I've been fighting and killing my entire life."

Quist looked up as the room began shaking again and a loud crashing sounded from high above.

"This is long overdue," said the she wolf, flexing her claws.

"Oh, I can't tell you how much I'm going to enjoy this."

The building lurched sickeningly, the ground opened beneath her and Adler let out a guttural screech before vanishing into the deep fissure taking one of the Persian rugs with her. The rumbling above became deafening, alerting Quist to the castle turrets and upper stories collapsing onto the floors below. He shot across the remains of the floor in two swift leaps, diving headfirst through a window in an explosion of glass, as the chandelier and the ceiling came down behind him.

The wolf plunged into the freezing sea and surfaced to the dramatic sight of the entire fortress crumbling. With powerful strokes, he quickly swam out of range of the destruction and turned to watch the balconies fall, the outer walls crumple inwards and showers of masonry tumble into the water. It took less than fifteen seconds before the Jacobean splendour of Ravenspoint Castle had been replaced by a mountain of rubble enveloped in a billowing dust cloud.

"So, Colonel..." he muttered, treading water. "Did you enjoy that as much as you anticipated?"

Fires had broken out in various parts of the debris, as electrical mains shorted out and gas pipes ruptured and ignited. Quist gazed at the erupting flames, then swam to the rocks and climbed out of the waves, pausing to vigorously shake his soaking fur like a wet dog. Through the swirl of choking dust he could see how various sections of the village perimeter wall had fallen. He clambered over the stones in the closest gap and glanced to his right as a terrace of nearby houses came noisily down, more gas fires blazing up in the resulting ruins.

Quist slowly surveyed the destruction, shaking his head grimly. *To cause this much damage, the elemental must have been twisting and writhing violently as it left in its energy vortex. It was as if someone had constructed a house of cards on a blanket and then allowed two snakes to fight each other underneath it.*

Jumping down into the castle courtyard from the heap of stones, the wolf prowled around sniffing at the people who sprawled dead and dying on the cobbles. Some had already deteriorated fully, the way Oliver Tarrant had done in the York hospital, leaving behind puddles of gelatinous brown sludge. The courtyard wall and its barbican entrance tower had also collapsed and more bodies lay in the neighbouring marketplace. Several decrepit villagers staggered about, resembling white-haired extras in a zombie movie, their skin wrinkled and ulcerated.

"Good Lord," gasped Quist, reeling with shock on seeing the kilt and realising that one of the shambling figures was Reginald Mulgrave.

The wolf looked up as flakes began to drift down all around. At first he assumed it was dust particles from the destruction, but no, they were snowflakes. A festive shower of snow had begun to fall, providing quite a contrast to the horrors in the square. Avoiding the huge cracks, the wolf padded over to the Laird, noticing how his beard and most of the lustrous red hair had turned grey and fallen out.

"Who's there?" croaked Mulgrave, sensing his closeness. "I can't see. What's happening to me?"

"You're aging," said Quist. "I can only presume the older you are, the faster it will happen."

"*What?*" Mulgrave's breath came in laboured gasps. Feeble as it was, the panting still had the power to blow out his loose front teeth. "I don't understand."

"That's because your brain is decaying too." The wolf wrinkled its nose at the stench. "You told me you wouldn't last more than a few weeks away from the Fountain, but your longevity was supernatural and that time will be reduced now that it's gone. It will be the same for everyone here of advanced age." He looked around at the decomposing villagers in the square and winced to see Mulgrave's melting features. "*Vastly* reduced, apparently."

"You have to end it," pleaded the Laird. "I've seen your claws and you could stop this pain with one quick swipe of them." He stumbled to his knees, moaning as one of the bones in his left leg snapped and tore through his parchment skin. Bodily fluids began to ooze from opening sores. "Do it, please, I beg you. Do it now and stop this agony."

"I'm sorry," murmured Quist, turning to walk away through the falling snow. "I'm sure Colonel Adler would have been happy to oblige you, but I'm unable to help with that. I can't take a human life."

* * * *

Chapter 32

Snow was falling steadily on the dark headland road outside Ravenspoint village, the drifting flakes settling on the clumps of gorse bush and the windscreen of Quist's parked car. Waiting anxiously in the driving seat, Watson jolted as a sudden loud clicking broke the tense silence. He yelped with fright to see glowing eyes at the side window and a furry, taloned finger tapping at the glass.

Fortunately, there were *two* eyes and they were amber, not red.

"I really wish you'd stop scaring me like that." The young man unlocked the doors and shuffled across from behind the steering wheel as the beast shapeshifted. "First the bedroom window and now here. Are you okay, Guv? What happened?"

"It's finished," said his boss, opening the rear door. "This nightmare is finally over."

Watson checked the mirrors. "Is anyone following you?"

"That's highly doubtful." The detective retrieved his leather overcoat from where he'd thrown it earlier and pulled it on to cover his nakedness. "The banishing worked and the elemental has gone."

"The Fountain has left the building?" The youth laughed nervously. "Wow! So does that mean the villagers…"

"They're deteriorating and dying," said Quist, jumping into the car. "All of them, at different rates depending upon their age. I have to say, it isn't pretty."

"Is Adler dead too?" asked Watson, hopefully.

"That's rather difficult to ascertain with a castle on top of her."

"Whoo, that sounds like it was a hell of a party." The youth gave a low whistle. "I heard the loud rumbling and I guessed it was buildings falling. So, the castle actually *collapsed* and you're saying she's underneath it? But Adler's a werewolf like you, so can she survive that?"

"I don't know," admitted the detective. "I suppose the falling and sliding masonry could have decapitated her, and ruptured gas piping has caused several fires in the rubble, but who knows? One thing is for sure, she's completely entombed beneath hundreds of tons of stone and her lupine strength will be useless down there."

"Bloody hell." Watson pictured this macabre scenario and shuddered. "I can't get my head around the fact that all those people back there are dead."

"Including your new friend Brunton," said Quist. "I'm afraid he didn't leave any parting message for you."

"Shame." The youth turned in his seat to look back. "It's weird to think that an entire village has just been wiped out. Will the experts put it down to a freak earthquake or something?"

"They'll have little choice," said Quist. "It won't explain the missing population, of course. Whatever explanation the authorities come up with for *that* mystery, we both know it will be wrong." He noticed his assistant's troubled features. "By the way, compassion is something to be greatly admired, but you must know it's wasted on that particular community. You have to remember their actual ages and the horrendous things they were doing to selfishly maintain their miserable lives."

Watson nodded. "How about Ali Bongo the magician? He's away from the village, but will he be aging too?

"I presume so, but not Rachel Mulgrave." Quist started the car, his expression growing dark. "She's younger than the other villagers, so that means she'll survive this."

"But her home's gone and she no longer has the Fountain to keep her young and healthy, so she's finished."

"Well, of course she isn't." The detective let out a dry laugh. "Someone like *her* will definitely have planned for such an eventuality. Yes, Ravenspoint has gone, but I've no doubt she has a fortune stashed in offshore accounts." He punched the car dashboard. "The woman is a murderer. I can't imagine how many people she must have killed, or helped to kill, over the years, but she can't be allowed to get away with those crimes."

"Um, Guv?" Watson eyed the broken air blower. "Are you feeling a little…"

"Sorry." He gave the youth a tight smile. "It's just the moon plying havoc with my emotions, primarily my anger, as you can doubtless see. As I was saying, we need to find her."

"Okay," said Watson. "Do you remember me telling you I once had a girlfriend called Katie?"

"Er…" Quist looked blank. "I'm sorry, but *what*?"

"That's how I remembered the name of the company. The trackers they used were made by an electronic firm called KT."

"I don't see what possible use…"

"They put miniature transponders in our pockets," explained the youth. "That's how they knew we were running out on them earlier. Old Ali Bongo's taken a bit of a fancy to me and he gave me a big lovey-dovey hug before he left tonight. I managed to fish the tracker out of my jacket and drop it into *his* pocket without him noticing."

"I see," nodded Quist. "Good work, but surely we would need the serial number to locate it?"

"Yeah, and you have one in *your* pocket," said Watson. "They bought them together, so the chances are…"

"Ah, of course." His eyes widening, the detective searched in his coat and produced the tiny device. "The chances *are*, the one you planted on Crowley will be the serial number *before* this one, or the one *after*. Now if only we had a phone to track them with. They took mine when they…"

"You mean like *this*?" Watson held up his mobile. "I plugged it in to charge in the car and it was still here. I found the KT company on the internet and downloaded their tracker app while I was waiting for you."

"Good Lord, young man." The detective shot him a look of admiration. "Outstanding. I'm definitely awarding you a *Quist Gold Star* for this."

"Oh, lovely." Watson nodded. "So is that similar to a large pay rise?"

* * * *

Chapter 33

Aleister Crowley stared wistfully over the River Tyne, his hands submerged in the warm pockets of a black cashmere overcoat. Newcastle was further south than Ravenspoint, and the snow that had begun to fall on the Craggan headland had yet to reach here. Many believe the Tyne flows *through* Newcastle, but the river actually flows *past* it, forming a natural boundary with the city to the north of the water and the town of Gateshead to the south. The Sage dominates the southern embankment, the enormous glass complex rising 150 feet beside the iconic Tyne Bridge and spreading along the waterfront like some gigantic snoozing armadillo. Bustling with excited crowds and media vehicles, this futuristic music and culture centre prepared itself for the Saturday night televised finals of *Dance Away*.

The Hilton stands nearby and Crowley leant on his BMW bonnet in the hotel car park. Rachel realised he wasn't following her across the tarmac and returned to the vehicle with a puzzled frown.

"So what's wrong?" she quizzed. "Are you coming to check in, or what?"

The girl wore a snow leopard coat and buttoned it up against the cold. The fur rarely attracted the contempt or anger it deserved, as the majority of people who saw it were unable to conceive that it was genuine.

"I'm sorry," said Crowley. "But I was lost in thought there. Something isn't right and I feel quite *different*. It's a strange, ethereal sensation that I can't manage to pin down and I..." Shaking himself, he checked his watch. "Listen, we don't have to be at the event just yet, do we? Why don't we leave our bags in the car and take a short walk first?"

"A spot of exercise?" Rachel followed the magician to where the main road turned left onto the Tyne Bridge. Masses of arched metalwork rose in front of them. "Well, *this* is certainly a new one."

"What can I say?" He smiled dejectedly. "I suppose I just need to clear my head. It isn't just this peculiar sensation I'm feeling. It's almost eight o'clock and your father and the others will soon be in the cellar with Bernard."

"That's true," she smiled. "Dinner time in the dungeon."

"Unlike you, I'm unable to find any humour in what they're about to do."

Crowley looked over the handrail beside him to see that the land beneath the road had fallen steeply away to the river. Negotiating the four lanes of evening traffic, he crossed the bridge and strode along the wide pavement on the opposite side, gazing at the view to the east. The brightly-lit Sage lay to his right and the lively modern quayside on the left was busy with restaurant and bar nightlife. The Millennium footbridge linked the two riverbanks and pleasure boats passed ninety feet below, the large vessels hosting night cruises, wedding parties and corporate Christmas functions.

"I really don't understand your problem," laughed Rachel. Lighting two cigarettes, she passed one to the magician. "Quist is a werewolf, just like the other two. I remember you couldn't care less when we gave *them* to the Fountain."

"No, there's a whole world of difference," snapped Crowley. "Surely you're able to see that? The first two were evil creatures. Both of them were killers like Adler."

"Yes, you were fine with the idea of feeding *her* to the Fountain."

"Exactly," he nodded. "The woman is a despicable murdering psychopath. If everything had gone to plan and we'd managed to contain her, I would have had no objection to *her* death, but Bernard Quist is very different. He's never killed anyone, and he lives to help others with…"

"He *lives*?" repeated Rachel, blowing cigarette smoke. "Oops,

I think you might be mistaken there." Holding up her wrist and allowing him to see her watch, she giggled. "Sorry, Aleister, but eight o'clock has just passed."

* * * *

"Ali Bongo still hasn't moved, Guv." Watson sat in the passenger seat of Quist's speeding car, staring at the transponder app on his phone. "We're coming to the Tyne Bridge and his tracker signal is right in the middle of it. He's been there for the past few minutes, so maybe Rachel's with him."

"They're clearly on foot," said the detective. "To keep the traffic flowing, parking won't be allowed on the bridge." He turned into the grounds of the Newcastle Hilton and spotted a black saloon. "Yes, I deduced they'd be spending the night in the closest hotel to the Sage and I was right. There's Crowley's BMW."

"AC 666." Watson read the registration as he jumped out of the car. "Yeah, you can say what you like about people with private plates, but I still reckon that's a pretty cool one."

Leaving the Hilton car park, he followed his boss over the main road and onto the Tyne Bridge pavement, the pair breaking into a jog towards the two figures who leant on the handrail. Night traffic with glaring headlights rushed past behind Crowley and Rachel as they gazed across the river in conversation.

"It's a spectacular city view," said Quist, approaching them. "But I thought you two were taking part in a dance competition?"

Rachel turned, freezing momentarily in disbelief, before quickly composing herself. "And I thought *you* were treating the Fountain to an eight o'clock snack," she sneered, her conceited brashness returning. "So you somehow managed to escape? How clever of you."

"It's so good to see you, Bernard," enthused Crowley, with a genuine smile. "I can't imagine how you accomplished it, but I'm relieved that you're here. As you know, I was never happy with their decision to harm you."

"*Harm* me is putting it rather mildly," snarled Quist.

"That's true," admitted Crowley. "Because, of course, your death would have been pointless; the Mulgrave Ritual works perfectly well without that quite horrible addition. As I keep telling them, there isn't any..." He paused, peering curiously at the detective's bare legs and feet. "Good Lord, are you naked under that coat?"

Rachel smiled tartly. "So how *did* you get away. Come to that, how did you know we were here on the bridge?

"That isn't important," said Quist. "You need to listen to me, because..."

"Oh, I really don't think so," she broke in, checking her watch. "This unexpected reunion has been fun, but, as you've pointed out, we're due in the Sage for the *Dance Away* finals. We have a rumba to perform and a competition to win. I'm sure your Colonel friend and Richard Brunton will listen to you when they track you down and..."

"Afraid not, luv," said Watson. "If I were you, I'd hear what he has to say. Adler and Brunton have both gone and so has your Fountain."

"What's *that* supposed to mean?" snapped the girl.

"The Fountain's *gone*," he repeated. "Gone for good, along with your castle. It turns out your pet monster was pretty much supporting the building. Proper stone foundations might have been a better idea than a supernatural starfish."

"Don't be ridiculous," she laughed. "Do you think I'm going to believe that shit."

"No, he's speaking the truth," said Crowley, quietly. "I told you how I've been sensing a huge ethereal change and this is obviously why. Our paranormal link with the entity has been severed." He grabbed the detective's arm. "I've only just strengthened the Fountain with the ceremony so *how* can it have gone? What on earth did you *do*?"

"I banished it." Quist shrugged off the magician's grip. "You really shouldn't have used that hypnotic enchantment on Watson. You opened his mind and allowed the elemental to communicate with him. It explained how I could return it to its own plane of existence. It turned out to be quite an easy task."

"That mindless creature?" Rachel laughed again. "It spoke to you? Are you serious?"

"Hardly mindless," corrected the youth. "I can't imagine it on a stage giving university lectures, but yeah, it was able to talk to me just fine."

"Like Watson says, your castle has gone," confirmed Quist. "It's rubble. Most of your community are dead too, including Brunton and your father. Within minutes of the elemental vanishing, the villagers began to age and decompose."

"My home has gone?" Rachel trembled with rage, her teeth tightly clenched. "You're telling me *everything* has gone? Because of you, my life there is finished?" She fell silent for a moment, before forcing a sarcastic smile. "Well, let's face it, Daddy was getting a little old and I suppose he had to go sometime. I suppose it's just as well that I'm the youngest person in Ravenspoint, so I won't be affected."

"That's right," agreed Quist, his anger rising. "You'll age at the normal human rate… but you'll be doing it in a prison uniform. I don't know how many murders you must have committed over the years, but I watched you kill those two young men earlier tonight. You actually laughed as you kicked one of them down the well and you need to answer for that. Believe me, you *will* answer for it."

"Well, there isn't much in the way of proof," snorted Rachel. "We've always been adept at covering our tracks and the Fountain never left anything behind in the way of evidence. It was a good little elemental and it always cleared its plate at meal times. Also, I can't help wondering how the police would view your crackpot fairy stories about supernatural monsters eating people."

Crowley cleared his throat. "The full moon is angering you, Bernard," he said. "It's clouding your judgment, and Rachel *does* have a point. The police won't believe a word about…"

"You could be right," snarled Quist. "But why don't we find out?"

The girl looked over her shoulder.

"Seriously?" The detective shook his head. "You must be aware of my speed and strength, even in human form. You couldn't possibly outrun me."

"I've no intention of running." Rachel shrugged off her fur coat to reveal a red mini dress and, with graceful agility, sprang up onto the waist-high bridge parapet. "I much prefer swimming."

"Don't be bloody daft," gasped Watson. He turned to the passing traffic, but none of the motorists had noticed the girl's dangerous balancing act. "Have you seen how high you are?"

"Yes, exhilarating, isn't it?" Kicking off her shoes, she glanced at the black water ninety feet below, before smiling triumphantly at Quist. "Right now, you're angry enough to hand me over to the cops. I don't know whether they could charge me with anything, but I've no intention of letting it happen."

"Come down from there." The detective sighed irritably. "You'll end up killing yourself."

"Not a chance," she laughed. "I'm an expert diver and no one will see me leave the river downstream at night. I've always had a lucrative escape plan ready for just such an occasion and it's time to put the wheels in motion. You won't be seeing me again. Goodbye, Aleister, it's been fun."

"We had our moments." Crowley gave her a thin smile and a small wave. "Do what thou wilt, my dear."

Flipping backwards, Rachel twisted in the air and plummeted

in a perfect dive… straight onto the prow of a brightly-lit pleasure cruiser emerging from beneath the bridge. Her upper body slammed into the front deck, exploding her head.

"*Fuck!*" whispered Watson, peering over the parapet with Quist and Crowley. "What in the name of… *fuck.*"

More of the boat appeared, revealing a stunned hen party of twelve girls spattered with blood and brain matter. The traumatised bride looked up, her white face and penis-shaped balloon dripping with scarlet gore.

Watson peered back in open-mouthed shock, before some bizarre compulsion forced him to blurt: "Hey, if he stands you up at the altar, luv…"

His boss dragged him back from the handrail as a cacophony of terrified screams erupted below.

* * * *

Chapter 34

"Well…" croaked Crowley, gesturing shakily to the bridge parapet. "That was somewhat unexpected, wasn't it?"

"You don't say," stammered Watson, horrified.

"So, I'm thinking…" The magician gave Quist an awkward grin. "Very shortly, this bridge will be swarming with police. As I'm often in the habit of saying, do what thou wilt, but in *this* particular case, *do what thou wilt* should perhaps involve you allowing me to leave?"

"*What?*" barked the detective. "After everything you've done?"

"Well, I think we can all agree that I'm no angel." Crowley smiled ruefully. "However I've never killed anyone. Well, apart from helping to dispatch a couple of werewolves in 1906 and 1947, but in my defence, they were very *bad* werewolves and not at all like you, Bernard. You know that I argued with the Mulgraves to release you and…"

"You may not have killed anyone yourself," said Quist. "But you watched the murders and did nothing to prevent them. I saw you performing one of your rites when they killed those two men earlier tonight. You benefitted from all of those deaths, just like the Mulgraves and the rest of the village."

"Er, Guv…" Watson gulped uneasily. "You know those girls on the boat will be ringing the cops right now?"

"He's right." Crowley looked both ways along the road. "I'm sure we could discuss these matters all night long, but none of us want to be here when the authorities arrive. They may think we threw Rachel off the bridge, especially when the boat party make their statements." He nodded to Watson. "When they tell them how our young friend here was looking over and shouting jokes immediately after her fall."

"His *joke* was an involuntary response to the shock," said Quist.

"True." The youth let out an anxious laugh. "But let's face it, no one is going to believe she was crazy enough to jump up there and dive off *herself*."

The detective grimaced, his acute hearing picking up the distant sound of a police siren.

"We both have secrets that we need to protect," said Crowley. "Who I am and my true age. *What* you are and your true age. We both have our reasons to remain anonymous in this world."

"He's right, Guv," agreed Watson. "You definitely don't need any awkward questions."

Quist hesitated for several moments, glaring at Crowley, before finally nodding. "Go on," he snapped, bitterly. "Get out of here."

"A very wise choice," sighed the relieved magician. "Believe me when I tell you it was a great pleasure to meet you both." He smiled warmly at Watson before turning to go. "Take care, young man, and always remember my personal maxim: *do what thou wilt shall be the whole of the law*."

"I'll be honest, mate, that's a really crap motto," shouted Watson, watching as he hurried away along the bridge pavement. "You should change it to *my* personal favourite: *if it's not Yorkshire, it's shite*."

"Time to go," said Quist. Peering up at the illuminated metalwork overhead, he set off at a fast marching pace to follow Crowley. "Fortunately there are no CCTV cameras." He grabbed his assistant's arm, slowing him a little. "No, don't break into a run – witnesses remember the unusual, such as people running when they're clearly not dressed like runners. The drivers who are passing by are concentrating on the road and the other traffic. They're not looking at pedestrians, so hopefully there will be no evidence that we were ever here."

"You did the right thing letting him go," said Watson as they neared the Hilton.

"I know," admitted his boss with a sigh. "He was right; anger *was* clouding my judgment and I couldn't possibly have answered the police questions."

"Yeah," smiled the youth. "Plus you won't have to explain why you're stark bollock naked under that coat." They arrived at the car park in time to see the black BMW leaving. "Hey, there goes Ali Bongo."

Crowley dropped the side window. "I'm sorry," he said. "I forgot to wish you both a merry Christmas. If ever I need the services of a detective agency, I certainly know where to call."

Watson watched the BMW speed away. "Funny, isn't it?" he murmured, with a curious frown. "I mean, I don't want to sound morbid or anything, but shouldn't he have turned into sludge by now?"

"Yes, I wondered about that myself," admitted Quist, jumping into his own car. "He wasn't showing any signs of deterioration, was he?"

"Maybe he's used some of his abracadabra stuff?" suggested Watson, climbing in beside him. "So what about Irana Adler? Aren't you worried she might not be dead?"

"I won't be losing any sleep in the near future." The detective pulled out of the car park and onto the main road. "Dead or not, she's currently entombed beneath a thousand tons of stone. I don't know how long it would take to remove all that rubble, if indeed it ever *is* removed."

"Yeah, how would you get bulldozers through those narrow twisting streets?"

"Most of the streets have *also* collapsed," pointed out Quist. "The tip of the Craggan headland is undermined with dangerously

248

unstable tunnels. Plus, of course, the owners of the castle have unexpectedly vanished. There's no one to authorise what would definitely be a vastly expensive clean-up operation. The community has mysteriously disappeared and I suspect the questions and legal wrangling will last for years."

"That entire village has gone." Watson shook his head as the enormity of this sank in. "Most of Ravenspoint has been demolished and all the people are dead. When you think about it, that's some seriously mind-blowing, fucked-up shit."

"The exact words that I would have used." Quist smiled thinly, switching on the windscreen wipers as flakes began to settle on the glass. "Ah, look, the snow has reached Newcastle. Tomorrow is the 22nd, so Christmas is only three days away. I wonder if we're in for a white one this year?"

"Oh, come on." The youth laughed. "I know the only reason you're only saying that is to take my mind off all that death and destruction."

"Now didn't I say you were astute?" The detective nodded. "So is it working?"

"I only remember *one* white Christmas," said Watson. "It was a few years ago when I was a little kid. Some of the weather stations dotted around the country reported falling snowflakes in the early hours. None of it settled, of course, but it was kind of nice to know that we'd had one"

"Ah, yes, I'm forgetting..." Quist nodded. "Yes, that's the modern classification used by the Met Office – falling flakes have to be officially registered on the 25th. Of course, back in the days of Charles Dickens, who, by the way, was a thoroughly nice chap, we had a white Christmas every year. I remember the snow being four feet deep on the Christmas Eve that I went skating on the frozen Thames with Oscar Wilde and..."

"Unbelievable," gasped Watson, astounded. "Talk about

topping someone's story. I remember a few crappy flakes and you remember *that*. If I've been to Tenerife, you've probably been to Eleven-erife."

"Well, it's often difficult to avoid." The detective laughed. "I don't know if you've noticed, but I'm a little older than you."

"Really? I hadn't realised." Watson laughed too. "Merry Christmas, Guv."

"Merry Christmas," said Quist.

The End

Milton Keynes UK
Ingram Content Group UK Ltd.
UKHW021430210923
429112UK00013B/538

9 781804 242353